Praise for the novels of Sheila Roberts

"Crisp, charming and amusing storytelling.... A well-crafted plot and distinctive, genuine and endearing characters.... Roberts will delight and charm with her special brand of heartwarming romance."
—*RT Book Reviews* on *Starting Over on Blackberry Lane*

"It's always great to go back to Icicle Falls.... Sheila Roberts has created a magical place where friendship and love abound, and you never know who's going to turn up here next. Another enchanting tale."
—*Fresh Fiction* on *Starting Over on Blackberry Lane*

"The latest in Roberts completely charming Icicle Falls series is both a delightful celebration of the joys of small-town life and a richly rewarding romance sweetened with just the right dash of bright humor."
—*Booklist* on *Home on Apple Blossom Road*

"Engaging, sweet, and dusted with humor, this emotional romance tugs at the heartstrings."
—*Library Journal* on *Home on Apple Blossom Road*

"Roberts engages readers from the first page with her colorfully distinctive characters and her amusing storytelling. She expresses the pitfalls that occur through the holiday season with flair and fun. A delightful read."
—*RT Book Reviews* on *Christmas on Candy Cane Lane*

"*The Lodge on Holly Road* is the ultimate in feel-good family drama and heart-melting romance."
—*USA TODAY*

"The common thread and theme of making changes in your life for the better serve as an inspiration and make this novel a real page-turner."
—*RT Book Reviews* on *The Cottage on Juniper Ridge*

SHEILA ROBERTS

CHRISTMAS
in Icicle Falls

mira

mira

ISBN-13: 978-0-7783-3079-0

Recycling programs
for this product may
not exist in your area.

Christmas in Icicle Falls

Copyright © 2017 by Sheila Rabe

For questions and comments about the quality of this book, please contact us at
CustomerService@Harlequin.com.

www.MIRABooks.com

Printed in U.S.A.

For Sandy and her ugly tree.

Dear Reader,

Thanks so much for joining me once more in Icicle Falls. This will be our last visit to my favorite mountain town, and I have to admit, I'm a little sorry to say goodbye to all those characters who have become so real to me.

But we're going out with one final Christmas celebration and a few final pearls of wisdom from our resident wisewoman, Muriel Sterling. Muriel herself is going to learn a few things in this book and I hope you'll enjoy watching her story unfold. Of course, she's not the only one who's going to have a sharp learning curve. Muriel's old friend Olivia is going to learn an important lesson and maybe so will Sienna Moreno, a newcomer to town who's got to deal with her grumpy neighbor, a modern-day Scrooge.

So, grab a cup of your favorite holiday tea, and let me spin one final Icicle Falls adventure for you. I hope you enjoy the ride. Merry Christmas and, as Tiny Tim once said, God bless us, everyone!

Sheila

CHRISTMAS
in Icicle Falls

Chapter One

This is the time of year to offer thanks for all the wonderful people in our lives.
　　—Muriel Sterling, *A Guide to Happy Holidays*

Thanksgiving, a day to spend with family, to give thanks for all your blessings, to...have a close encounter with your cranky neighbor's shrubbery. Oh, yes, this was how Sienna Moreno wanted to start her day.

Why, oh, why, had she ventured out in her car on an icy street to go to the grocery store for more milk when she could have asked her cousin Rita Reyes to bring it? Rita's husband, Tito, worked at the Safeway meat department. He could have picked up a gallon.

But oh, no. She had to go out on her cheap no-weather tires. She should have stretched her budget a little further and gotten those snow tires like Rita had told her to do. "Here in the mountains, you want snow tires," Rita had said.

Yes, she did, especially now as she was skidding toward Mr. Cratchett's front yard.

"We're gonna die!" her nine-year-old son, Leo, cried,

clapping his hands over his eyes as they slid up and over Mr. Cratchett's juniper bush. Sienna could hear the branches crunching under them, the bush equivalent of breaking bones. *Madre de Dios!*

The good news was the bush brought her to a stop. The bad news was she was stopped right in front of Mr. Cratchett's house.

Maybe she hadn't damaged the bush too much. "It's okay, honey. We're fine," she assured her son and got out of the car on shaky legs. She probably couldn't say the same for Mr. Cratchett's landscaping.

She was barely out of her car before her neighbor stormed down the walk, an ancient navy pea coat thrown on over pajama bottoms stuffed into boots, a knit cap pulled over his sparse gray hair. He was scowling. Great.

"What have you done to my juniper bush?" he demanded.

"I'm so sorry, Mr. Cratchett. I hit a slippery spot."

"You shouldn't be out if you don't know how to drive in the snow," Cratchett growled.

She wasn't sure how she'd learn to drive in the snow if she didn't get out in it but she decided this wasn't the time for that observation.

He leaned over the bush like a detective examining a corpse. "This thing will never come back. You've damaged it beyond repair."

"I'll buy you a new one this spring," Sienna promised.

"You certainly will," he snapped. "If you don't, you'll be hearing from my lawyer. You're becoming a real nuisance."

"So are you," she muttered as she got back into her car.

"He's mad," Leo observed.

There was an understatement. "It's okay," she said as much to herself as her son. She put the car in gear, held her breath and inched toward their driveway. The car swayed as they turned in. *Ooh.*

"I want to get out," Leo said.

"Stay put. We're fine." She bit her lip as she braked—oh, so gently—and the car fishtailed to a stop right before she hit the garage door.

She let out her breath. There. Something to be thankful for.

She could see Cratchett standing on his front walk, glaring at her. "You shouldn't be driving," he called.

Yeah, well, neither should he. She'd seen him behind the wheel and he was scary even when there wasn't snow. Honestly, what had she ever done to deserve inheriting him?

"Just lucky, I guess," teased her cousin Rita Reyes later as Sienna recounted her day's adventures to her family over their evening Thanksgiving feast.

There were plenty of people present to enjoy it—Rita, her husband, Tito, and their toddler, Linda, were present, along with Sienna's *tía*, Mami Luci, and Tito's sister and brother-in-law and their two small children. It was Sienna's first holiday celebration in her new house and she loved being able to fill it with company.

Especially on Thanksgiving, which was her favorite holiday. The food—turkey and pork, tamales, Mami's *arroz con gandules*, *coquito* and flan for dessert; the music—salsa, merengue and *bachata*; and, of course, time with family. With her parents and two brothers still in LA, it was a comfort to be able to have her aunt and cousin living in the same town. It was also nice to have them right here to complain to.

No, wait. No complaining on Thanksgiving. She was simply venting. Justifiably venting. "I mean, it's not like I meant to run over Mr. Cratchett's juniper bush."

"You didn't exactly get practice driving in snow down in LA," Rita said consolingly. "That man." She shook her head in disgust as she helped herself to more fruit salad. "Neighbors should come with a warning label."

"This one should have," Sienna said. "He shouldn't be allowed to have neighbors. He should be a hermit. Actually, he's already close to one. He hardly ever comes out of that big, overgrown house of his except to yell at me." Okay, maybe that was a slight exaggeration.

Or not.

"Mr. Cratchett's mean to me, too, Mommy," put in Leo.

Tito shook his head. "Threatening to call the cops over a baseball through the window."

"I didn't do that," Leo declared hotly. "It was Tommy Haskel. Tommy said it was me."

Poor Leo had taken the fall and Sienna had bought Mr. Cratchett a new window.

"*Culo,*" muttered Tito. "I should have come over and taken a baseball to the old dude's head."

Tito's sister pointed her fork at him. "Then he really would have called the cops."

"He's been there, done that," Sienna said. "Remember?"

"Yes, making such a stink when we had your house-warming party," Rita said in disgust. "Too loud, my ass. It was barely nine."

"Maybe that's what got us started on the wrong foot," Sienna mused. That had been back in the summer. Even after all those months it would appear she and her crusty neighbor still hadn't found the right foot.

Tito shook his head. "No. The dude's a *cabrón*."

"Oh, well. Let's not think about him anymore," Sienna said. There were plenty of nice people in town to make up for her unneighborly neighbor. She liked Rita's boss, Charley Masters, who owned Zelda's restaurant, and Bailey Black, who owned a tea shop, was quickly becoming a good friend. Pat York, her boss at Mountain Escape Books, was great, and Pat's friends had all taken her under their wings.

"Good idea," agreed Rita. "Pass the tamales."

Venting finished, Sienna went back to concentrating on counting her blessings. So she didn't have husband. Who wanted a creep who walked away when the going got tough, anyway? She had her family, new friends, a wonderful job and a pretty house that she'd been able to purchase from the previous owner on a private contract with a very minimal down payment. It wasn't as big as Cratchett's corner-lot mansion—nobody's was—but it had three bedrooms, two baths and a kitchen with lots of cupboard space, and it was all hers. Or it would be in thirty years. And she had the sweetest son a woman could ask for. Her life was good, so there'd be no more complaining, er, venting.

Olivia Claussen's feet hurt. So did her back. For that matter, so did her head. Serving Thanksgiving dinner to all her guests at the Icicle Creek Lodge was an exhausting undertaking, even with help.

Thank God she'd had help. Although one particular "helper," her new daughter-in-law, had been about as useful as a roadblock.

"I was a waitress at the Full Table Buffet," Meadow had bragged when Olivia had asked if she'd be able to give her a hand with the holiday dinner service. "No problemo."

She'd showed off her experience by setting the tables wrong, spilling gravy in a customer's lap and then swearing at him when he got upset with her. She'd capped the day off by leaving halfway through serving the main course.

"Meadow doesn't feel good," Olivia's son Brandon had explained.

Meadow didn't feel good? Olivia hadn't felt so good herself. She'd been nursing a headache for days. Perhaps it had something to do with the arrival of her new daughter-in-law? But running an inn was not much different from show business. The show must go on.

And so it had, but Olivia was still feeling more than a little crabby about the performance of one particular player. "Whatever did he see in her?" she complained to her husband, James, as he rubbed her tired feet. Besides the obvious, of course. The girl was pretty—in a brassy, exotic way. Brandon had always dated good-looking women.

James wisely didn't answer.

Olivia had been longing to see her baby boy married for years, but she hadn't expected him to sneak off to

Vegas to do it. She certainly hadn't expected him to commit so quickly, before anyone really had a chance to get to know this woman. Before *he* really even had a chance to get to know her!

Brandon had met Meadow when he was skiing. She'd been hanging out at the ski lodge at Crystal Mountain after her first ski lesson and there was poor, unsuspecting Brandon. They'd wound up having dinner together and then spent the night partying, which led to private ski lessons followed by private parties for two. And then it was "Oops, I'm pregnant." And that was followed by "Surprise, we're married!" This sudden turn of events had taken place quite clandestinely. He'd known this girl only a few months. Months! And had never said anything about her. Now suddenly they were married. And, well, here they were.

Not that Olivia wasn't happy to have her wandering boy home again, ready to help run the family business. It was just that the woman he'd brought with him was taking some getting used to. Actually, a lot of getting used to.

The couple had started married life in Seattle, and Brandon had settled down and gotten a job working for a large company that was slowly taking over the city. The benefits were great, but the hours were long and Meadow had complained about not seeing him enough. So he'd called his mom and suggested coming back to Icicle Falls. Olivia had loved the idea of her son coming home. The bride, not so much. But the lodge would be passed on to him and Eric eventually anyway, so of course, she'd gotten a little suite ready for them, one similar to what her older son, Eric, and his wife had, making them all one big, happy family.

With a cuckoo in the nest.

"She tricked him into marrying her, I'm sure," Olivia said to James.

"Now, Olivia, you don't really believe that, do you?"

"I can't help but wonder."

Her second son had always been a bit of a ladies' man, but she'd never known Brandon to be irresponsible. The idea that he'd gotten someone pregnant— someone he barely knew and who was so clearly not his type—didn't make sense to her at all. It was just so *unlike* him. In fact, the more she'd thought about it after hearing the news, the more she couldn't help the sneaking suspicion that the whole pregnancy thing had been a ploy to chain Brandon down. Olivia's suspicion only grew when, just a few weeks after they were married, they'd told her the pregnancy had ended. It was a terrible thing to think, and yet Olivia couldn't shake the feeling that there probably hadn't ever been a baby— only a trashy girl looking to snag a good-looking man and some financial security.

Okay, she had to admit that Brandon did seem smitten with Meadow. So there had to be *something* hiding behind the revealing clothes, the lack of manners, the self-centeredness and the haze of smoke from her electronic cigarettes. Such a filthy habit, smoking, and so bad for your health.

"I'd rather smoke than be fat," Meadow had said to Olivia when she—politely—brought up the subject.

"And if I didn't do this, I'd be eating all the time instead."

Olivia was a little on the pudgy side. Was that a slur?

Not only did Meadow appear to disapprove of Olivia's looks, she obviously disapproved of her decorating skills. The first thing out of her mouth when she'd seen the lodge had been "Whoa, look at these granny carpets."

Granny carpets indeed! Those rose-patterned carpets were classic, and they'd cost Olivia a small fortune when she first put them in. Plus, they complemented the many antiques Olivia had in the lobby and the guest rooms. Well, all right. So the girl had different tastes. Obviously, she wouldn't know an antique if she tripped over one. But did she have to be so…vocal about them?

She'd hardly raved over the small apartment that Olivia had given her and Brandon when they arrived. She'd walked into the bedroom and frowned. "Where's the closet?"

Olivia had pointed to the antique German pine armoire and said, "This is it. It's a *schrank*."

"A what?"

"For your clothes."

"I'm supposed to fit all my clothes in there?"

Taking in Meadow's skimpy skirt and midriff-bearing top, Olivia had doubted that her clothes would take up much room. "I'm sure Brandon can remodel for you," Olivia had said stiffly.

"I hope so." Meadow had drifted over to the window and looked out. "Wow, that's some view."

At least she'd appreciated something.

"It's gonna be really cool living here," she'd said and

Olivia almost warmed to her until she added, "Once we fix this place up."

"So what do you think of Meadow?" Brandon had asked after he'd brought her home to meet Mom.

By then they were already married. It had been too late to say what she really thought. Instead, she tried a gentler approach. "Wasn't this a little fast? I always thought we'd have a wedding." *I always thought you'd pick someone we wanted you to marry.*

That was when he'd blushed and confessed that they were pregnant. They'd wanted to get married anyway, so what the hell?

What the hell indeed.

"Dear, this isn't like you," James said, bringing Olivia out of her unpleasant reverie. "You're normally so kindhearted and welcoming."

"I've welcomed her," Olivia insisted. She'd given Meadow a home here at the inn with the rest of the family. That was pretty welcoming.

But you haven't exactly taken her in with open arms.

The thought gave her conscience a sharp poke and she squirmed on the sofa. Her cat, Muffin, who'd been happily encamped on her lap, meowed in protest.

"If only she was more like Brooke," Olivia said as if that excused her attitude. "At least Eric got it right." Brooke was refined and well educated and appreciative. She loved the lodge, granny carpets and all. Not only did she truly want to be helpful, she actually was. She and Olivia were on the same wavelength.

James couldn't help smiling at the mention of his daughter. It had been Brooke who was responsible for

James and Olivia meeting. "No one's like Brooke," he said proudly.

"She is one of a kind, just like her daddy."

James, who had spent most of his life playing Santa Claus, was as close to the real deal as a man could come. With his snowy white hair and beard, husky build and caring smile, he embodied the very spirit of Christmas.

"Thank you, my dear," he said and gave her poor, tired foot a pat. "But, getting back to the subject of Meadow, I'm sure she has many redeeming qualities. All you have to do is look for them."

"With a magnifying glass."

"Olivia," he gently chided.

"You're right. I'm just having such a hard time warming to the girl."

"I know. But this is the woman Brandon has chosen."

Olivia sighed. "Yes, and you're right. I need to make more of an effort for his sake."

And she would. Tomorrow was another day.

Another busy day. They'd be decorating the lodge for the holidays. Meadow had been excited over the prospect and assured Olivia she loved to decorate. Hopefully, she'd be better at that than she was at helping serve food. And maybe this time she wouldn't ditch them halfway through the job.

The next morning Eric was knocking on the door of Olivia's little apartment in the lodge. "We ready to do this?" he asked James.

"Yep. Let's start hauling up the holidays."

And there was plenty to haul up from the huge basement storeroom where Olivia kept the holiday decorations—ornaments to go on the eight-foot noble fir they'd purchased for one corner of the lobby, as well as ones for the tree in the dining room, snow globes and red ribbons for the fireplace mantel and, of course, the antique sleigh that would sit right in the center of the lobby. It was a favorite with their guests and people were constantly taking pictures of it. There were stuffed teddy bears and antique dolls to ride in the sleigh, mistletoe to hang in the hallways and silk poinsettias to be placed on the reception desk. Decorating the inn was an all-hands-on-deck day.

"Where's your brother?" Olivia asked as he set down the box of toys for the sleigh.

"He's coming. Meadow's just now getting up. They closed down The Man Cave last night and she's pooped."

So, she'd recovered from her earlier illness. How convenient. "Maybe she's too tired to help," Olivia said hopefully. Playing pool all night could be exhausting.

No such luck. Fifteen minutes later Olivia and Brooke were sorting through the first bin of decorations when Meadow dragged herself into the lobby accompanied by Brandon. She was wearing tight ripped jeans, complemented with a sheer blouse hanging loose over a low-cut red camisole that perfectly matched the patch of hair she'd dyed red. The rest was a color of blond that made Olivia think of light bulbs. Olivia could see the butterfly tattoo Meadow had over her right breast fluttering over the top of the camisole. Her holiday look was completed with a ring through her nose and one through her eyebrow. She made a shocking contrast to

Brooke, with her soft brown hair and tasteful clothes. Now almost eight months pregnant, Brooke was wearing a long gray sweater accented with a blue silk scarf over her black maternity leggings and gray ankle boots. Meadow even looked like a total mismatch with Brandon, who was in jeans and a casual button-down black plaid shirt.

"I feel like shit," she confessed. "I think those fish tacos were off." She shook her head. "Now I know what they mean when they say 'toss your tacos.'"

The queen of refinement this girl was not. To think Brandon could have had sweet little Bailey Black if only he'd gotten with the program. Bailey had carried a torch for him for years. Too late now. She was happily married. And Brandon was…trapped. So were the rest of them.

You're going to have to make the best of it, Olivia reminded herself. Her son loved his new wife. He'd obviously seen something in her. She probably would, too. If she looked harder.

James and Eric arrived in the lobby, bearing more decorations. "You're just in time," Eric told his brother. "You can help me haul in the sleigh."

Brandon nodded and followed the men back out.

Olivia pasted a smile on her face. "Well, girls, let's get started."

"All right. This is going to be fun," Meadow said eagerly and opened a bin.

Eager and excited to help—that was commendable. And surely this was bound to go better than Thanksgiving dinner.

Meadow pulled out a pink ribbon ball holding a sprig of silk mistletoe and made a face. "What the hell is this?"

"It's mistletoe," Olivia explained.

"Mistletoe." Meadow said it as if it were a foreign language.

"You've heard of mistletoe, right?" Brooke prompted and Meadow shook her head.

Both Olivia and Brooke stared at her in amazement. "So, what is it?"

"You hang it up and then when you catch someone under it, you kiss him," Brooke explained.

Meadow shook her head. "Why do you need a plant for that? If you want to kiss a guy, just kiss him!"

Good Lord. The child was a complete philistine.

Brooke smiled. "It's a fun little tradition people enjoy."

"Whatever," Meadow said, unimpressed.

She was impressed with the sleigh, though. "Wow, that's epic." The minute the men had set it down, she climbed into it and tossed Brandon her cell phone. "Take my picture, babe," she commanded and struck a rapper-girl pose, complete with the weird finger thing and the pout.

An older couple was walking through the lobby, and the husband stopped to enjoy the moment. "Now, there's my kind of Christmas present," he joked.

His wife, not seeing the humor, grabbed his arm and got him moving again. "Tacky," she hissed.

Meadow flipped her off and Olivia's cheeks heated. This girl was like a puzzle piece that had wound up in the wrong box. However were they going to get her to fit in?

Dear Santa, please bring me an extra dose of patience. I'm going to need it.

Sienna was still smiling when she went into work on Friday, remembering her fun evening of feasting, laughter and dancing. While the day had gotten off to a bad start, happily, it had ended on a positive note. And now she got to go to a job she loved. She had so much fun at Mountain Escape Books that her time there never felt like work, even when things were at their busiest.

The store was especially busy this day. In addition to shoppers enjoying Black Friday bargains, Muriel Sterling was there, signing copies of her newest book, *A Guide to Happy Holidays*.

Sienna took advantage of her employee discount and bought one. "I hope I can write a book someday," she confessed to Muriel. *I want to be just like you when I grow up. Gush, gush.*

"We all have a story to tell," Muriel said.

"I don't know what mine would be."

"You have lots of time to figure it out," Muriel assured her. "You're still young."

"I keep telling Muriel to write a book about Icicle Falls," said Pat, who was stacking more books on the table where Muriel was seated. "Maybe you'll be the one to do that, Sienna."

"Yeah," put in Dot Morrison, one of Muriel's friends who'd come in to purchase a book and offer moral support. "Or...why don't you write a juicy novel with lots of sex? And a murder. You can set it right here in Icicle Falls."

"If you need characters for a book, there's your girl," Pat teased, making Dot frown.

Known for her crazy sweatshirts, Dot was definitely a character. Today's offering said Apologies to Anyone I Haven't Offended. Please Be Patient. I'll Get to You Shortly.

"Murder in Icicle Falls?" Muriel gave a mock shudder.

Dot shrugged. "Yeah, I guess that wouldn't work. Who would you murder?"

"Your neighbor Mr. Cratchett?" Pat suggested to Sienna.

"Well…" Sienna regretted having told Pat about her problem neighbor. Complaining to family was one thing. Complaining to other people was plain old badmouthing. Although if anyone deserved to be badmouthed, it was Cratchett.

Dot gave a snort. "That old grump. Don't mind him. He's lived here forever. Comes into my restaurant every once in a while. Never leaves my gals a tip. You could bump him off in a book. Put him in my place and have someone slip poison in his coffee. The way he gripes about it, you'd think it *was* poisoned."

"There's probably more to Mr. Cratchett than what you're seeing," Muriel said.

"As in, you can't judge a book by its cover," said Pat.

"Not even in a bookstore," Muriel added with a smile.

Sienna had seen enough of Mr. Cratchett and she didn't want to read any further.

"We shouldn't be too hard on the poor man. Maybe he's got a good reason to be so grouchy. He's a widower, after all," Muriel said in Cratchett's defense.

This produced another snort from Dot. "I've been a widow for years. You don't see me whining about it." She shook her head. "Men. They're the weaker sex."

At that moment a member of the weaker sex came into the store, needing help finding the latest Suzanne Selfors book for his daughter, and that broke up the confab as Sienna went to help him and Pat moved to ring up a sale.

Business remained brisk for the next two hours, with townspeople popping in to get signed copies of Muriel's book. Her daughters Samantha and Cecily both came by, bringing treats from their sister Bailey's tearoom. And Vance Fish, one of the town's older single men, stopped in to say hi to Muriel. He owned a bookstore in Seattle but he always came by Pat's when she had a special event going on.

"We indie booksellers have to stick together," he said.

While he was there, two women came in looking for the latest Vanessa Valentine book. Sienna had heard a rumor that Vance Fish himself was really Vanessa Valentine. She'd worked up her nerve to ask him once. He'd laughed and replied, "Do I look like a Vanessa Valentine to you?" So much for that rumor.

Muriel's book signing ended, but before she left the store, she handed out invitations to her ladies' Christmas tea the next Sunday afternoon.

"It's a tradition," Pat told Sienna. "She does this

every year for her girlfriends and daughters, so make sure you line up your cousin to watch Leo, because you won't want to miss seeing Muriel's place all fixed up for the holidays."

She wouldn't want to miss seeing Muriel's place, period.

The rest of the day sped by and before Sienna knew it, it was quitting time. She picked up her car from Swede's Garage, where they'd put on those snow tires she'd been postponing purchasing. Then she fetched Leo from Rita's house, which was his home away from home when Sienna was at the bookstore. It was a good arrangement. Rita worked nights at Zelda's, so she was home during the day and was happy to have Leo around, as he kept little Linda entertained. Plus, the price was right: free—always a good thing for a single mom who had stretched her budget to buy her house. Child support from the creep only went so far.

"How was your day?" Sienna asked, hugging her son.

"I helped Tía Rita make cookies," he told her.

"You did?"

He nodded eagerly.

"He's very good at stirring," Rita confirmed.

"That's nice to hear. You're a good helper," Sienna said and mussed his thick, dark hair. "Come on, handsome, let's go home and make some hamburgers."

"Hamburgers, yes!" Leo cheered and raced for the door.

"Why don't you let Tito watch him tonight and you come to Zelda's for a while?" Rita suggested. "There's a new band playing in the bar."

"I'm too tired," Sienna said. "We had a busy day at the bookstore."

"Tired," Rita echoed in disgust. "You're too young to be tired. You're only thirty-five."

"Well, tonight I feel like I'm eighty-five. And my feet hurt."

Rita frowned. "You gotta get out, *chica*. You need a life. You need a man."

"I have a life with Leo, a perfectly good life."

Rita rolled her eyes. "All men aren't like your ex, you know. Look at Tito."

"Clone him and then we'll talk," Sienna said and followed Leo out to the car. The weather was still cold and the roads slushy from the earlier snowstorm. More snow was predicted for late that night and she was ready to go home and get tucked in before everything got icy.

It was an exciting Friday night, hamburgers followed by Leo's favorite movie, *Cars*. They'd watched that movie so many times she could say every line of dialogue right along with Lightning McQueen and Strip Weathers. Yes, this was what her life boiled down to— work and Pixar movies.

And hamburgers and time with her sweet son, who still thought it was cool to snuggle on the couch with Mom and watch an animated movie. So there wasn't a man in her life. She could live with that.

A good thing, since she was probably going to have to. Lonely after her divorce, Sienna had looked for a good man, but in the end she hadn't found anyone worth keeping. There'd been Manny, who'd proved to be more of a child than Leo, wanting nothing more out of life than to go dancing and work on his car. He'd yelled at her son when Leo was assisting him in changing the oil and accidentally dropped the oil pan, calling him *estúpido*. That had been the end of Manny. Gregory had liked Leo just fine…as long as he didn't have to hang out with him. Gregory hadn't lasted long, either. Those had been the best of the bunch. Sadly, there weren't a lot of men out there who wanted to take on a woman with a kid, especially a woman with a kid who had some challenges.

And Leo did have challenges. While most kids his age were reading small chapter books, he was struggling with simple words like *cat* and *bat*. He still didn't know all his colors. Everything was either red, blue or yellow. And math completely overwhelmed him. Trying to master new information often drove him to tears and tantrums. So when the men Sienna dated got a look at life with Leo—when they realized every day wasn't going to be smooth sailing—they bolted.

But what had she expected? Her own husband hadn't been able to cope. "I can't deal with this anymore," he'd said only six months after Leo had finally been tested and diagnosed with a learning disability. She'd tried to convince Carlos that, together, they could deal with anything, but her pep talk hadn't done any good. "I'm sorry, Sienna. I want a divorce."

Sienna hadn't known which had been worse, his initial harshness and impatience with Leo or the ensuing coldness to the little boy, who only wanted his love.

Well, new town, new start. She and Leo would manage fine on their own, and even though she missed her parents and brothers, she knew she'd done the right thing coming here. She was happy with her new job and her new friends. And, most important, Leo was happy with his new teacher. Really, the only fly on the frosting was her neighbor.

After Leo went to bed, she settled in with Muriel Sterling's new book. *There's something about the holidays*, Muriel wrote.

> The wonderful message of redemption, the time with friends, the treats, the sights and sounds and smells.
>
> But perhaps you're finding it difficult to experience the joy of the holiday season. I hope my suggestions will help you find your way to a wonderful Christmas that's not only merry but also meaningful. My wish for you is that no matter who is in your life, no matter what is going on, you'll be able to make the days merry and bright—for yourself and others, too!

A very noble sentiment, Sienna thought. And she intended to do just that. No matter how many unpleasant encounters she had with old, cranky Cratchett, she was going to find a way to have a merry Christmas.

Chapter Two

Giving is one of the joys of the season. Be enthusiastic whether you're on the giving or the receiving end of the gift.

—Muriel Sterling, *A Guide to Happy Holidays*

Muriel Sterling-Wittman often met her old friend Arnie Amundsen for breakfast at Pancake Haus. If Olivia and James Claussen weren't busy, they'd usually join them. Dot Morrison, the owner of the restaurant, frequently sat in on the conversation for a while, too.

A flood of tourists was in town for the long holiday weekend and the snow, and the restaurant was packed this Saturday morning with people enjoying German waffles, pancakes and eggs. The smell of coffee and sugary treats greeted Muriel as she stepped inside. Voices and laughter came at her from all sides, telling her this was, indeed, the place to be.

"He's back there," Dot said with a nod toward a back booth as she hurried past Muriel to pour coffee for a table of young women.

Yes, Muriel could see him. All by himself, he stood out in the mob of families and couples.

She'd known Arnie most of her life and he hadn't changed much since high school. He was still as thin as he'd been back then and still wearing the same style of glasses. About the only change was a few more wrinkles and a heavy salting of gray in what was left of his once-sandy-colored hair.

Of course, Muriel's hair was now heavily salted as well, but she wasn't letting anyone know that. Thank heaven for her stylist at Sleeping Lady Salon.

He'd been watching for her and waved discreetly when they made eye contact. Her late husband would have stood and called her over, but that had been Waldo, larger-than-life. Arnie was...well, Arnie. Quiet, soft-spoken, unremarkable. But solid, steady and sweet.

And a terrible dresser. She took in the Christmas-red sweater he was wearing over his shirt and the red bow tie. She'd bought him neckties for Christmas the last few years as a subtle hint and he'd worn them to please her, but in the end, he always reverted to his bow tie addiction. The red sweater didn't do much for him, either. He'd look so much better in blue. It would show off his blue eyes. Maybe she'd give him a blue sweater for Christmas this year.

He greeted her with a smile as she slid into the booth, seating herself opposite him, and informed her that he'd taken the liberty of ordering her usual cheese-and-mushroom omelet.

"No James and Olivia today, I figured," he said as he took a sip of his coffee.

"You're right. She's busy at the lodge. How was your Thanksgiving?"

"All right," he said with a shrug. "At my sister's again this year."

Sometimes Muriel felt downright guilty about Arnie's lackluster life. He'd loved her since they were teenagers. Sadly, she just hadn't felt the same about him. Other men had come along to steal her heart. Still, Arnie had remained her steadfast friend, seeing her through the loss of two husbands. Arnie was a dear.

"How was the gathering of the Sterling clan?" he asked.

"Chaotic, noisy as always."

"In other words, a good time was had by all."

"Yes, that sums it up," she said with a smile.

Dot appeared with her coffee carafe. "I hope you two aren't in a hurry today," she said as she filled Muriel's mug. "As you can see, we're slammed."

"That's okay, we're not in a hurry," Muriel assured her. "Unless... Arnie?"

"I can stay as long as you want me to," he said.

What a sweetie. It was a shame to see such a nice man single.

"Good," Dot said and hurried off.

They filled in the time with small talk as they waited for their orders. Arnie wanted to know how Muriel's book signing had gone. "Sorry I missed it," he added.

"You've attended more than your share of signings," she said.

"Yeah, but I like to support you."

"You're the most supportive friend I have," she told him, and it made him beam with pleasure.

Talk turned to plans for the holidays. "I've booked a cruise," he announced.

"Really? Where are you going?"

"To Germany."

"Germany, how lovely."

She'd always dreamed of going there. That had yet to happen. With her first husband, Stephen, she'd been busy raising a family, keeping things together on the home front while he ran the family chocolate business. She and her second husband had talked about taking a trip but then Waldo had been diagnosed with Lewy body dementia, and that had been that. She couldn't help feeling a little wistful. She would've loved to have seen some of those German towns after which Icicle Falls had been modeled.

"It's a river cruise and we'll be stopping at all the famous Christmas markets—Nuremberg, Bamberg, Heidelberg."

Heidelberg. She'd always wanted to see the castle ruins.

He pulled out the brochure with its glossy pictures of outdoor markets, smiling couples leaning on the railing of the river barge, lit-up cities. It all looked so romantic.

"Joe, from the Yakima branch of Cascade Mutual, invited me. He had a group from the bank going and a couple of them had to cancel at the last minute. I was able to book their staterooms."

"How fun! Good for you," Muriel said, impressed. Arnie was rarely spontaneous and always careful with his money. It was nice to see him taking a step toward living large.

"Actually, I'd like you to go with me. You'd be back in time for Christmas with the family," he hurried to add.

"With you?" she repeated. Like a couple? But they weren't a couple. They were simply friends. Good friends, dear friends. But that was all. She'd never thought of Arnie as anything else. Besides, at this point in her life, after being widowed twice, she had no intention of starting anything with anyone. "Oh, Arnie, I couldn't."

His smile flipped upside down.

"It's a lot of money," she explained, trying to soften the blow of her refusal.

"Muriel, you don't think I'd ask you and then expect you to pay," he said, shocked.

She couldn't let him spend that kind of money on her even though she knew he had it to spend. "It's sweet of you, but…I can't." She'd feel like she was using him. He'd get his hopes up. It would get awkward.

Dot had returned with more coffee to tide them over as they waited for their food. "Can't what?" she asked, having caught the tail end of Muriel's rejection. "Arnie, you look like you've got indigestion and your food hasn't even come yet. What's going on here, you two?"

"Arnie's taking a river cruise in Germany," Muriel explained.

"Go, Arnie," Dot said encouragingly.

"I wanted Muriel to come with me," he said, and Muriel felt the weight of his disappointment settling over her. Their waitress arrived with their breakfasts and he moved his plate away.

Oh, dear. Muriel felt awful about upsetting him. "Arnie, I'm sorry."

"I know how much you always wanted to see Germany," he said, his expression wistful.

"I do." *But not with you.* She bit her lip.

"Seriously, you don't want to go?" Dot asked, and she and Arnie exchanged glances. Muriel, the ingrate.

"I have too much going on. The new book and everything," Muriel added feebly. It was a flimsy excuse and they all knew it.

"I guess I should have checked with you before I bought the tickets, but I needed to act fast," Arnie said. Then he added, "I was sure you'd be all over something like this."

"You should still go," Muriel said, not wanting to be responsible for spoiling her old friend's good time, not to mention being responsible for him losing money. At such a late date, he'd never be able to get a refund.

Maybe she should go, if only not to have his money go to waste. She'd make it clear that they were going only as friends...

"Yeah, Arnie," put in Dot. "That's a once-in-a-lifetime trip." She shook her head at Muriel. "You're crazy not to go, Muriel. I'd be all over that like white on rice."

Now there was an idea. "Maybe *you* should go," Muriel suggested. Dot was single, Arnie was single—they could become travel buddies.

Except now she'd just put Arnie on the spot. She looked to see how he was taking her suggestion.

He did blink in surprise, but before he could say anything, Dot settled herself next to Muriel and set down
her carafe. "What do you say, Arnie? Would you like
some company?"

"Well," he said slowly, the gears turning as he
worked to keep up with this sudden change in his
plans.

Now Muriel regretted her impulsive suggestion.
How could poor Arnie be honest about whether or not
he wanted to bring Dot along with her sitting right
there?

"How much did that extra stateroom cost? I'll write
you a check today," Dot said.

"So you're serious?" Arnie asked.

"Sure. Why not?"

"Well," he said, hesitating. He was probably looking
for a polite way to get out of this, the same as Muriel
had just tried to do with him.

"We'll have fun," Dot assured him. "Unlike Muriel,
I can get away for a couple of weeks.

"We can do our Christmas shopping over there.
Talk about ringing in the holidays. This is a great idea,
Arnie!"

Yes, it was, wasn't it? Muriel looked at the excitement
in Dot's eyes and suddenly felt the stirrings of regret.
Maybe she should have said yes...

"I thought so," he said. The look he gave Muriel
showed how disappointed he was that she hadn't taken
him up on his offer.

"You know, I've always wanted to see Germany,"
said Dot.

"Same here," Arnie said.

"Well, then, let's do it. You only live once. Anyway, I bet you can't get your money back at this point, so you may as well go and let me pick up the tab for the other half."

He nodded thoughtfully. "Good point."

"So, what do you say? Shall we see how the other half lives?"

Her last argument about saving some money seemed to have tipped the scale and he gave a decided nod. "Why not?"

Arnie's smile returned and suddenly he was digging into his pancakes, and he and Dot were deep in discussion about their upcoming adventure. How much currency to convert into euros, flight departures, how early they needed to get to the airport. Did either of them have a window seat on the plane?

"There's a whole group of people going," Arnie told Dot, "so we'll be partying our way across Germany."

"I like the sound of that," she said.

The discussion continued. What should they pack? What was the weather doing over in Germany? They'd have to try a real German schnitzel so they could see how the schnitzel served at Schwangau measured up. In all their excitement, neither urged Muriel to change her mind and come along.

Arnie chuckled as Dot demonstrated what little German she knew, holding up two fingers and saying, *"Zwei bier, bitte."* Oh, yes, Dot would be the life of the party. In fact, it looked like the party was already starting right here in Pancake Haus.

Muriel smiled and nodded as the two continued their conversation. Of course, she was happy for them. Arnie would have a companion on his trip and Dot would enjoy a well-deserved vacation. She hadn't taken one in years. They'd both have a lovely time together and Muriel could be relieved that she hadn't spoiled his vacation by turning him down. Yes, she'd been positively inspired to suggest Dot go in her place.

Arnie certainly hadn't mourned being turned down for long. Muriel's omelet suddenly tasted a little off. She set down her fork.

"Something wrong with your breakfast?" Dot asked, pointing to the half-consumed meal.

"No, I guess I'm not very hungry," Muriel said. She looked at her watch. "You know, I should get going. My new Christmas tree is due to arrive this morning."

"Oh, okay," Arnie said. "I'm sorry things didn't work out for you to go, Muriel."

"Yeah. This is exactly the kind of trip you'd love," Dot said.

It was true—this was her dream vacation, and she'd been so quick to set boundaries with Arnie she hadn't taken much time to think of the experience she'd be missing. Maybe she should reconsider and come along.

"But oh, well. We'll be thinking of you," Dot said.

Would they? Muriel wanted to say, "Wait, I've changed my mind. I'm coming!" Now it seemed too late, as if she'd be crashing the party.

Maybe Dot had more than a friendly interest in Arnie and wanted him all to herself. She certainly managed to find time to join them whenever Muriel and Arnie came in for breakfast. Now here she was, with the restaurant packed and her waitresses running in circles, sitting around happily making plans for an international getaway with him.

Well, if that was the case, good for Dot. She'd worked hard, running her business and raising her daughter single-handedly. Arnie had been thrifty all his life and spent very little money on himself. It was time they both got out and had some fun. Good for them.

She said her goodbyes and made her way home to her little cottage next to Ed and Pat York's vineyard feeling a little less cheerful than she had an hour ago.

She'd always wanted to see the vineyards in Germany.

You had your chance. Reminding herself didn't exactly restore her cheery mood.

But then she pulled up in front of the cottage and was cheered by the sight of a big box sitting on her front porch. Wonderful! Her new artificial tree had arrived. Arnie and Dot were off to Germany but she would enjoy life here in Icicle Falls as the holidays approached. And she had a new tree. A woman could always find something to be happy about, she told herself as she hauled it into the house.

When she'd seen the tree on an online site, she'd hardly been able to believe her eyes. It was beautiful, with lots of full branches. And so realistic looking. A perfect replacement for her old, tired tree, which she'd taken to the Kindness Cupboard. On sale and with free shipping, too. Of course she'd purchased it immediately. It would be the perfect centerpiece at her annual holiday tea party.

Filled with anticipation, she opened the box and lifted out...a sad, bald poor excuse for a tree. What on earth? She looked inside the box, hoping to find, what? A note that said "Ha, ha. Your real tree is coming"?

"I've been had," she muttered. She stood the tree up against the living room wall, feeling cranky. This was not going to work. No way could she display this pitiful excuse for a tree. It was an insult to Christmas, not to mention an insult to trees.

It served her right. She should have purchased her new tree from Ivy Bohn over at Christmas Haus. Well, it wasn't too late. She dialed Ivy's shop.

Ivy answered, sounding almost breathless. Hardly surprising considering how busy the shop got this time of year.

"Ivy, I won't keep you long," Muriel promised. "But I'm wondering if you have any artificial trees left."

"Gee, I'm sorry, Muriel. Our last one just walked out the door."

"Already?"

"I know. Go figure."

Muriel looked at her ugly tree and frowned. "Will you be getting more in?"

"I hope so, but I'm not sure. We've been having some problems with our supplier."

Muriel had experienced a problem with her supplier, too.

"I'm sorry. If you'd told me you wanted a tree, I'd have set one aside for you. But you're usually all set for

Christmas so far ahead of time—I'm surprised to hear you don't already have one."

Ivy was right. This was definitely unlike her. Christmas was hands down her favorite holiday. She'd pull out all her favorite cookie recipes and bake up a storm, putting together gift boxes of cookies for all the Sweet Dreams employees, always making sure to bake Arnie's favorite fruitcake cookies for him. She loved to entertain and always threw herself into decorating. In her mind, setting a festive backdrop for gatherings was a must. She was sure that beautiful surroundings sent a subliminal message that life was beautiful and being together was worth rejoicing in.

"That's okay," she told Ivy. "I'll work something out."

"You can always get a live tree."

Yes, she could but, much as she loved that wonderful fragrance, she preferred an artificial tree that she could put up right after Thanksgiving and leave up until after New Year's Day. Besides, getting a live tree home and set up wasn't a job she liked to tackle alone, and she hated to bother the kids.

She thanked Ivy and ended the call and returned her attention to her ugly tree. "Someone didn't spend much time or love on you," she informed it. Poor Ugly Tree.

What to do now? She absently ran a finger along one of its branches. Maybe, with enough ornaments… She had three boxes of silver balls that she'd purchased on sale the year before and some silver garlands. And she could pull out those pinecone-shaped lights, buy a few red cardinals at Christmas Haus. Maybe she could fix up her ugly little tree and make it into something pretty. Maybe it was salvageable. It was worth a try.

Always make the most of what you have, even if it isn't much. She'd said that in one of her books. It was time to take her own advice.

"We have a week to get you gorgeous," she told her ugly tree. "Let's see what we can do."

She could almost hear the poor thing saying, "Yes, please. Don't give up on me."

She'd barely determined her course of action when one of her grandmother's favorite sayings came to mind. *You can't make a silk purse out of a sow's ear.* Maybe her grandmother was wrong. Maybe you could. She certainly hoped so.

Her daughter Samantha wasn't so sure she'd succeed. She dropped by later with Muriel's three-year-old granddaughter, Rose. "That's the most pitiful tree I've ever seen," Samantha said.

"Did you go to the woods, Grammy?" Rose asked, cocking her head and staring at the tree.

"No, sweetie. This is a pretend tree," Muriel explained.

The child wrinkled her nose. "It's ugly."

"It's not pretending very well," Samantha agreed. "Is that the one you found online?"

Muriel sighed and nodded. "The picture looked much better."

"Ivy's probably got some."

"I called. She's sold-out already."

"Wow, not even December 1 and there's a run on trees. Do you want us to cut you one when we go to the tree farm?"

Freshly cut, the tree would last. Her son-in-law would set it up for her. The whole house would smell woodsy.

Except Samantha and Blake weren't going to put up their tree for another two weeks and Muriel wanted hers up for her party. "No, that's okay. I think I can make this little tree look good. Anyway, it doesn't seem right to toss the poor thing without at least giving it a chance."

Samantha rolled her eyes. "It's not like it's got feelings, Mom."

Yes, it was silly, but somehow Muriel felt like there was a principle at stake here. "I can dress it up."

"Well, if anyone can do it, you can," Samantha said. "If you change your mind, though, the offer still stands."

"I won't, but thanks." It was game on now. Somehow, she was going to make that tree lovely.

And maybe if she stayed busy with the tree and all the other Christmas preparations she loved, she wouldn't have time to think about Arnie and Dot having fun in Germany without her. Maybe.

Chapter Three

Look for the good in everyone and every day, and
you can't help but be happy.
      —Muriel Sterling, *A Guide to Happy Holidays*

Come the afternoon of Muriel's party her tree was, indeed, beautiful. The bald spots had been filled in with
the ornaments she already had as well as some elegant
filigreed silver bells she'd found at Christmas Haus. The
red cardinals were a brilliant addition, if she did say so
herself. They added a splash of vivid color, backed up
by the pastel colors of the lit pinecones. The silver garlands finished it all off nicely. Poor Ugly Tree was now
a thing of beauty. It just went to show you what lavish-
ing a little love could accomplish.

She checked her makeup and adjusted her long green
scarf, then got busy setting out her refreshments: red
velvet cupcakes, peppermint fudge from Sweet Dreams,
brie cheese baked in puff pastry, crudités, prosciutto-
wrapped asparagus and her favorite holiday punch. And
of course, her signature chocolate-mint tea. She started

some Christmas music playing, lit her fresh balsam-scented candle and she was ready to go.

Her dear friend Pat York was the first to arrive, along with Dot. "Good Lord," Dot said, taking in the table centerpiece of red Christmas balls nestled among greens and the array of red candles and pine boughs marching across the mantelpiece. "Martha Stewart lives. Sometimes I really don't like you."

Muriel was used to Dot's sense of humor. She merely smiled and took Dot's coat.

Her daughters came in one big group, bringing laughter and plates of food. "Everything looks wonderful, Mom," said Cecily, her middle child.

Samantha nodded in the direction of the tree. "I should have known you'd pull it off. The tree looks great."

More people began to arrive—Pat's new employee, Sienna Moreno; Charley Masters, her daughters' good friend and owner of Zelda's restaurant; Beth Mallow; Cass Masters; Stacy Thomas; Maddy Donaldson; and of course, Muriel's other close friend, Olivia Claussen—and Muriel's little cottage began to hum with conversation.

"Your tree is gorgeous," Olivia raved as the women settled in the living room with drinks and plates of goodies.

"You should have seen it when she first got it," Samantha said and shook her head. "It was pathetic."

"It was pretty sad," Muriel admitted. "But I hated to simply get rid of it."

"I would have," Dot said. "That looks like way too much work. I'm not even bothering with a tree this year."

"You have to put up a tree," Olivia said, shocked.

"No, I don't. I'm old," Dot retorted. "Besides, I'll be gone for a good part of December."

"Where are you going?" asked Beth.

"I'm off to Germany," Dot said. "Arnie Amundsen and I are doing one of those Christmas cruises."

"You and Arnie?" Pat looked surprised.

"Yep. I'm moving in on Muriel's man," Dot teased.

Muriel was aware of all three of her daughters looking at her curiously. *Arnie didn't ask you?* She smiled to show she was perfectly all right with this. Arnie needed a life.

"When did you and Arnie become a couple?" Olivia asked, and she, too, shot a look in Muriel's direction.

"Since Arnie had an extra stateroom," Dot said. "We're just going as pals. There's a whole group of us. It's going to be a blast."

"Wow," said Beth. "I'm jealous."

Muriel was *not* jealous. She forced her smile to stay in place.

"By the time I get back, there'll be no point in bothering with a tree," Dot continued. "I'll just come over and enjoy Muriel's if I need a fix. I'll bring my own punch, though. This needs booze."

"If you drink and drive, Tilda is bound to catch you," Olivia told her.

"That'd make the paper," Pat joked. "Cop Locks Up Pain-in-the-Neck Mom for the Holidays."

"Hey, room service and no cleaning?" Dot retorted. "Sounds good to me."

Pat shook her head and returned her attention to Muriel. "Anyway, the tree is fabulous."

"Thank you. I'm glad I didn't give up on poor Ugly Tree," Muriel said. She was also glad that the conversation had moved on to a new topic.

"I guess you just proved that anything can be made pretty if you put in the effort," Pat said.

Cass shook her head. "I don't know. I've had some cakes that I had to completely give up on."

"But I bet they still tasted good," Muriel said to her.

"True," Cass admitted.

"I think a few little flaws can add charm," said Stacy Thomas. "You wouldn't believe how much fine china I sell in my shop even if it has a chip. The Royal Albert Old Country Roses pattern is always in demand."

"Do you think it's the same with people?" Maddy Donaldson mused. "Because when it comes to charm, my mother-in-law still has a long way to go."

"I bet most of us have people in our lives who are a lot like Ugly Tree, maybe not so lovable sometimes," Muriel said. "It can be hard to see anything good in them. But, really, don't you think there's something good in all of us?"

"No," Dot said, and Muriel frowned at her. Honestly, sometimes Dot could be so...irritating. What had Muriel subjected poor Arnie to?

"I don't know," Sienna confessed. "I'm having a hard time seeing anything good in my neighbor. I think he might be the meanest man in Icicle Falls."

"Yes, but what made him that way?" Muriel countered. "Sometimes people go through hard times and it takes the shine off their smiles."

"He has no smile," Sienna said.

"I guess that's when you've got to walk a mile in his snow boots," put in Bailey, and Muriel beamed approvingly at her youngest daughter.

"No, thanks," Sienna said with a shudder.

Olivia sighed. "All this talk of seeing the good in people has really convicted me of the bad attitude I've had lately."

"What are you talking about? You never have a bad attitude." Dot scoffed. "You need bad-attitude lessons."

Olivia shook her head. "Not where some people are concerned."

"Oh," Dot said slowly as realization dawned.

Olivia didn't have to say any more. Her close friends knew exactly to whom she was referring. Poor Olivia. Sadly, a woman had no control over who her children married. All she could do was hope and pray they used good sense when they picked. Fortunately for Muriel, all three of her daughters had.

"I'm sure you'll find something you can appreciate in your new family member. And under your tutelage, she's bound to turn into a wonderful woman," Muriel said in an effort to encourage her.

Olivia sighed. "If only it was as easy to fix up a person as it is a tree."

"People often respond to how we see them," Dot said, surprising Muriel with her insight. Dot was such a character that it was sometimes hard to remember that she had some depth to her. She was older than Muriel and she, too, had racked up a good share of life experiences. Like Muriel, she was a widow twice over.

"Good point," Pat said. "Maybe this holiday season we should all look for people who need a little extra love and reach out to them."

Dot rolled her eyes. "You sound like a greeting card commercial."

"Not a bad idea, though," said Cecily.

"Yeah," Samantha agreed. "I can think of a certain supplier who could use some buttering up."

"I don't think there's enough butter in the whole state of Washington for Mr. Cratchett," Sienna said with a frown.

"I'm not sure we should be thinking in terms of buttering people up," Muriel said.

"Muriel's right," said Pat. "I'm talking about being kind simply for the sake of being kind, seeing the best in people no matter what."

When had all of Muriel's friends gotten so wise? And why hadn't she thought to suggest that? "I think it's a lovely idea," she said.

"Although I'm not sure how easy it will be to execute, at least for me," Pat said. "The only person I can think of is Harvey Wood, and it's hard to see the good in a landlord who keeps raising your rent and never fixes anything in the building. If the toilet in the employee bathroom makes it through to the New Year, I'll be amazed."

"Maybe if you give him some Sweet Dreams chocolates, he'll get with the program and get you a new toilet," said Dot.

Pat raised an eyebrow. "Do you really believe that?"

"No. Harvey's a cheapskate."

"I know who we should work on showing kindness to," Cecily said to her sister.

Samantha looked at her warily. "Please don't say who I think you're going to say."

"Priscilla Castro?" Bailey guessed and snickered.

"There's an ugly tree," Samantha muttered.

"Who's Priscilla Castro?" asked Sienna.

"She runs the office at city hall. Every year she does her best to hold up permits for the chocolate festival," Cecily explained. "I'm afraid she and Sam have been rivals ever since high school."

"She was a mean girl in high school," Samantha added. "Nothing's really changed."

"Except her name," Bailey added. "Her friends used to call her Prissy. Everyone else called her Pissy. It kind of stuck."

"*Pissy* definitely suits her better," Samantha said.

"She hasn't had much success in life," Muriel reminded her daughters. "I'm sure that has a lot to do with it."

"I have my hands full working on my own success. I don't have time to help Pissy find hers," Samantha replied, obviously not on board with the idea.

"I think she needs love," Cecily mused. "She's been pretty bitter since her divorce."

"If I'd been married to Pissy, I'd have left, too," Samantha said.

"Samantha," Muriel scolded.

"Okay, then see what you can do," Samantha told Cecily, dumping the problem of Priscilla in her sister's lap.

"I just might," Cecily replied with a grin.

"What if we all tried to see people in a whole new light?" Muriel suggested.

Dot rolled her eyes. "Sorry, I'll miss it."

Muriel frowned. Wasn't it time for Dot to leave?

"We can start with looking for something beautiful in you," Pat said, pointing a finger at her.

"I'm already a thing of beauty," Dot said and struck a pose.

"Well," Olivia said, "I'm up to giving it a shot. I definitely need to work on my attitude."

"When it comes right down to it, we can all use some work on our attitudes," Muriel told her. Herself included. Hers toward Dot was certainly shifting into ugly gear, which was pathetic considering the fact that she'd suggested Dot take her place on the cruise.

"I know mine sucks," Sienna admitted.

"You've got a challenge," Pat said to her.

"It *is* the season for peace on earth, goodwill toward men," Muriel added. *And irritating friends.*

"So—" Pat raised her punch cup "—here's to the ugly trees in our lives. Let's see what we can do with them."

"To the ugly trees," repeated Olivia.

"To ugly trees," the others echoed.

Conversation moved on and so did the afternoon. Toward the end of the party Muriel drew a name to win a small gift basket she'd put together, containing a candle, a box of Sweet Dreams chocolates and a copy of a Christmas novel by RaeAnne Thayne.

Sienna was thrilled when she won it. "Thank you so much," she said to Muriel before she left. "My son is going to love helping me eat the candy and I know I'll enjoy the book. I'm reading your new one right now. Maybe it will inspire me to have a better attitude about my neighbor," she added.

"I hope it will," Muriel said. "Next time you see him, think of my tree."

The other guests began to depart soon after Sienna. "Great party," Dot said as she and Muriel hugged each other. "Be sure to tell me what you want me to bring you from Germany."

Muriel set aside her earlier irritation. One of Dot's sterling qualities was her generosity. "I will. And you have fun."

"Oh, I will. I'll be sure to drink some *glühwein* for all of you," Dot said to the group in general.

"Don't drink too much and fall off the boat," Samantha teased.

"Not me," Dot said and then, with a wave, was out the door.

Olivia was the last of Muriel's friends to leave. "I guess I should get home and try to figure out where to start with my own little ugly tree. I do hope this idea works and I can start seeing the good in her. I know I need to, for Brandon's sake."

Muriel hugged her. "You will."

With the last friend gone, Muriel joined her daughters, who were in no hurry to leave and still relaxing in her living room. It was only the four of them now, and much as Muriel enjoyed entertaining her friends, moments like this were what she cherished most, when it was just her and her girls.

"Poor Olivia," said Samantha.

"Meadow is pretty tacky," Bailey said. "But then, Brandon never did have the best taste in women."

"Otherwise he'd have picked you," said Samantha.

Cecily shook her head. "They were never a match."

Cecily, who had an uncanny gift for seeing who should be with whom, would know, thought Muriel. Although it had certainly taken her long enough to figure out who her own ideal man was.

"Speaking of matches," said Samantha, "what's with Dot and Arnie going to Germany? Why didn't he ask you, Mom?"

Muriel could feel her cheeks warming. She picked up her cup and took a sip of tea. "He did. I turned him down."

"You did?" Samantha looked at her as if she were crazy. Maybe she was.

"Why, Mom? You guys would have had a great time," Bailey said.

"It didn't seem right," Muriel explained. "I didn't want to raise false hopes."

"He's had false hopes for years," Samantha pointed out. "So what's the difference if he's having them here or in Germany?"

"The difference is that I'd have been taking advantage of him."

"Mom, taking advantage of someone is doing things with an ulterior motive, letting them always do things for you without getting anything in return," Samantha argued. "You and Arnie don't have that kind of relationship. You're always making him cookies or feeding him dinner."

"Poor Arnie," Bailey said. "I bet he feels really bad."

Muriel had seen how bad he felt. "Believe me, he got over my rejection in record time. He's perfectly happy going with Dot." In fact, the two of them were downright ecstatic. Muriel was suddenly aware of Cecily studying her. She smiled as if nothing at all were bothering her—because, really, nothing was—and finished her tea.

"I'm wondering if perhaps Arnie is your ugly tree, Mom. Maybe you've never really *seen* him," Cecily said.

"I see the good in Arnie," Muriel insisted. "We've been friends for years."

"You could be more," Cecily suggested.

More, after all those years? "Well, honestly, a woman can't manufacture attraction. You of all people should know that."

Cecily shrugged.

"I don't know why all three of you couldn't have gone," Samantha put in.

They could have, probably. If Dot was paying her own way anyway, there was no reason Muriel couldn't have just bought an extra ticket and truly made this a trip among friends. Really, though, it was better this way. Arnie needed to expand his horizons, do more things with other people. "I think he and Dot will have fun."

"Maybe something will happen between them," said Bailey.

"Oh, I don't think so," Muriel was quick to say. "Arnie and Dot are two very different people." Arnie was quiet and refined; Dot was outrageous and often uncouth.

"Opposites attract," pointed out Samantha.

"Not those two opposites," Muriel said firmly. Samantha and Cecily exchanged smiles and that annoyed her. "I don't know what you two are smirking about," she said irritably, and all three of her daughters grinned.

"Mom, I'm beginning to suspect you don't want to share your special friend," Samantha teased. "I wonder why."

"Don't be ridiculous," Muriel snapped. "I was the one who suggested they go together. There's nothing between Arnie and me. We're good friends and that's all we'll ever be." She wasn't attracted to Arnie. Dot could have him!

"Okay, whatever," Samantha said. "But I think you should have gone to Germany."

Yes, she probably should have. Was Arnie interested in Dot?

Sienna normally worked Mondays, but it was parent-teacher conference week and her conference was scheduled for early Monday afternoon, so Pat had given her the afternoon off. She'd promised Leo that after her meeting with Mrs. Brown he could help her put up Christmas lights. He'd also begged to watch *How the Grinch Stole Christmas* and she'd agreed, hoping the

anticipation of a fun-filled afternoon would lift his spirits. His poor excuse for a father hadn't bothered to call
on Thanksgiving and it had left Leo feeling down.

He wasn't exactly happy that she had a conference
with his teacher, either. And once she sat down with
Mrs. Brown, she knew why.

"Leo is a sweet boy," Mrs. Brown began. "He always
wants to help. He loves to help me collect and pass out
papers, but..."

Oh, no. Here came the *but*.

"...we need to work on his concentration. He'd much
prefer to clown around and put pencils up his nose or
talk to his neighbor than work on his addition and subtraction."

Addition and subtraction. Other kids Leo's age were
on to multiplication and division and Leo was putting
pencils up his nose. This behavior wasn't anything new
but it was still disheartening. Sienna heaved a sigh.

"This is not unusual," Mrs. Brown said gently. "Children with special needs often prefer to ignore dealing
with unpleasant tasks. As do most of us," she added
with a smile.

"I know. And I have talked to him in the past. I'll
speak with him again."

"He is making some progress," Mrs. Brown assured
her. "If you could work with him a little more at home,
that might help."

"I'm doing all I can, Mrs. Brown, believe me."

The woman gave her a sympathetic nod. "I know.
It's hard. Don't give up. And remember, he needs con-

crete examples and step-by-step direction. I'm sure you have other aspects of his life where you have to do this."

As a matter of fact, she did. Even simple tasks like taking a bath could get complicated. Leo needed to be reminded that washing his hair required another step beyond simply sudsing up his scalp. When she forgot to remind him to rinse it out, he often wound up crying with soap in his eyes. Setting the table was done with everything mapped out and she still had to stand over him when he loaded the dishwasher and supervise the process.

"We have a lot of the school year left," Mrs. Brown assured her.

Sienna wasn't sure whether to be grateful for that or depressed by it. She thanked the teacher and left.

She saw Leo standing at Rita's living room window when she went to pick him up, but by the time she got inside, he was hiding behind the couch. Rita had her toddler on her hip, and at the sight of Sienna little Linda squealed happily and reached for her, crying, "Si-si."

"Hello, my beautiful niece," she said and took the child. She would have loved to have had another child, but that probably wouldn't happen now with no husband in the picture. As a single parent, she felt that one child was all she could handle, especially when that one child had special needs.

Still holding Linda, she walked into the living room. "You can come out now."

Leo's head popped around the corner of the couch. "Hi, Mama."

"Have you been behaving yourself for Tía Rita?"

He nodded but still stayed behind the couch.

"How'd it go?" Rita asked.

Leo's head disappeared.

"It could have been worse." Sienna kissed the toddler's head. "Your teacher says you're a sweet boy. Is that true, my son?"

Leo peeked around the corner of the couch and made a silly face.

"And she says you're a clown."

"I like clowns."

"That's nice, but you can't be a clown when you're supposed to be doing your schoolwork," Sienna told him.

He frowned.

"Tito will be disappointed if he hears you're not paying attention in school," put in Rita.

The frown dug deeper.

"But we're going to work on that, aren't we?" Sienna said cheerfully.

Leo went back behind the couch and now Sienna frowned.

"Remember, the teacher said what a sweet boy he is. I know a lot of parents who'd give anything to hear that from their kids' teacher," Rita said. "Come on out to the kitchen, have a cup of coffee."

"No, we should get going. The snow's starting to stick and I want to get home."

"You're good to go now. You've got snow tires."

"I also want to get my lights up before it gets dark."

"Okay, fine. Linda and I both should take a nap, anyway."

Sienna gave back the baby and summoned her son, and he reluctantly came out of hiding. She felt as though she should give him a stern talking-to on the way home and insist that there would be no more showings of *Cars* until he stopped clowning around in class. But really, clowning was preferable to tears. So instead, she hugged him as they walked down her cousin's front walk and told him she loved him.

"I'll try harder, Mamacita," he said softly.

"You just try your best. That's all anyone can do."

When she'd first left for her conference, only a few little snowflakes had been drifting lazily toward the ground. Now an entire army of flakes was falling, quickly smothering the street and adding to the thick blankets on the lawns.

"It's snowing!" Leo announced.

Brrr. Maybe she'd rethink hanging her Christmas lights.

Except Leo hadn't forgotten that decorating the house was on the agenda. "Can we do our lights now?"

"Yes, on one condition. You have to promise you'll try to have a good attitude about schoolwork tonight."

Leo frowned. "I promise," he said reluctantly.

Once they got home, she fetched the boxes of lights she'd purchased earlier in the week. "This is going to look like Disneyland," Leo predicted as he followed her out onto the front yard.

Hardly, but it would look nice.

The new snow had lured out many of the neighbor kids and they were racing back and forth through yards, throwing snowballs at each other. She caught Leo watching them, yearning to be a part of the fun. The last time he'd joined in, the fun had involved a baseball sailing through Mr. Cratchett's living room window and it hadn't turned out so well.

Jimmy Wilson, a nice little boy who lived a few houses down, came running up to them. "Can Leo play?"

Jimmy was one boy in the neighborhood who was kind to Leo, who didn't see him as different. Jimmy was seven and Leo was nine. The age difference worked to Leo's advantage.

"Yes!" Leo cried. "Can I go play?" he asked Sienna.

"Of course," she said. Snowball fights were infinitely more exciting than putting up Christmas lights.

The words were barely out of her mouth before he and Jimmy were charging off across the lawn. As far as Leo was concerned, snow was one of the Seven Wonders of the World.

Sienna smiled until she heard a boy call, "Here comes the retard."

Her jaws clamped together and her good mood evaporated. When Rita had suggested she leave LA and move to Icicle Falls, it had seemed like a good idea. Leo had been having trouble in school and she'd grown weary of the traffic, pollution and worrying about staying in a neighborhood that was becoming increasingly more populated with unsavory characters. A move to her cousin's idyllic mountain town had seemed like the best solution, especially when Rita had painted a glowing picture of Icicle Falls. Gorgeous scenery, clean mountain air and a good school for Leo, friendly people.

But Sienna had quickly discovered that a small town could be just as hard on a child's psyche as a big city. It hadn't taken the other kids long to figure out that Leo wasn't as mentally sharp as the rest of them. Then the bullies had surfaced and the name-calling had begun, leaving him hurt and angry.

She'd love to have aimed a snowball at whoever had just called out those hurtful words.

"I am not a retard," Leo cried hotly.

Sienna turned to summon him back just in time to see Mr. Cratchett checking his mailbox, kids racing past him down the sidewalk. And here came Leo after the biggest one, a scowl on his face and a tightly packed snowball in his hand. He hurled it with all his might.

And missed.

His target danced away, laughing, even as the icy weapon beaned Mr. Cratchett on the head. Sienna watched in horror as Cratchett blinked, staggered and lost his balance, stumbling backward onto his lawn.

Chapter Four

Be sure to include that new family member in
your holiday preparations.
—Muriel Sterling, *A Guide to Happy Holidays*

Laughing and whooping, the herd of boys moved on,
taking their snowball fight to the other end of the street.

Leo's friend Jimmy stood for a moment, wide-eyed,
and then he bolted.

Leo simply froze in the street, staring in horror.

"Leo, get out of the street!" Sienna called as she
rushed to help Mr. Cratchett.

An approaching car honked and Leo jumped and
moved out of the way. He slowly approached Cratchett,
who was struggling to his feet, and said in a small voice,
"I'm sorry."

"Are you okay, Mr. Cratchett?" Sienna asked as she
bent to help him up.

He waved away her hand. "I'm fine, no thanks to
your son. I could've broken my hip. As it is, I think I've
sprained my wrist."

Oh, no. What if he had? What if he expected her to
pay the doctor bill?

Now he was upright again and brushing the snow off his backside. Leo tried to help him and was promptly told to keep his hands to himself. "You'll get the doctor bill for this," he informed Sienna. Of course she would.

Just what she wanted for Christmas. "Absolutely," she said. "I'm really sorry."

"You're lucky I don't sue you," Cratchett added.

Oh, Lord. She wouldn't put it past him.

"I didn't mean to hit you," Leo told him.

"Well, you did. Didn't you?" Cratchett snapped.

"I didn't mean to," Leo repeated, tears beginning to make their appearance. "I was trying to hit Tommy Haskel."

"It's okay, sweetie," Sienna said, patting her son's arm.

Cratchett glared at her. "It is not! These kids run around throwing snowballs every which way, hitting innocent bystanders, and then you coddle them."

"He said he was sorry," Sienna snapped, her mama-bear side showing itself.

Now Leo began to cry in earnest and she hugged him.

"You should be ashamed of yourself," Sienna scolded Cratchett.

"Me?" he protested. "Who's the one who got hit?"

At that moment a red truck pulled up to the curb. A large man with a dark beard wearing jeans, boots and a black parka stepped out of it. "Hey there, uncle. Making friends with the neighbors?" he said with a smile.

Cratchett told him he was a smart-ass and stomped back up his front walk.

This man was related to Mr. Cratchett? Poor him.

"Don't tell me, let me guess," said the man. "You must be the killer of the juniper bush." He had a deep voice and a nice smile.

But Sienna was in no mood to smile back. "Your uncle is…impossible."

"Yes, he is," the man agreed.

"He's made my life miserable ever since we moved in." Why was she complaining to this man? As if he had any control over his uncle's behavior?

"It's a gift." The man held out a gloved hand. "I'm Tim Richmond."

She took his hand and shook it. His big hand swallowed hers and she felt a little tingle in her chest. *Tingle bells, tingle bells… It's been way too long.*

Oh, stop, she commanded herself. Anyone even remotely related to Cratchett wasn't worth getting stirred up over. He was probably married, anyway. If he took off his glove, she was sure there'd be a sign of ownership there on his left hand.

"Sienna Moreno," she said, all business so her hormones would get the message. "This is my son, Leo."

"I saw him in action when I was coming up the street. That's quite an arm you've got on you, son, if you can knock a grown man over," Tim said with a wink.

Leo looked at the man suspiciously and wiped his runny nose with his coat sleeve. "I didn't mean to hit him."

"I know you didn't. Don't mind the old guy. He gets grumpy sometimes."

Sienna cocked an eyebrow. "Sometimes?"

"Well, okay, a lot of times."

Now Cratchett had his front door open. "Are you going to get in here and fix my sink or just stand out there jawing all day?" he hollered.

"I'm coming. Keep your shirt on," Tim hollered back.

"His shirt is on," Leo pointed out.

"So far," the man said. He had a nice smile. He opened the passenger door of his truck, reached inside and pulled out a toolbox. "Don't mind my uncle. He's got issues."

As if that excused his behavior? "Well, I'm going to have issues before he's done with me. Anyway, that's no excuse for being rude to a child."

"He's mean," put in Leo.

"Yeah, sometimes he is."

"Are you coming?" roared Cratchett.

Tim scowled in the direction of his uncle's house. "Shut the door, unc'," he yelled. "I'll be with you in a minute." Cratchett's door slammed shut and Tim turned his attention back to Sienna. "Nice to meet you. Maybe next time it will be under better circumstances."

"If your uncle's around? I'm not holding my breath," Sienna replied. "Maybe you can give him kindness lessons," she said, adding a smile to show her grumpiness wasn't directed at him.

"Trust me, I keep trying." He gave a friendly nod and then made his way up Cratchett's front walk.

Wouldn't it be nice to get someone like him for Christmas?

Sienna pushed away the thought. Her life was full enough with Leo and her family and friends. Besides,

Cupid hadn't exactly come through for her lately. After her ex and the losers she'd dated since her divorce, she didn't trust the little guy.

"Come on," she said to her son. "Let's finish stringing our lights."

Putting up the Christmas lights was enough to make Leo forget his earlier misery. His sunny disposition quickly surfaced once the front porch and windows were glowing with multicolored bulbs.

Sienna, too, was pleased with how pretty their house looked. There were certainly benefits to living in a gorgeous small town like Icicle Falls, and the home she was able to provide for her son was one of them.

An older couple from the neighborhood strolled by and waved. "Your house looks lovely," the woman called.

"Thanks," Sienna called back.

At least most of her neighbors were nice. If only the Grinch would come along and steal Cratchett. Then they'd have peace on earth.

Once the guests had checked out, Mondays were often a quiet day at the Icicle Creek Lodge, and Olivia took advantage of that to run errands or go shopping in nearby Wenatchee. She usually tried to buy from her fellow business owners in town, but many of those shops were closed on Mondays and Tuesdays. In addition to that, while the town was filled with charming specialty shops that catered to tourists, as well as a grocery store and drugstore, it was lacking the malls or department stores the larger cities boasted. When a woman wanted new underwear or a nightgown, she had to look elsewhere.

Today Olivia was in need of a new bra. She also wanted to do a little Christmas shopping, and this was as good a time as any to slip away and do it.

She mentioned her intention to scoot off while she and Brooke were in the kitchen cleaning up after breakfast.

"Would you mind if I come with you?" Brooke asked. "Eric needs some new jeans and I want to pick up a few things for the baby."

"Of course not. I'd love the company."

She always enjoyed spending time with Brooke. Her daughter-in-law was sweet and generous and she shared Olivia's love of elegant home furnishings, fancy soaps and all things lavender, especially the lavender lemonade and lavender cookies to be had at Bailey Black's tearoom.

When they'd first met, Brooke had been mourning the loss of her mother and hadn't been enthused about another woman taking her mom's place in her father's heart. But in the end she'd been happy to see both James and Olivia find love again, and while Olivia knew she could never take the place of Brooke's mother, she and her stepdaughter had become good friends.

Once the last guests departed, Olivia and Brooke left, also. "We've been so busy it seems like we've hardly had any time together, so this is a real treat," Olivia told her as Brooke drove them down Highway 2 out of town.

"Yes, it is," Brooke agreed. "Gosh, I wonder if Meadow wanted to come with us."

Olivia should have asked her, but really, she'd been looking forward to getting away from the girl for a while. "I'm sure she and Brandon are going skiing today," she said airily, determined to silence the nudge from her conscience.

"I thought that was tomorrow."

"Was it?"

"Should we go back?"

"They probably have plans. After all, they're still newlyweds." And brides wanted to spend time with their husbands. This bride did, certainly. She was always there. Every time Olivia hoped for a moment to enjoy her son's company, along came Meadow, demanding attention, wanting him to go somewhere with her, needing Brandon's advice. Sometimes Olivia thought the girl was jealous of the relationship she had with her son.

Who else is sounding a bit jealous? Olivia pushed the thought away, consigning it to a far corner of her mind, right along with her earlier vow to look for the good in her new daughter-in-law.

With all guilty thoughts gone, she enjoyed her afternoon with Brooke and got most of her holiday shopping done. She still had to think of something for Meadow. What would the girl like? Olivia had no idea. Well, she still had plenty of time until Christmas. She'd figure out what to get later.

"That was fun, Mom. Thanks," Brooke said as they walked back into the lodge, laden with packages.

"Yes, it was," Olivia agreed. The words were barely out of her mouth when she caught sight of Meadow on the first stair landing, looking down at them, the hurt plain on her face.

Oh, no. Olivia could feel her cheeks go hot with shame. She should have asked Meadow to join them.

Meadow whirled around and vanished down the hall and Olivia was aware of Brooke looking at her with concern. "I'd better ditch your father's present before he returns from his errands," Olivia said and beat a hasty retreat. There was going to be fallout from this.

Sure enough, she was barely done putting away her purchases when her son came to the apartment looking for her. It didn't take a psychic to know why he was there.

She gave him a kiss and forestalled the unpleasant conversation by asking if he'd like a cup of coffee.

"No, thanks." He wasn't smiling.

"Were you and Eric able to fix those burned-out lights on the trees out front?" A silly question. She'd seen the two firs out front when she and Brooke returned and all the lights had been working fine.

"Yeah. Mom."

Here it came. Olivia retreated to her kitchenette in search of coffee, Muffin, the cat, following in the hope of getting more cat food.

"Meadow's feeling left out. She'd like to have gone shopping with you and Brooke."

They should have gone back and invited Meadow. Wicked Mother-in-Law of the Year, that was her.

"It was a spur-of-the-moment decision, dear, and she was nowhere in sight." Olivia took a mug from the cupboard, keeping her back turned to her son.

"Would you have asked her if she was?"

She wasn't that awful. "Of course."

He frowned. "Mom, I know you don't like her."

Olivia focused her attention on putting a pod in her Keurig. "Don't be silly. Of course I like her." Oh, what a whopper.

"Is that why every time you smile at her, you look like you've got gas?"

"Don't be crude."

The scold didn't sidetrack him. "You spend time with Brooke. You've got her doing a lot of stuff around here. Meadow could help, too."

Ah, now here she at least had a leg to stand on. "She did on Thanksgiving Day, and I had her help decorate on Saturday." Not content with being a handicap in the kitchen on Thanksgiving, Meadow had managed to drop a box of imported glass balls the day they decorated, breaking several. She'd been quick to point out that they hadn't been very well packed. "Really, Brandon, what more do you want?" Olivia hoped he'd realize that was a rhetorical question.

He moved to her side and put a hand on her arm. "I want you to give her a chance. Can you do that, Mom? For me?"

Of course, she had to. If she didn't, she'd lose her son. She turned to face him. "I'll try. But honestly, I don't know what you saw in this girl," she couldn't help adding.

His eyes narrowed and a muscle in his jaw twitched. "Try harder—then maybe you'll see."

Okay, she deserved that. Even so, her son's displeasure stung. She managed a nod.

Brandon's expression softened. "She's got a good

heart, Mom, and she really wants to be part of the family."

"I want her to be, too." Another lie, but at this moment honesty would not be the best policy.

"Good, because otherwise it's probably not going to work out for us to be here."

The ultimatum made her blink, but she knew she shouldn't be surprised by it. When it came to picking sides, a wise man sided with his wife. Sad for her, but that was how it should be. *What God has put together, let no mother-in-law put asunder.*

Anyway, a man shouldn't have to choose. It was wrong of her to put her son in that position. "Darling, I really will make more of an effort, I promise," she said with tears in her eyes. The thought of him leaving so soon after he'd decided to move back in with them was not one she wanted to consider.

He came around the counter and hugged her. "Thanks, Mom. I knew I could count on you."

Theoretically. So far she hadn't been very reliable. And that was hardly to her credit.

"I don't think she's got a good relationship with her mom," he continued. "She could use someone in her corner."

He was right. Olivia would do better. She'd try harder. "Maybe Meadow would like to help with breakfast. We only have a few guests checking in later today, so tomorrow will be easy."

"Good idea," he said, grinning.

That settled it, then. "Tell her to be in the kitchen tomorrow at six."

"How about you tell her?"

After that moment in the lobby Olivia wasn't particularly excited about facing her daughter-in-law, but she nodded. "All right."

She didn't exactly receive a warm welcome when she went to her son's little suite at the opposite end of the lodge. The look Meadow gave her shot her back to an incident in her childhood when she and a friend had snubbed another little girl on the playground at lunch. The hurt had come off the child in waves and Olivia hadn't been able to concentrate on anything the teacher said the whole rest of the afternoon. Those same waves were coming at her now.

"May I come in?" she asked.

Meadow nodded and moved aside, opening the door farther.

Olivia stepped in. The TV was on. Dr. Phil was working with a dysfunctional family. Olivia could almost hear him saying, *You're next, Mrs. Claussen.* She cleared her throat. "Meadow, I'm sorry I didn't think to invite you to come shopping with me today." *And sorry I didn't want to think to!*

Meadow studied the roses on the carpet. "It's okay."

Of course, it wasn't, and the fact that Meadow was so quick to forgive only shone a spotlight on Olivia's lack of kindness. "Maybe we can fit in an outing, just the two of us." *Penance.*

Meadow's gaze lifted and the gratitude Olivia saw in her daughter-in-law's eyes made her feel small. "Yeah?"

"Yes. Meanwhile, I could use some help at breakfast tomorrow. Would you be up for that?"

The girl was beaming now. "Sure. What time?"

"We start serving at seven, so I need you in the kitchen at six."

Meadow's eyebrows shot up. "Six?"

"If that's too early for you…" *I'll be off the hook.*

"No, I can do that," Meadow said gamely. "I'll tell Brandon we have to wait and go night skiing."

"Oh, if you had plans…"

"No, no. I'll be there."

"Are you sure? Because if you're already busy…"

"I can change my plans. Really. I want to help."

Olivia smiled weakly and tried not to think about the so-called help Meadow had been with the Thanksgiving Day meal. Well, they weren't serving gravy at breakfast, so maybe it would be okay.

"If you're sure," she said in a last-ditch effort to give Meadow an out.

Except the one she was trying to give an out was herself. Once more that spotlight exposed Olivia's own ignoble attitude. Who was the real ugly tree here?

"Oh, yeah," Meadow said, still smiling. "I'm sure."

Okay, the girl did seem to have a good heart. "Wonderful," Olivia said. And darn it all, she was determined to mean it.

Chapter Five

The important thing to remember this time of year
when things get a little awkward is that we're all
different.

—Muriel Sterling, *A Guide to Happy Holidays*

Come six o'clock Olivia and Brooke were in the
kitchen, ready to go, Olivia in her dirndl and Brooke
in a maternity-friendly version of the classic German
garb. No Meadow.

The two women got busy filling bread baskets with
Olivia's eggnog muffins, setting fruit on trays and putting out hot water and coffee. Still no sign of Meadow.
Olivia put her breakfast casserole in the oven to bake
and started cooking sausages.

It was now six twenty. Meadow had obviously overslept. She was probably rushing around the apartment
right now, throwing on clothes and brushing her teeth.

Or not. By ten after seven the first guests were ac-
cumulating in the dining room but there was still no
sign of Meadow.

Fortunately, Olivia's midweek crowd was sparse,

so the extra help wasn't needed. Still, it irked her that she'd given Meadow a chance to be involved and, after her enthusiasm of the day before, the girl hadn't bothered to show up. Meanwhile, here was Brooke, eight months pregnant but happily pitching in, keeping the cold-cereal dispenser and the pitchers of juice filled and chatting with the guests.

By eight James, too, was on deck, clearing tables. "No sign of Meadow?" he asked Olivia as he headed for the sink.

"No." So much for her wanting to be a part of things.

"Maybe she overslept."

At that moment Brandon came into the kitchen.

"Where's Meadow?" Olivia greeted him.

"She doesn't feel good. She said to tell you she's sorry. She'll be down as soon as she can."

Sick. *How convenient*, Olivia thought but said nothing.

"Nothing serious, I hope," James said.

"I don't think so," Brandon said. "You got any of your casserole left, Mom?"

"I do," she said and pulled a second pan from the oven.

"I always loved this one," Brandon said as she cut him a large piece. "Thanks, Mom," he added and gave her a kiss on the cheek.

The smile that had been dodging her all morning made its appearance. She so loved her boy, and just a simple compliment from him was enough to fill her with happiness. It kept her in a good mood clear through the rest of the breakfast hour.

It was edging toward ten and the last guests were strolling out of the dining room when Meadow made her appearance, wearing fashionably torn jeans and a long-sleeved black top. She hurried over to where Olivia sat at a corner table, ready to take a coffee break.

"Sorry I'm late. Did Brandon tell you I was sick?"

She didn't look sick now. "He did," Olivia said and took a sip of her coffee. "Are you feeling better?"

"Yeah. I'm ready to help."

Now that the guests were all done eating... But there was still plenty to do. "Why don't you spell Brooke and help James with the cleanup?"

"I can do that," Meadow said with a nod.

Olivia watched as she scooped up several plates from a nearby table and moved off to the kitchen. Okay, she was willing to pitch in. Maybe she really hadn't been feeling well. Maybe she had a little low-grade...something.

Olivia ate one of the muffins she'd served herself and continued to observe her new daughter-in-law as she bustled in and out of the kitchen, clearing away dirty dishes and silverware, empty pitchers and serving bowls. Perhaps Olivia had misjudged her, thinking she was a slacker. She wasn't slacking now.

Brooke came to the table with a glass of milk and a muffin and joined Olivia. "This is my second muffin. I need to stop."

"Well, you are eating for two," Olivia said.

"More like eating for three. I'm getting as big as a house."

"You'll take it off after the baby comes," Olivia assured her. Not that she had managed to do that but oh, well. She'd been carrying those extra pounds for years and they had made themselves happily at home.

Lucky for her, James thought her figure was just fine the way it was.

"You're not going to have many left for tomorrow," Brooke said. "Sorry."

"That's okay. They're best when they're fresh." Which was why she'd helped herself to three.

"That's what I told Meadow," Brooke said with a smile. "She's eating one now."

Yes, a very short-lived sickness.

"She says it's helping settle her stomach."

Whatever. Olivia didn't say anything, just smiled and took another sip of her coffee.

Soon Meadow joined them, sitting down next to Olivia and facing her. "Okay, the kitchen's all clean."

"That was fast," Olivia said.

"James had most of it done already," Meadow admitted. "What else can I do?"

"Well…"

"I don't want to just sit around and eat muffins and get fat."

Two muffins still sat on Olivia's plate. She frowned.

"So, tell me what to do."

"We need to put out silverware and napkins for breakfast tomorrow," Olivia said.

"Okay." Meadow jumped up.

"And replace any stained tablecloths."

"I can do that."

"I'll help you," Brooke said and got up.

"No." Meadow waved her back down. "You've been working all morning. I can do it."

Meadow was certainly on her best behavior now.

Olivia let her go at it, knowing James was still around and could answer any questions she had.

"I guess I'll run back to the apartment and throw in a load of laundry," Brooke said to Olivia.

Olivia, too, got up and returned her cup and her un-eaten muffins to the kitchen. "See you later," Meadow called as she walked by, bearing a bundle of dirty tablecloths.

Brandon was manning the front desk when Olivia got there. "How'd Meadow do?" he greeted her.

"Fine." Of course, he wanted to hear more than that. He wanted to hear approval. "She's working hard."

He beamed and that made Olivia feel good.

"I can take over here now," she said.

"Thanks. I need to get out and help Eric shovel the walkways."

Yes, it was nice to have her boy back home. He gave her a quick kiss on the cheek and left, and she settled in behind the front desk, feeling happy with her life and the world in general. She had just finished checking out a young family when Meadow joined her.

"Dining room's all ready for tomorrow," she reported.

"Good. Thank you."

"Stuff sure starts early around here," Meadow said and leaned on the desk.

"That's how it is in the hospitality business," Olivia said.

Meadow wrinkled her nose. "Who the hell wants to eat at seven in the morning when they're on vacation?"

"A lot of people like to eat early."

"I don't see why. Nothing much opens up around

this town until ten. We should wait until eight to serve breakfast."

In some ways that sounded perfectly logical, but Olivia had been running her lodge for many years and she knew that people expected to be able to eat early if they had plans to get on the road. Or if they were just plain hungry.

"I guess," Meadow said dubiously after Olivia had explained. "Running a motel is kind of a pain in the butt, isn't it?"

"This is a lodge," Olivia corrected her.

Meadow was not impressed. "Lodge, motel, what's the difference?"

"Ambiance. This is more of a resort, a specialty kind of place with a garden and grounds around it."

"Oh." Meadow thought on that a moment, then shrugged. "It's still kind of a pain in the butt. I mean, look how hard you guys all work."

"Well, yes, we do. But we're working at something worthwhile. We're providing people with a nice place to stay, helping them make memories. We're offering more than rooms here, Meadow. We're offing hospitality."

"Hmm. Never thought of it that way. Kind of cool."

Yes, it was.

"Pretty cool that Brandon will own all this some-day," she added.

Spoken like a true gold digger. The feeling of warmth that had started in Olivia's chest cooled.

"So, what do you want me to do now?"

Go away? "Oh, I can't think of anything."

"There must be something. It's a big place. Brandon

says you guys all take turns working the front desk. I can do that."

Thank you, Brandon. About the last thing Olivia wanted was her daughter-in-law showing off her lack of social graces at the front desk. "That's kind of you to offer, but you don't need to."

"Hey, I'm family, right? Gotta pitch in. Anyway, I think it will be fun to help people check in and out."

"Meadow, I'm not sure that particular job would be a fit for you."

Meadow's sunny expression clouded over. "Why? It can't be that hard. And I'm not stupid," she added. "I did two quarters at Seattle Community College."

"It's not a matter of intelligence," Olivia said. "It's a matter of fit."

Olivia could hardly say she thought Meadow was uncouth. She was about to finesse the truth with a little speech about how different temperaments were suited for different jobs, but Meadow dashed in a literal direction before she could get the words out.

"Fit for what? Oh, clothes?"

Olivia grabbed on the flimsy excuse. "You do need a dirndl."

"Like what you've got on." Meadow made a face.

"This is a German-themed town. Business owners dress the part," Olivia said firmly. And if a certain ripped-jeans wearer didn't want to do that, it wasn't Olivia's fault.

Meadow ditched the frown and shrugged. "Okay, then. I'm up for it. How about we go get one today?"

Olivia tried a new tack. "Are you sure you want to

do this? Manning the booth requires a certain amount of…" *couth* "…patience and diplomacy."

"Sure," Meadow said. Brandon chose that moment to come inside and she called, "Hey, babe. I'm gonna learn how to work the front desk."

"You'll be great," he called back.

Olivia sincerely doubted it. Here was proof positive that love was blind.

She'd give the girl a chance, though. Everyone deserved a chance. But if Meadow got lippy with a customer, she'd be back to bussing tables.

The lodge wasn't that busy and check-in wasn't until three. Das Dorf, which carried all manner of German items, including dirndls, was open on Tuesdays. Irmgard Schultz, the owner, would be more than happy to help Olivia outfit Meadow.

"All right," Olivia said. "How about we go after lunch?"

And with that it was settled, so at one in the afternoon Olivia and Meadow walked into the German shop that sat right in the middle of Center Street, the main drag, where some of the town's most popular shops could be found.

"I haven't been in here yet," Meadow said as they entered the shop. "Whoa, look at these." They were barely in the store when she stopped in front of a display case filled with Hummel figurines. "Look at that cute one with the umbrella—wow." This was quickly followed by wide eyes and a muttered "Shit."

"What?" Olivia asked.

"Those things are expensive," Meadow whispered, pointing to the price tag at the figurine's feet.

"Hummels are. You have expensive tastes."

"I guess. Who knew I had such good taste? Well, except that I picked Brandon. He's got a lot of class."

Something you either had or you didn't, and Meadow didn't. She had, however, shown good taste in marrying Brandon. There was no denying that.

Irmgard came toward them now. She was in her late sixties, with a round face and an equally round figure to match. Her light brown hair was ratted into a style left over from the early '60s and she wore a green dirndl.

"Olivia, it's been ages," she said. "And who is this with you?"

"This is my new daughter-in-law, Meadow."

"Ah, I heard Brandon got married. Such a lovely girl," she said, looking Meadow up and down. "But much too skinny. Don't worry, though. Your mother-in-law can make strudel almost as good as mine. She'll get some meat on your bones in no time."

Meadow's brows shot up. "Uh, thanks. I think."

"We need a dirndl for Meadow. She's going to be helping out at the lodge," Olivia explained.

"Of course she is. Families stick together."

A not-so-subtle message from the universe?

"Well, they should, anyway," Irmgard continued. "My daughter—" here Irmgard gave a sorry shake of the head "—she married a man from Texas. Texas, can you imagine? It's so hot down there. And they all speak with an accent," she added in her clipped Germanized English. "Now it's only me here. Olivia, you don't know how lucky you are to have both your boys with you. And now a new daughter-in-law. Oh, how I wish my Alfred would get married and move up here."

Be careful what you wish for.

"And now that you're working at the lodge, you're truly part of the family," Irmgard said to Meadow. "So, let's see what we can find you. I think something in blue. Don't you, Olivia? Blondes always look pretty in blue."

"Yes, blue," Olivia agreed.

"What size are you? I'm guessing a six?"

Meadow nodded and trailed Irmgard over to a rack of dresses. A few moments later she had an armful and Irmgard had sent her to a changing room.

"What a lovely girl," she said to Olivia.

"She's very pretty," Olivia agreed.

"And so sweet—and wanting to help out with the family business. Ah, you are so lucky."

She's right, Olivia reminded herself. Both her boys were back home. She had one daughter-in-law who was perfect and another who…wanted to be here. That counted for a lot. So what if that daughter-in-law wasn't exactly her cup of cocoa? Meadow loved Brandon and wanted to be part of things. Surely that balanced out laziness, crudeness and a lack of tact.

The little dressing room curtain parted and out stepped Meadow in the blue dirndl, a very odd match with her overdyed hair and the butterfly tat that soared up over the neckline.

"Oh, doesn't she look pretty?" gushed Irmgard.

"I look stupid," Meadow muttered, pulling at one of the puffy sleeves.

This was not the time to agree with her daughter-in-law. "You've got the perfect figure for that dress," Olivia said. It was true. Meadow was slim and pretty in her own flamboyant way. "But maybe you'd like a different color."

Meadow looked like she'd just eaten a rotten nut. "I don't think that'll make any difference."

"We can find other things for you to do at the lodge if you don't want to wear it," Olivia offered. She could tell Brandon she'd tried. *Meadow didn't want to wear the dress.*

"No, no," Meadow said quickly. "I'll get it."

Olivia had to admire her for her willingness to step outside her comfort zone just to be part of the family operation. *Give her a chance. She might surprise you.* "All right. It really does look beautiful."

A few moments later Meadow was back in her clothing comfort zone and Olivia was pulling out her credit card to purchase the dirndl. "Actually, we'd better get two so you have one to wear when that one's getting washed."

"Okay," Meadow said. "But I'm paying."

"Oh, no. This is my treat."

"I really don't mind. Anyway, I've got some money left from my mom's—um, that my mom gave me."

Interesting. What had she been about to say? Her mom's what?

"What a good daughter-in-law," said Irmgard.

"Let me buy these for you," Olivia said to Meadow. As if buying a couple of dresses would make up for her unmotherly attitude.

"No, I've got it," Meadow insisted and handed over three large bills. "I'll take the red one, too."

Mission accomplished, the two women drove back to the lodge. "Thanks for taking me," Meadow said.

"Not much thanks needed since you wound up paying for the dresses yourself." Olivia really should have insisted on paying for them.

"It's okay," Meadow said. "I didn't mind. And now when we get back, I can work the front desk," she added cheerfully.

"This will be a good day to start," Olivia said. Check-in time was right around the corner and they had some guests arriving that afternoon. It being early in the week, there wouldn't be so many that Meadow would get overwhelmed as she learned the ropes.

If Meadow could master some social graces, it would be good to have an extra pair of hands. Now that December had arrived, the lodge was going to be full on weekends clear into the New Year.

So would every B and B and motel in town. This was peak tourist season thanks, in part, to a yearly town tradition that had quickly become a tourist attraction. Now, every weekend during the month of December Icicle Falls hosted a tree-lighting ceremony and people came from all over the country to join the locals to watch the big tree in the center of town and all the surrounding buildings come alive with colored lights. The ceremony preceding the big moment was usually brief, but people loved it since it included caroling and a visit from Santa, who had plenty of grown-up helper elves on hand to pass out mini candy canes to all the children. The partying started well before the ceremony began, with vendors selling everything from roasted nuts to hot chocolate, local artisans displaying their works and, of course, a German oompah band playing. Skaters enjoyed the little ice rink in the town-center park, while shoppers swarmed the specialty shops and restaurants. It was a mob scene, with the streets and sidewalks packed, but that didn't stop people from coming in droves. And the residents of Icicle Falls welcomed it because it kept their local economy humming.

It didn't take Meadow long to change into her new dress and when she reported for duty at the desk, she was smiling. "Brandon thinks I look hot in this," she announced, clearly feeling much more confident in the outfit than she had in the store.

"Well, that's…good," Olivia said. For such a slender little thing Meadow certainly had cleavage and, yes, the low-cut neckline showed it to advantage.

"So, what do I have to do?" Meadow asked.

"Make sure you swipe the guests' credit cards when they come in. We don't charge them until checkout but we keep the card information. We have our guests fill out this little form with contact information and their driver's licenses. Each couple or family checking in gets two room-key cards. Oh, and we always tell them the hours breakfast is served."

"I can handle that."

"And, of course, we greet everyone with a smile. If a guest has a complaint, we're always sympathetic. We never get upset."

Meadow frowned. "I know what you're thinking

about. It's not like I spilled gravy on that man on purpose. Sheesh. He was a shit."

"I know. Sometimes people can be unreasonable. But we're in a service industry. Serve is what we do. Our job here is to keep our guests happy. So, if anyone ever comes to the desk with a complaint you feel you can't handle, don't get upset with them—just come find me. Okay?"

Meadow nodded. "Fine with me. I don't like dealing with shits."

Hopefully, no shits would cross Meadow's path when she was on duty. Olivia vowed right then to limit her time at the desk as much as possible.

Their first guests arrived right at three o'clock, the official check-in time. They were a middle-aged couple, the woman bundled in a faux-fur coat, leggings and boots, her silver hair stylishly cut. Her husband, swarthy and handsome, wore a parka and jeans.

"Fortelli," he said, stepping up to the desk. "We're booked for the week."

Meadow smiled at him. "Nice to have you, Mr. Fortelli."

Mrs. Fortelli, who was standing right next to him, frowned.

"And Mrs. Fortelli, too," Olivia added.

"Oh. Yeah. Of course," Meadow said and gave the missus a smile, as well. The missus almost returned it.

"So," Meadow said briskly, shoving a form at him, "give us your car license number and all that good stuff. And we'll need your credit card. But don't worry. We won't charge you until you leave." The man handed over his credit card. "Fortelli, that's a cool name. It's, like, Italian, isn't it?"

"Yes, it is," he said.

"Have you been to Italy?" she asked, and Olivia felt rather pleased with Meadow's attempt at pleasant small talk.

"Several times," said Mr. Fortelli.

"I've always wanted to go to Italy," Meadow said. "Somebody told me Italian men pinch you," she added with a grin.

Mr. Fortelli handed back the completed form. "Italian men do appreciate beautiful women," he said. Now there wasn't even a hint of a smile on Mrs. Fortelli's face.

"Oh, yeah? Then I definitely need to go. Make my guy jealous." Meadow dealt efficiently with the credit card, then handed it back. She leaned on the desk, giving Mr. Fortelli a close-up view of Butterfly Mountain. "So what's the best city to go to in Italy? Where would you tell me to go?"

"To a guidebook," the missus said, her voice frosty.

They were wandering far from standard check-in procedure at this point. "How about getting the Fortellis' key cards, Meadow?"

"Oh, yeah." Meadow straightened up but Mr. Fortelli remained fixated on her boobs.

"So, are you folks are up here from Seattle?" Olivia asked, hoping to distract him.

"We are," the husband said, making himself the official spokesperson for the Fortelli family.

"Is it your first time here in Icicle Falls?" Olivia asked his wife.

"Yes, it is," the woman said, frowning at Meadow.

"I'm sure you'll enjoy it. We have some wonderful shops and restaurants. And Currier's Tree Farm offers sleigh rides."

"They do? I'm so making Brandon take me on one," put in Meadow. "I bet you'd like a sleigh ride, huh, Mr. Fortelli."

Fortelli was obviously enjoying the attention. He smiled at Meadow as if they were in a bar working toward hooking up.

"A very romantic thing to do with your husband," Olivia said to his wife, who was looking as if she'd like to run over Meadow with a sleigh.

"You should take your wife," Meadow added. She gave Mr. Fortelli the room-key packet. "You're on the second floor. Breakfast is from seven to ten. Meanwhile, if there's anything you need, just let us know." She gave the man a playful finger point. "We're here for you."

"Let's go," his wife snapped, snatching the key-card envelope from his hand. She turned and marched toward the staircase.

"What's her problem?" Meadow asked as the couple crossed the lobby.

"I think she didn't like all the attention you were giving her husband."

Meadow's eyes widened. "Seriously? I was just being friendly—like you told me. And he was the one doing all the talking."

"You should still address all your remarks to both when it's a couple."

"Okay, fine. But I was just being friendly," Meadow repeated.

"Next time don't be quite *so* friendly," Olivia advised. "Wives don't like it."

"Insecure," Meadow muttered.

"Most of us are."

Meadow heaved a long-suffering sigh. "Okay, fine. Whatever."

Another couple arrived, this time a slightly younger pair with a teenage boy in tow. The boy, who hadn't looked all that thrilled when they entered, instantly appeared happier at the sight of Meadow.

But this time Meadow was all business. "Welcome to the Icicle Creek Lodge," she said, her lips a straight line. "Have you got a reservation?"

"Barrows," said the man.

Meadow nodded. Still no smile. "Fill out this form. We need your car's license number. And I need a credit card."

Okay, now the pendulum had swung too far in the other direction. "Where are you folks from?" Olivia asked as the man handed over his Visa.

He began working on the form and his wife said, "We're from San Diego."

"My, you're a ways from home," Olivia said.

"Oh, yes," the woman replied cheerily. "We wanted a taste of snow. And friends had been telling us what a cute town this is."

"We're proud of it," Olivia said as an unsmiling Meadow handed over the key cards.

"You're in 306. Breakfast is from seven to ten. Enjoy

your stay," Meadow said. Her sober expression added, *Good luck with that.*

"And let us know if there's anything you need," Olivia said, adding the smile her daughter-in-law was missing.

"Okay, how was that?" Meadow asked as the family made their way up the stairs.

"Well, it was good. But you can smile. Be a little friendly."

Meadow rolled her eyes. "Well, shit. I was friendly before and you got on me!"

Argh. "It's okay to smile, but when it's a couple, make sure you smile at both of them. And talk to both of them. And no *shit*s in public."

"Okay. Got it," Meadow said. After a moment she added quietly, "I don't know why I can't just be myself."

"Of course you can be yourself. I just want you to be a better version of yourself."

That hadn't come out right. Meadow frowned. "Whatever."

"She'll get the hang of it," Muriel assured Olivia later when she met her friends at Bailey's tearoom for an afternoon cup of tea and some red velvet cake.

"I have my doubts," Olivia said. "The girl is just so…unpolished."

"She may never get polished," Dot said. "She's not you. You're going to have to accept that."

"I know," Olivia said. Did she sound petulant?

"I don't think this whole getting-her-trained thing is the real problem," Dot continued. "What's really bugging you, Liv? Is it the fact that they didn't have a wedding or that Brandon didn't marry a carbon copy of you?"

Dot's words shed unwanted light in corners where Olivia didn't want to look. "Neither," she insisted.

Dot shrugged. "If you say so. But if there's more going on here, you know we'd understand. We always want our kids to do exactly what we would do. We want them to be a mini-me."

"There's no danger of that," Olivia said with a scowl. "I'd have never picked someone with nose rings and tattoos."

Dot frowned at her. "Have you been living in a cave? Almost all the younger generation has that these days. It's their way of being creative. Hell, Tilda has 'To Serve and Protect' tattooed on her leg." She shook her head. "Our kids have their own ideas of what their lives should be like, and as long as they're not turning into criminals or drug addicts, we shouldn't take it personally when they go their own way. It's their story to live. Anyway, you raised Brandon well. Have a little faith in him."

"Wow. When did you get so smart?" Pat teased.

"When my kid became a cop instead of going into the restaurant business."

"Things will work out," Muriel assured Olivia. "Remember our ugly-tree vows."

All easier said than done. "Bah, humbug," Olivia muttered.

Sienna had barely gotten home from work when a delivery from Lupine Floral arrived at her door. The arrangement was done in the shape of a tree with greens, red roses, baby's breath and tiny silver balls.

"A Christmas tree!" cried Leo. "From Santa."

"Santa doesn't come for a while yet," she told him.

Who had sent her flowers? She took the card and read, *Apologies for my uncle.* It was signed from Tim Richmond. How sweet! The man sure was nothing like his uncle. Maybe Cratchett was adopted.

She needed to thank Tim. She found a Richmond listed in nearby Cashmere. That had to be him. She called the number but got only voice mail. "I hope I'm calling the right Tim Richmond," she said. "If I am, I just wanted to thank you for the lovely flowers. You certainly didn't have to do that, but I'll enjoy them, anyway." Suddenly out of words, she said, "Well, um, thanks again. Have a nice day."

She would now. She couldn't remember the last time someone had sent her flowers. Her ex never had. There should be more Tim Richmonds in the world.

And why couldn't she have lived next door to Tim rather than his uncle? If he was sending flowers, he was obviously single. This surmise led to a pleasant fantasy of her and Tim Richmond strolling down a snowy country lane hand in hand.

Leo interrupted her reverie. "I'm hungry."

Back to reality. The rest of the evening was taken up with dinner, the usual table-setting lessons and then the unpleasant fun of dealing with math homework, which ended in a tantrum that took a while to deal with. After hugs and encouragement and a reminder that someday Leo was going to get this math stuff and make her very proud, she popped him in the tub, reminding him to rinse his hair after he washed it.

By the time Leo was in bed, Sienna was exhausted herself. And depressed. She hated to see her boy struggling so hard. Was she doing enough for him?

Her mother chose that moment to call. "How are you doing up there, *hija preciosa*? Are you ready to move back home?"

No phone call from her mother was complete without this question. "No, but I'm ready for you and Papi to move up here."

"We'll never get your *papi* out of LA," her mother said in disgust. "You know that. He's been here all his life. Oh, I wish you hadn't moved so far away. How's Leo doing?"

"He's doing well." In spite of the mean boys who teased him, Leo liked Icicle Falls and loved having a big backyard to play in—something they hadn't had, living in an apartment.

"I don't know how he can do well so far from his grandparents," said her mom.

"You'll come up and visit this summer," Sienna reminded her.

Right now, summer seemed a long way away. Sienna knew she'd made the right move, but she was close to her parents, and talking on the phone with her mother wasn't the same as having her just a few blocks away, ready to make tamales or *tres leches* cake together or go shopping. Or getting a hug from her father, who was always quick to tell her how proud he was of her.

Ah, well. She had Rita and Tito. And Leo would

enjoy experiencing his first-ever white Christmas. Not for the first time, she told herself that she'd done the right thing moving up here.

"Meanwhile," she said to her mom, "keep an eye out for your Christmas presents. I already put them in the mail." She'd sent her mother a copy of Beth Mallow's cookbook and one of Muriel Sterling-Wittman's books, which she'd bought using her employee discount. Her father would be receiving Sweet Dreams chocolates and a T-shirt that said *Wilkommen* to Icicle Falls.

"Oh, you shouldn't spend the money," her mother protested.

"I won't if you won't," Sienna teased.

Her mother gave a snort of disgust. "As if we wouldn't make sure you had presents under the tree. Are you driving all right in the snow now?"

Sienna decided not to tell her about the close encounter with Cratchett's bush. "I'm getting better at it all the time," she lied, then quickly changed the subject. "I got flowers today."

"You did? From who?"

"From a man I met the other day."

"You met a man?" Now Mama sounded suspicious and Sienna regretted opening her big mouth. She should have known it would get Mama worked up. "You be careful, Sienna. You know what kind of luck you've had with men. You don't want another Carlos."

"Don't worry, Mama, I—"

Mama kept talking. "Or Manny. Or Gregory. Or Juan."

Sienna needed eggnog. She poured herself a tall glassful. "Okay, I get it." One thing her mother was really good at was pointing out her daughter's mistakes. Maybe there were some things she didn't miss about living so close to her parents. "Look, Mama, I've got to go. I'm glad you called." *Sort of.* "Tell Papi hello."

That had not been one of her more enjoyable mother-daughter conversations, she thought as she ended the call. But her mother had made a good point. When it came to men, Sienna was a lousy judge of character. With her luck, Tim Richmond would probably turn out to be as flawed as the other men she'd dated. She simply hadn't found his flaw yet.

She had stretched out on the couch with her eggnog, ready to distract herself with whatever she could find on TV, when he called.

"So you like the flowers?" She could hear the smile in his voice, and she couldn't help smiling in response.

"I do. It was nice of you, but you didn't need to."

"I think you needed some proof that not everyone in my family is a jerk."

"You proved it."

"Good. Maybe next time I'm over your way, I can prove it some more."

That low voice swept over her like a caress. "Maybe you can," she said, wiping the memory of her past romantic mistakes from her mental hard drive. New town, new beginnings.

The short conversation lifted her spirits. Life wasn't all bad. You struggled to do what was right for your child, you worked hard and tried to get along with your neighbors, even the undeserving ones. And sometimes, just when you needed it most, God whispered in someone's ear to send you flowers. Surely a man who would send flowers to make up for his uncle's shortcomings couldn't be all bad? She went to bed with her mood much improved.

The good mood was still with her when Tim's holiday bouquet sitting on the kitchen counter greeted her the next morning. Leo had forgotten his misery of the night before and she got him off to school feeling just as happy as she did.

"Do your best," she told him, channeling Muriel Sterling, "and have a smile for everyone."

He nodded. "I will."

"Then I know you'll have a good day."

With Leo out the door she had a few minutes before she had to leave for the bookstore. She settled on the couch with Muriel Sterling's book. The flowers had certainly brought some joy into her life. What could she do today to keep that going?

Look outside your window, Muriel advised from the pages. *The world can be a beautiful place if you look with the right attitude. What do you see? A snowy lawn? A cardinal perched on a tree branch? Your neighbor's Christmas lights?*

Sienna looked out her living room window. There were the snowy lawns and houses with their roofs all frosted white.

And Mr. Cratchett, bundled up in his hat, winter coats and boots, a determined look on his face, marching up her front walk bearing a shovel full of what looked like...

Dog poop?

Chapter Six

This is the season to reach out in love.
——Muriel Sterling, *A Guide to Happy Holidays*

What on earth? Sienna scrambled off her couch and got to her front door just in time to see Cratchett marching back down the front walk. There on her front porch sat a freshly made pile of unpleasant, half of which looked like it had been mashed with a boot.

"What are you doing?" she yelled.

"Returning the present your dog left on my front walk," he called back over his shoulder.

"I don't have a dog!" she shouted at him. He kept walking and she slammed her front door. This man was impossible. She was never going to be able to see the good in him. There wasn't any.

She threw on her coat and got a baggie for doggy-doo pickup. Once on her front porch, she was strongly tempted to go right on over to Cratchett's place and return the gift.

But did she want to start a war? World War Poop.

That would be what she'd have if she lowered herself to Cratchett's level.

Knowing him, he'd call the police and she'd get another visit from Tilda, the cop, like she'd had when she'd first moved in and he'd sicced the Icicle Falls Police on her for having the nerve to host a noisy barbecue on a Saturday night. It had been only nine at night but he'd insisted the police come talk to her about turning down the music.

"Turn it off by ten or we'll be back," Tilda had said. "And welcome to Icicle Falls."

Welcome, indeed! Cratchett had been a nail in her flip-flop ever since.

She scooped up the mess, sealed it and deposited it in her trash can, then soaped up a rag and scrubbed away the remnants. There. Problem solved.

For the moment. Somewhere nearby she heard the sharp bark of a small dog. She'd never seen any of her neighbors out walking one. Who had the pup? Whoever it was, she hoped that person kept a closer eye on it in the future.

It was now time to leave for work, so she left Muriel's book sitting on the couch. She was in no mood to read it now, anyway. *Thank you, Mr. Cratchett. I hope Santa brings you a gigantic lump of coal for Christmas. And if he's not sure where to put it, I'll be glad to make a suggestion.*

She frowned her way to work, but once she got inside Mountain Escape Books, it was impossible to stay grumpy. The store looked so cheerful. The ends of the bookshelves had been made to look like giant presents, covered with red paper and topped with fat green ribbon and large matching bows. Two little trees made of book pages, which Sienna had created for Pat, looked on as customers purchased their books. The place smelled like fresh pine thanks to the room freshener Pat had sprayed and Christmas music played softly in the background—a sample from one of the CDs for sale. Customers were browsing and everyone was smiling. Yes, this was how the holidays should be.

"You look happy," Pat greeted her.

"I'm always happy to be here," Sienna said. "This is the best job in the world." Best job and best employer. It went a long way toward making up for having the world's worst neighbor.

She hung up her coat in the back room and then got busy helping customers find the books they wanted. And even some they didn't know they wanted.

Sienna's other next-door neighbor, Mrs. Zuckerman, came in around eleven. She was a pretty woman, maybe at the end of her sixties or beginning her seventies, slender with short snowy white hair, always fashionably dressed. Today she wore snow boots and leggings and a long winter coat accented with a red wool scarf.

"I need some books for the grandchildren and my little great-granddaughter," she told Sienna. "One married, two in college and a three-year-old. Do you have any suggestions?"

"I think I can help you," Sienna told her.

"Good, and then when we've taken care of them, I think I'll buy a little something for myself. I love books. In fact, I can't think of a better Christmas present. Can you?"

"Books are the best gifts," Sienna agreed.

"Speaking of gifts, my son and daughter-in-law surprised me with an unexpected one when they were over this weekend and you'll never guess what it was."

"A smart TV?"

"No. There's not much worth watching on TV. I'd rather read. But I was saying only the other day how empty the house feels sometimes and so what did they do but go out and get me a dog."

"A dog?" A wandering, pooping dog?

"Yes, he's the cutest thing—Alaskan malamute and Border collie. Black-and-white and he has the softest fur. It's black around his eyes and he looks like a little bandit, so that's what I named him. He's a few months old and full of energy. I'm afraid he got loose earlier this morning and I had to chase him down and lure him back with a piece of bacon. He is a little rascal."

"I'll bet," Sienna said. Now the mystery of the dog was solved. She hoped it stayed away from Mr. Cratchett's place. He'd have the dogcatcher after it in a heartbeat.

Arnie dropped by Muriel's cottage on Wednesday evening. It was the first she'd seen of him since the morning he and Dot decided to take the Christmas cruise together.

"I haven't heard from you since breakfast at Dot's," she greeted him. That sounded rather accusatory. "I guess you've been busy," she hastily added.

"I have," he agreed but didn't go into details.

"I imagine you and Dot have been making plans," she continued as he settled on her couch. Here she was fishing. For what, she wasn't quite sure.

"We've had a few things to talk about," he said with a smile.

Obviously, he and Dot were becoming buddies. Nice for both of them.

"Good thing we both already had passports."

Muriel remembered the discussion around the Pancake Haus table earlier in the year. The Claussens had joined Arnie and Muriel for breakfast and Dot had sat down for a chat, as well. The subject of travel had come up, and everyone had agreed that it would be a good idea to do so while they were all in good health. They'd all decided to take the first step and get passports.

Arnie had been the first to get his, followed by the Claussens, who had used theirs for a trip to London. Muriel had gotten hers and done nothing with it. And the last time the subject had come up, Dot hadn't even gotten around to getting one. "Too busy at the restaurant," she'd said. So, when had she found the time?

"Muriel?"

Arnie was looking at her in concern and she realized she was frowning.

She wiped it off and donned a more friendly expression. "How about some coffee?"

"Sure," he said.

"And some fruitcake cookies to go with it?" she suggested.

"You know I love your fruitcake cookies."

"You love everything I bake," she teased.

"True."

And Dot can't bake at all. Don't forget that.

There was a petty thought. Where on earth had that come from? She immediately shoved it away.

She returned with the coffee and the cookies and Arnie was quick to help himself to one. "These are my favorites."

"I know," she said. "That's why I make them."

He looked surprised, then smiled. "Really?"

"Really. The kids aren't all that fond of them."

"I never knew that. Here all these years I thought you were giving them to me to get rid of them."

"That, too," she joked. She studied him as he helped himself to a second cookie. Arnie was kind of cute in a nerdy sort of way. *Hmm, speaking of nerdy...* "Where's your bow tie?" Today he was wearing a shirt under a black sweater and his usual slacks. But no bow tie.

He made a face. "Dot said I look like a dweeb in it. She threatened to throw me overboard if I wore one on the cruise."

The bow tie had come along with his job at the bank many years ago. Even after Arnie had taken early retirement, the bow tie had remained. Now here he was, sans tie. Her subtle hints with the neckties hadn't gotten the message across, but all it had taken was a word from Dot and they were gone.

"Arnie, if you like wearing bow ties, then you should."

What kind of silly advice was this? Muriel knew exactly. Whatever Dot had said, she'd be contradicting it. *Shame on you*, she told herself. How perverse she was being. It was as if she were a teenage girl again, feeling threatened by a rival.

But she wasn't a girl anymore. She was a grown woman, and Dot was a friend, not a rival. There was no need for this petty jealousy.

There may have been no need, but she was feeling it, anyway. She wasn't jealous of Dot, though. Why should she be? She was simply envious of all the fun Dot was going to have. Fun that she could have had.

"No, I think maybe Dot was right," Arnie was saying. "Who wears bow ties these days, anyway? I like being more casual."

"Casual is good," Muriel said.

"I kind of like the new me."

So did Muriel. How much did Dot like the new Arnie?

"I'll send the rest of those home with you," she said as he helped himself to a third cookie.

"Great. We can eat them on the plane. We're leaving tomorrow"

Yes, she knew. She forced her lips to stay curved up.

"What would you like me to bring you back from Germany?"

"I'd love a table runner."

"Done," he said with a nod. "What else?"

"Oh, that will be more than enough. And if they're too expensive, don't bother."

"Muriel, I was ready to pay for your trip. I think I can afford a table runner."

"Thank you. That's awfully sweet of you." She should have let him pay for the trip. She should have gone.

"I'm happy to do it."

Arnie was such a kind and generous man. She couldn't help thinking about how good he'd been to her over the years. When her first husband had died, he'd helped her sort out the legal and financial matters when she'd been completely overwhelmed by the loss.

"I don't know how I'll live without Stephen," she'd told Arnie at the memorial service. She'd felt so alone, so unequal to the task of raising her girls without their father. Her own father had promised to step back in and run the company, but his health had been poor and she'd worried about him working so hard.

Arnie had hugged her and said, "You'll manage, Muriel. You're a strong woman."

But she wasn't really. She'd managed to raise her daughters only because Arnie had been there by her side, helping her when she snarled her finances—something she did on a regular basis—stopping by the house with little gifts for the girls, taking them all out to eat at Herman's Hamburgers after church on Sundays. After her father died, he'd taken a hand in helping her keep the company afloat, advising her every step of the way. Actually, when it had come right down to it, he'd made a lot of her decisions for her, helping her hold the company in trust until Samantha, her oldest, could take over.

Once, he'd tentatively broached the subject of love, asking her if she'd ever be open to having another man in her life.

"I couldn't," she'd said. "There was only one man for me and he's gone."

And she'd truly felt that way…until Waldo came along.

* * *

Muriel had stopped at Bavarian Brews on her way to the Sweet Dreams office. It was a beautiful spring morning and she'd enjoyed her walk into downtown. A pleasant walk on a nice day, a sweet coffee drink— it was on days like this that she found it very easy to count her blessings. Yes, she still missed her husband after all these years, but in spite of that, life was good.

She ordered her mocha, then realized that she'd forgotten to put her credit card in her sweater pocket.

"Don't worry, Mrs. Sterling. I know you're good for it," the barista assured her.

"I'll be happy to pay for the lady's drink. Put it on my tab," a deep voice behind Muriel said.

She turned to see a tall man with broad shoulders and an equally broad smile and she felt the same fluttering in her chest as what she'd felt the first time she'd seen Stephen.

"There's no need," she protested.

"But I want to. It's not every day a man meets such a beautiful woman. Tell me you're not married." He took her left hand and examined it. "Ah, lucky me."

"I'm a widow," she said, withdrawing her hand. Thinking of Stephen, her one true love, she felt guilty for her reaction to this stranger.

He sobered immediately. "I'm so sorry. I know just how you feel. I lost my wife three years ago. I was like a crazy man. I didn't want to go on living. But of course, you have to, don't you? Especially if you've got kids. Do you have kids?"

And that was how the conversation began. Of course,

she had to tell him about her children and he had to tell her about his daughter. It turned out he was in Seattle with his brother's family and they'd all decided to come to Icicle Falls to enjoy the hiking and the scenery.

"The prettiest scenery is right here in this coffee shop," he said.

And there went the flutters again. Next thing she knew, Muriel had a lunch date with Waldo and his brother and sister-in-law. And then she had a dinner date. And then Waldo was extending his stay in the Pacific Northwest.

"What do you know about this man?" Arnie demanded when Muriel told him she'd met someone. "What's his financial situation?"

"I don't know and I don't care. I think I love him, Arnie." Hard to believe it could happen twice in one lifetime and so quickly, but it had.

The news did not sit well. "You shouldn't rush into anything," Arnie cautioned.

"Why not, if it's something wonderful?" she countered. "I'm lonely, Arnie. I'm so lonely it aches."

"You're not alone. You have your friends. You have me."

"I know and I'm grateful. But it's not the same. You don't understand. You don't know what it's like to have loved someone and lost them."

"Maybe not. But I know what it's like to love someone and never have had her."

The simple statement filled her with guilt, but it didn't change their situation. "Arnie, I'm sorry. I can't help the way I feel." And she couldn't.

He sighed. "I know. If this is what you want, Muriel, then I'm happy for you."

That had always been Arnie's attitude. His love had been constant and selfless. He'd remained her friend and extended that friendship to Waldo, as well. And when Waldo died, Arnie had, once more, been there for her.

She'd taken his devotion for granted all these years. He'd always been a part of her life, an important part, and yet she'd viewed him more as scenery, two-legged background for the life and loves of Muriel Sterling-Wittman.

Now the background was walking offstage, starting to write his own story, and this new chapter didn't include her. It felt wrong.

Arnie finished the last of his coffee. "I'd better get going. I've got to get home and start packing."

"Then let me box up the cookies for you," Muriel said and hurried to the kitchen. Come tomorrow, Arnie and Dot would be off to Germany. Castles and museums and open-air markets, *glühwein*. Good times. It all could have been hers.

Arnie could have been hers.

You don't want him, she reminded herself. If she had, she could have done something about it years ago.

She returned with his cookies. "Here you go."

"Thanks. We'll enjoy these."

He made it sound as if he and Dot were some old married couple. "I wish I was going with you." Fine time to say it, right before he left.

He looked at her in surprise. "You were too busy," he reminded her.

She couldn't think of any reply for that. "Yes, well, have fun."

"We will."

She watched him make his way down her front walk, his boots crunching on the snow. He was whistling. Arnie Amundsen was a happy man.

Muriel shut the front door and returned to her living room couch and picked up her laptop to distract herself from the regrets that were creeping up. She needed a new book idea. So far nothing had come.

She stared at the blank screen, willing herself to have something profound or encouraging to say. The screen remained blank.

Maybe she should write about friendship. How to be a good friend? How to get past hoping your friend falls overboard?

Her green eyes were green in a whole new way now. But she had no excuse for this bout of jealousy. No one had deliberately excluded her from that holiday cruise, no one but herself. And just because it looked like Arnie and Dot were becoming good friends, it didn't mean she was being pushed out of the circle. Honestly, how old was she, twelve?

Muriel scowled at the screen. She didn't want to write about friendship. Right now, she didn't want to write about anything. Writer's block, that was what she had. She'd heard about it but never experienced it before.

Maybe this was more than writer's block. Maybe she had nothing left to say. Oh, there was a cheery thought.

"You need to take a break," she told herself and went in search of chocolate. Tomorrow she'd start fresh.

Tomorrow Arnie and Dot were flying off to Germany.

Muriel ate an entire sampler box of Sweet Dreams chocolate truffles.

As usual, Carlos was late with his child support. Sienna wished she didn't need it, wished she could shove her ex off the face of the earth and throw his money after him. But she couldn't. And anyway, it wouldn't be right to let him off the hook. Leo was his son and she wasn't about to let him forget that fact and skate off, free of doing what was right. But, oh, how she hated dealing with him when he did this to her. She hated having to go to him as a supplicant when caring for the child he'd fathered was part of his responsibility. She had other friends who were divorced. Their husbands paid child support and were involved in their kids' lives. A mother shouldn't have to hound her child's father to act like a father.

Carlos's behavior was a disgrace—to his family and to men and fathers everywhere. She was well rid of him. She only wished she didn't need his money.

Maybe someday, like Muriel, she'd write a book, perhaps one about a woman with a deadbeat husband, a woman who overcame all obstacles and rose to be governor of her state. No, make that president of the United States. Yes, a Latina woman president. It would be a bestseller. She'd become rich, go on talk shows, warn women to get a character reference from a man before marrying him.

After Leo was asleep, she called Carlos's cell, fully expecting to get voice mail, because Señor Poop was not only selfish but also a coward. Whenever he got behind on his child support payments he became conveniently unavailable.

She was surprised when he answered. "I know I'm late," he said. "It's coming."

"So is Christmas, but I need the money before then."

"I said it's coming, Sienna. I had some unexpected bills this month."

She knew he had a new woman in his life. "If you're spending my child's support money on that *puta*..."

"Hey, watch your mouth."

"You won't have to listen to my mouth if you man up and do what you're supposed to do," she retorted. "If it wasn't for you, I wouldn't have a bad mouth." The man brought out the worst in her.

Funny how when they were first together and happy, she'd thought he brought out the best in her.

Unbidden, words from Muriel's book slipped into her mind. *When dealing with those difficult people that you're able to avoid the rest of the year, try to keep your encounters brief. Stay positive and find one good thing about that person to focus on.*

But when it came to Carlos, Sienna couldn't. There was no good thing. Anyway, she wasn't in the mood. She'd already had to deal with Cratchett that day and that had been enough.

Remember, diplomacy is the key to a happy holiday.

Okay, okay, diplomacy. They weren't getting anywhere this way. "I'm sorry." He should have been the one saying this. She forced the thought aside and continued, "I don't like having to bug you for money."

"But you do, don't you?" he snapped.

"He's your son, Carlos."

"I know that," he said, his voice prickly.

"I'm sorry he's not going to grow up to be the superstar macho man you always wanted, but he's a human being. And if you ever made any effort to see him or talk to him, you'd see that he's a great kid with a big heart. He's still got your smile," she added. The same smile that had attracted her to Carlos in the first place.

"All right," he said. "I'm not trying to screw you, Sienna, even though you think I am. I've got overtime coming. I'll get the money to you as soon as I can."

"Thanks."

Always try to find something nice to say.

"I knew you'd do the right thing," she added, taking Muriel's advice. Actually, that was *tontería* to the max.

But it worked. "I'm trying to do my part."

Oh, yes. That was why there'd been no battle for custody, no father-son afternoons. His son was a failed experiment that he preferred not to see. "I know," she said and hoped at some point he'd work on making that a true statement. But she wasn't holding her breath.

They said their goodbyes and she tossed her phone on the couch and sat there, staring at Muriel's book. *A Guide to Happy Holidays.* Well, it had guided her to getting Carlos motivated and that was something.

She picked up the book and opened to the page where she'd left off. *Attitude is everything,* Muriel reminded her, *and happiness is a choice. Focus on good thoughts and you'll find your attitude changing.*

Okay, she was going to choose to be happy. There were too many good things in her life to let something as small as an ex-husband ruin her holidays.

And if Carlos didn't send that money, she was going to choose to sic her cousin Bruno on him. Bruno was a cage fighter.

Muriel was right. There was nothing like a good thought to improve your attitude.

Chapter Seven

One of the nicest presents we can give is to rejoice in others' good fortunes.

—Muriel Sterling, *A Guide to Happy Holidays*

Sienna arrived at work to find Pat on the phone with her landlord.

"Harvey, you have got to replace the toilet in the workroom," she said, gripping the phone as if it were Harvey Wood's neck. "No, we're not putting anything down it we shouldn't. We wouldn't dare. It would explode."

Sienna watched as her employer stood at the till in silence, her scowl carving deeper into her face by the minute. Harvey Wood was Pat's version of Mr. Cratchett. Harvey was a lousy landlord, but at least he wasn't cranky. Sienna would have swapped him for her neighbor any day.

"You've got to do something." Pat listened a moment and then sighed. "Look, I know what it's like to run a business. I know you have your expenses, but this is a problem that needs to be solved right away. So can you please send someone from Sound Plumbing over here? I'll share the cost with you. All right. Thanks."

"So, the toilet's getting fixed?" Sienna asked.

Pat nodded. "That's what Harvey says. He'd better come through."

"I thought you handled that well."

"I was on the verge of making more threats," Pat admitted. "But, really, what would that have accomplished? And, actually, proposing a compromise made all the difference in his attitude."

"It doesn't seem fair you should have to help pay for the toilet," Sienna said.

"No, it doesn't. But I am trying to put myself in Harvey's shoes. He owns a couple of buildings here in town and I know he had to put a ton of money into a new roof over on the Icicle Building. So maybe he really is strapped." Pat smiled. "Anyway, we're getting the toilet replaced and that's what matters. Life is about compromise."

"It stinks that you had to, though."

"You have to do what you have to do," Pat said with a shrug.

Sienna thought of her conversation with Carlos. *Yes, you did.*

"I'm trying to look for the best in old Harv, and I'd like to think that he wants to do what's right."

"If he did, the toilet would have been fixed by now," Sienna pointed out.

Pat gave a reluctant smile. "You could be right, but ugly doesn't become pretty overnight. Speaking of, how are you doing with your neighbor?"

Sienna rolled her eyes. "I think it's hopeless. He's always going to be an ugly tree."

"Oh, no. What's the old coot done now?"

Sienna related the latest offense. "If only he'd move," she finished.

"Don't hold your breath," Pat said.

"You're right. It's just frustrating sometimes, you know, having to deal with him on top of my ex," Sienna confessed. "But every cloud has a silver lining. I did get flowers out of the deal," she said, following Muriel's advice to focus on something good. Flowers were always good.

"Flowers from Cratchett?" Pat asked in disbelief.

"No, from his nephew," Sienna said and told her about Tim.

"Hmm. Is he single?"

"I'm not in the market," Sienna said as much to herself as Pat. "Anyway, I'd have to be crazy to want to get serious with anyone related to Cratchett." She shook her head. "If only the old grinch would move, then my life would be perfect."

"There's no such thing, believe me," Pat said.

"You're right. Well, then, better, at least. I sure wish I could find the secret formula for turning Mr. Cratchett into a normal human being."

As if on cue, Muriel walked into the bookstore. She wasn't wearing her usual serene smile, though. In fact, she looked like she'd been drinking from the same bahhumbug punch bowl as Cratchett.

"Let's ask the expert," Pat said, calling her over.

"Things are going from bad to worse with Sienna's neighbor. Have you got any advice?"

"I'm afraid not," Muriel said shortly. "Where are those books you need me to sign?"

Pat and Sienna exchanged puzzled looks. Sweet Muriel Sterling-Wittman had obviously been taken over by aliens.

"Is everything all right?" Pat asked her friend.

"Of course," Muriel said. "I'm in a hurry, though."

Muriel was never in a hurry. She always had time to visit, was always open to listening to a person's problems and offering a word of encouragement. Pat took the books from the shelf behind her and handed them over. Muriel silently checked the slip of paper in the first one and began inscribing the book to the requested name. Okay. So much for pearls of wisdom from the Muriel Sterling treasure chest.

A new customer came in, looking for an illustrated copy of *A Christmas Carol*, and Sienna got busy helping her. By the time she was done, Muriel, the town's wisewoman, had left.

"I was kind of hoping she'd have some advice for me," Sienna confessed.

Pat shook her head. "She's in a mood. Oh, well. I'm sure you'll think of something."

"Oh, I can think of lots of somethings, but none of them are very nice. Boy, I'd love to leave something icky on his porch like he did on mine. Except my mother taught me better."

"Now, there's an idea," Pat said. "Why don't you take something over to him? Something sweet—like cookies.

He's all alone. I bet he'd like some home-baked treats. It might be a nice peace offering."

"He should be bringing a peace offering to me."

"Yes, he should, but you know he won't. Anyway, my mother always said that a gift from the kitchen makes for good neighbors."

"Your mother never met Mr. Cratchett."

"True," Pat said with a chuckle. "Still, it can't hurt to try."

"I guess not," Sienna said.

So that afternoon, after she got home from work, she and Leo got busy making cookies. Snowball cookies— lovely little baked balls bulging with chopped walnuts and white chocolate chips, and rolled in powdered sugar.

Leo was happy to help with rolling the cookies into balls and setting them out on the cookie sheet…anything to put off his schoolwork. He was more open to digging out his math assignment when Sienna promised to save some cookies for him to devour while she went next door to make her delivery.

She set the cookies inside a festive holiday container that she'd bought at the grocery store on her way to pick up Leo, then donned coat and boots and went next door to Cratchett's house. It was now late afternoon and darkness had swallowed the sun, but she had enough light coming from the Christmas lights on her house and the streetlamps to see her way.

Of course, there was no holiday glow coming from Cratchett's place. His was the only house that remained untrimmed for the holidays and his porch light was off. That was hardly surprising, considering the fact that he probably never had company. She knocked on the door and waited there in the dark, the whole unwelcome vibe making her uncomfortable. There was no guarantee this encounter would be any more pleasant than their last one.

No one came to the door. She could hear the TV blaring from inside. Maybe he hadn't heard her knocking. She rang the doorbell.

It was cold out here on the porch. She pulled her coat collar closer and stamped her feet to keep the blood circulating. Still no sign of Cratchett. "I know you're in there," she muttered and rang the doorbell again.

Still the door remained shut. What was with this man?

She was about to ring the doorbell a third time when the door jerked open and Cratchett appeared in the doorway, wearing pajama bottoms, a faded black sweatshirt and an unwelcoming look on his face. "What?"

"I'm sorry about our misunderstanding earlier. I brought you some cookies," she said and held out the offering.

At first he almost looked pleased. At least, she thought he did, but she had such a fleeting glimpse of that near smile she couldn't be sure.

She could be sure of the suspicious expression he was wearing now. "What kind of cookies?"

Did it matter? They were free. She found herself frowning in true Bob Cratchett form. "They're snowball cookies."

"What's in 'em?"

"Flour, sugar, butter, chopped walnuts..."

"I'm allergic to nuts. Give 'em to someone else. Good night."

And with that the door shut. No "Thanks, anyway" or "Kind of you to think of me."

"Nice of me to go to all that trouble," she said to the closed door. "By the way, I really don't like you."

She turned and stomped down his front porch steps. What a waste of time it had been to be neighborly to him.

It seemed a shame to have gone to all that trouble for nothing. Surely someone in the neighborhood would like to have her cookies, not to mention a cute cookie container.

She knew exactly who. She hurried over to Mrs. Zuckerman's house. Mrs. Zuckerman always kept her front porch light on. And she answered the door only a moment after Sienna knocked.

"Sienna, come on in." She had a firm hold on her new dog's collar and Bandit was barking eagerly and wagging his tail.

Leo was probably distracted from his homework already. She needed to get back home and help him. Still, she couldn't resist Mrs. Zuckerman's warm welcome. "Just for a minute. I don't like to leave Leo unsupervised for long," she said, stepping inside. Bandit was thrilled to have company, still barking and jumping up and pawing at Sienna in the hopes of getting petted.

"Look at this little guy. He's so cute," she said, trying to get the dog to hold still long enough for her to give him what he wanted. "If you need someone to come over and play with him, I know Leo will be happy to volunteer." Leo had been lobbying for a dog lately. So far Sienna had resisted, feeling it would be better to wait for a while before giving her son that responsibility.

"He's welcome to take Bandit out in the backyard to play anytime," said Mrs. Zuckerman. "Once Bandit learns some manners. Now, down, Bandit."

Bandit barked again and pawed at Sienna's coat.

"When it comes to manners, I'm afraid he has a ways to go. I'm taking him to obedience school in the New Year." Mrs. Zuckerman gave the dog's collar a tug. "He'll settle down in a minute."

After a good deal of petting, followed by the distraction of a chew toy, the dog did happily settle down, lying on Sienna's foot as she sat on Mrs. Zuckerman's couch, drinking tea.

"These cookies look lovely. What a nice thought," Mrs. Zuckerman said, helping herself to one. "They're delicious. You're quite the baker."

"Not really," Sienna said.

"It's nice to see a young woman who likes to bake. So many women these days don't bother." Mrs. Zuckerman gave Sienna a sly look. "I'm sure there's some handsome man in your life who's looking forward to getting some of these."

"There is. I left some with Leo."

"Such a sweet boy. But you haven't met anyone here in Icicle Falls? You're such a pretty thing with those big brown eyes and that thick black hair. I'm sure you must have caught someone's eye."

A vision of Tim Richmond came ho-ho-ho-ing into

Sienna's mind. She told him to go ho-ho-ho somewhere else. "I've met lots of nice people. Including you."

"Oh, brother," Mrs. Zuckerman said, waving off the compliment. She took another cookie. "You know, I've made this cookie for years, but yours are a little different. I'd love the recipe."

"Of course." At least someone appreciated her cookies. Not only was Cratchett rude, he was an ingrate. Sienna suspected that if the gods came down from Olympus and offered him ambrosia, he'd shut the door in their faces, too. She set aside her tea and stood. "I'd better get back home. Thanks for the tea."

"Thanks for the cookies. I'll enjoy them," Mrs. Zuckerman said as she and Bandit walked Sienna back to the door.

At least Mrs. Zuckerman appreciated a kind gesture, and Sienna left her house in a much better mood than she'd been in when she'd first arrived. Her good deed hadn't been a waste of time after all.

And speaking of good deeds, she wasn't going to waste any more on Cratchett. For all she cared, he could die of Christmas-cookie cravings.

It was nine in the evening and Muriel was curled up on her couch with a book and a cup of cocoa when her phone pinged with a message. Arnie had sent a selfie of Dot and himself at the airport. They were both holding up one of Muriel's cookies and smiling. Waiting to board, he'd texted.

Waiting to have their big adventure. While Muriel was simply sitting around...waiting. It seemed like she'd put much of her life on hold since Waldo died, being content to merely write about living and go through her days as a spectator in her daughters' lives rather than strike out to make new memories of her own.

But, when it came right down to it, Muriel wasn't an adventurous woman. Her biggest adventure had been choosing her first husband, Stephen, when her parents hadn't approved of him.

Looking back, she could hardly blame them. He'd had long hair and had ridden into town on a motorcycle. Neither the long hair nor the motorcycle had been considered cool by the older generation back then, but she hadn't cared. He'd also been handsome and rugged and sexy—a man of the world and the most exotic thing she'd ever seen. Of course, she'd fallen hard.

Of course, he'd proved himself to be capable and responsible, eventually heading up the family chocolate company and making a success of it.

Waldo, on the other hand, had almost ruined the company, leaving it to Samantha to save. And during all this, Muriel had been stationed on the sidelines, coping with being widowed yet a second time. Now here she was, on the sidelines again while her friends flew off to Germany.

She studied the picture. Arnie looked so happy. Well, good. She was happy for him. Have a safe flight, she texted back. And let me know when you get there.

The next morning, thanks to the time difference, she awoke to find she had a new text from him, this time from Germany. We're here. Along with it came a picture of their cruise ship.

Soon there were more pictures, this time from Dot.

Check out the stateroom!

In addition to the large bed and requisite night-stands, the picture showed a room boasting a huge full-length French balcony that would frame shifting views of German towns and suburbs as the longboat made its leisurely way down the various rivers. Dot didn't stop there. She included shots of the view out the window, the TV, the bathroom. That was small, with a shower, toilet and very little counter space. Muriel consoled herself with the thought that it would have been difficult for two women to share.

Dot didn't stop with pictures of the room and the view it offered. More followed—one of the lounge area, all decorated for the holidays, and one of their lunch spread, a gourmand's delight.

Tomorrow we go to Nuremberg to our first Christmas market. Meanwhile, the food is great and Arnie and I are having a blast. Now don't you wish you'd come? Dot taunted.

Yes, as a matter of fact, she did.

Later came the text from Arnie.

Had my first taste of *glühwein*. You'd love it. Tomorrow we're off to Nuremberg. Meanwhile, tonight the boat is all lit up and on shore there's a light dusting of snow on the ground and the rooftops. Looks like a painting come to life.

What a charming description. Who knew Arnie was such a romantic? After all these years she should have known. After all these years she should have seen.

Muriel's ugly tree seemed to be mocking her. She picked up her laptop and moved from the couch, where she'd been trying once more to think of a new book idea, to the kitchen. The kitchen didn't hold any inspiration, either, but at least she didn't have to look at her tree.

Another couple of hours and she'd had enough of sitting around trying to come up with something positive and inspiring. She wasn't feeling either positive or inspired. She'd definitely had enough of seeing Arnie's and Dot's texts. She needed to get out…and leave her phone behind.

She rounded up Pat and Olivia and met them at her daughter Bailey's tearoom for lunch. The tearoom was looking festive with a flocked tree—decorated with pink bows, balls and tiny teacup and teapot ornaments—standing in one corner. Green linen napkins lay over lacy white tablecloths, and small arrangements of greens graced the center of each table.

Several other Icicle Falls residents were there, enjoying sandwiches or ordering Bailey's chocolate high tea, and Muriel waved hello to Janice Lind, who was seated with a friend at a window table.

"I love coming here," Olivia said after they'd been seated. "It's so pretty and girlie."

"I'm glad you supported her in opening the place," Muriel said. "It's been a perfect fit for her."

"So has he," Pat said as Bailey's husband, Todd, came

into the tearoom carrying their baby. They were both bundled up against the cold winter air, Todd in jeans, boots and a parka, and little Anna Louise all dolled up in a pink snowsuit complete with white faux-fur trim. At the sight of Muriel and her friends, he came over to the table, the baby enjoying the ride in her daddy's arms and looking eagerly around her.

Anna Louise was six months old now, taking in the sights and sounds of her first Icicle Falls Christmas with wide-eyed wonder. She gurgled happily at the sight of her grandma and bounced up and down in her daddy's arms.

"Kiss Grammy," he said, lowering her to Muriel. "Then it's time for your lunch and a nap."

The baby touched a slobbery mouth to Muriel's cheek, making all those happy grandma endorphins ooze every which way and wiping out all thoughts of the two adventurers abroad.

"And where were my darling and her wonderful daddy this morning?" Muriel asked.

"Out Christmas shopping for Mommy. Can I hide the present at your place? Bailey snoops."

"Of course," said Muriel.

Stephen had been a snooper, too, and she'd had a terrible time hiding presents from him. The memory made her wistful. She missed being married, missed the companionship, that feeling that she was important to someone. Of course, she was important to her children, but it wasn't the same thing. It wasn't the same as having that one special person in your life making the passage through time by your side, who made you feel like it mattered that you were alive.

Arnie had filled some of that gap, even though they'd been only friends. Was that all about to change now that Dot had stepped into the picture?

Bailey's server greeted them and handed out menus, and they placed orders for salads, which came with Bailey's popular herbed scones.

Bailey herself stepped out of the kitchen to say hello to her mother and the women who had been her adopted aunties for her entire life. "The place looks so pretty," Olivia told her.

"I'm pleased with how all my decorations turned out. By the way, guess what we just started serving for the holiday season. That bread pudding you gave me the recipe for. It's been a big hit already."

"I'm glad." Olivia beamed with pleasure, and Muriel, too, smiled. She was so proud of her girls and their accomplishments.

"Your daughter has got flair," Pat said to Muriel as Bailey slipped back into the kitchen.

"She does have beautiful taste," Olivia agreed. "If only my son had had the good taste to pursue her."

"He's happy with who he chose," Pat reminded her, and Olivia sighed and nodded.

"How are things going with your new daughter-in-law?" Muriel asked. Having a daughter-in-law you weren't happy with, now that was something to be depressed about. Muriel reminded herself she needed to count her blessings.

"A little better," Olivia said. "She still isn't much

help at breakfast. She's either claiming she doesn't feel well or she's oversleeping, but she does usually get downstairs in time to help with cleanup. And she enjoys checking in our guests. Of course, getting her trained to do that was an interesting experience." Olivia went on to recount the challenges of training the newest member of her family in social graces.

"Manners can be learned," Pat said. "And it sounds like she wants to."

"It looks that way. I think she's got it down now. In fact, she and Brooke are managing things at the lodge for me so I can get away."

"Speaking of getting away, have you girls heard from Dot?" Pat asked. "I have. She sent me a picture of their boat this morning."

"She told me they're already having fun," put in Olivia.

"I heard from her, too," Muriel said and left it at that. "Oh, look, here comes our lunch. I'm crazy about those herbed scones."

Her attempt to sidetrack the conversation failed. The minute their lunch was served, Olivia put them right back on the track. "Dot's been raving about what a sweet man Arnie is. Do you think she's interested in him?"

"No," Muriel said. "Of course not."

"I don't know," Olivia said. She took a bite of her scone. "Oh, these are heaven."

"Bailey created that recipe herself," Muriel bragged, happy to talk about something else besides Dot and Arnie. Anything else.

"You know," Olivia said slowly, "certain things are starting to make sense now."

"Like what?" Pat prompted.

"Like Dot always joining us whenever we're in Pancake Haus with Muriel and Arnie."

"That doesn't mean she has any interest in Arnie," Muriel said. "She's friends with all of us—why wouldn't she come over to join us? And besides, he's five years younger than her."

"At this point in life, who cares? And isn't that about the age difference they say you should have with your man if you're both going to grow old together?" Pat argued.

"No, that's seven," Olivia said.

"Well, it's still an age difference," Muriel said stubbornly and stabbed a chunk of her chicken salad with her fork. She was suddenly aware of both of her friends studying her. "What?"

"Arnie and Dot being on this trip, are you okay with that?" asked Pat.

"Of course I'm okay with it. Why shouldn't I be? I want to see them happy." She did. Really.

"You can't expect Arnie to carry a torch for you forever," Pat said. "Especially if you were never going to reciprocate."

Ouch. "I never expected him to," Muriel said and shifted in her seat. Although, maybe she had. As she examined her heart, it was looking more and more that way. Dog in the manger Muriel. She didn't want Arnie but she didn't want anyone else to have him, either.

"Anyway, they're only friends."

"Friendship often grows into more," Pat said. "Look at Ed and me."

Muriel didn't want to look. "That's different. You and Ed are a perfect match. Dot and Arnie wouldn't be right for each other."

"Muriel, you're jealous," Olivia said in surprise.

"I most certainly am not," Muriel snapped. "I'm happy for both of them and I hope they have a wonderful time." She was not jealous of her friend. She wasn't that petty.

The look Olivia and Pat exchanged showed how much they believed her. *In denial and in trouble.*

"Does anyone want dessert?" Chocolate. She needed chocolate.

Chapter Eight

Kindness is the key to happiness. No kind gesture
is ever wasted.

—Muriel Sterling, *A Guide to Happy Holidays*

Robert Cratchett had been trying to shovel his
front walk when Sienna left for work on Friday. He'd
looked—big surprise—irritated and more than a little
red in the face from the exertion. And no wonder. The
guy had to be in his seventies. He probably shouldn't
have been trying to do that on his own.

She wasn't going to be the one to help him, though,
not after everything that had happened in the last few
days. If he needed help, he could ask one of the other
people on the street. She was over trying to be neighborly. That was one ugly tree who would never look
good. No amount of cookies would ever sweeten him
up and all the kindness in the world would never pen-
etrate his crusty shell.

Anyway, she reasoned, she didn't have time for
Cratchett. She had to get to the bookstore. The old
grump was on his own.

She felt more than justified as she crept her way down the street, which had a new coating of snow... until her conscience kicked her.

He didn't want anything from her, she reasoned, kicking back. He'd made that clear. It wasn't her fault he was too stubborn to find a nice retirement home and leave the snow shoveling to someone else. Not that any retirement home would be nice once he arrived. So why bother?

She'd seen him again at the grocery store when she'd gone in on her lunch break to pick up some much-needed groceries. She'd started down the bread aisle only to discover him at the other end, inspecting a package of cinnamon rolls. She'd immediately turned her cart around and gone the other way.

"I think I truly hate the man," she said to Rita when she came to pick up Leo.

"You can't be hating anyone at Christmas. Santa won't bring you anything," Rita said and freshened Sienna's mug of tea.

"There's nothing I want, anyway," Sienna retorted.

Rita cocked an eyebrow. "Sex?"

"Overrated," Sienna scoffed. And then a vision of Tim Richmond entered her mind, and it was a vision to behold. There he stood in a pair of plaid pajama bottoms, that big chest bare. He smiled at her.

She realized she was wearing a goofy smile and quickly wiped it off her face.

Too late. Rita had seen. She shook her head. "Now you're lying. Boy, are you on the naughty list."

Yes, she was.

By Saturday morning she was feeling guilty about

her bad attitude regarding her neighbor. Muriel's book didn't help.

Kindness is the gift that keeps on giving, Muriel wrote. *Sadly, it's one thing we simply don't get enough of these days. Is there someone in your life who could use an extra serving of kindness?*

Yeah. Someone who didn't deserve so much as another single drop of that valuable commodity.

Not even the smallest kind gesture is ever wasted.

"It would be on Cratchett," Sienna muttered. She shut the book, tossed it next to her on the bed and snuggled back under the covers. Why did she keep reading this book, anyway?

Because Muriel Sterling was right. She sat up again and pulled the book back to her.

Remember, we all have people in our lives who stretch our patience and challenge our generosity. But I believe that God often brings those people into our lives for a reason. Sometimes it's so we can help them. Other times, believe it or not, it's so they can help us. When we rise above our petty dislikes and our hurt feelings, we become better people.

Sienna already had an ex to help her become a better person. She didn't need Cratchett for that.

Think of the oyster and the pearl it produces. The pearl starts out as a grain of sand, an unwanted irritant. But it's not going anywhere, so the oyster has to deal with it. Without that irritant the oyster wouldn't be able to make a pearl. You might have an irritant in your life.

There was an understatement.

But it could turn out that the very person who irritates you is exactly what is needed for you to produce something rich in your life.

Sienna sighed. "Okay, fine."

Although, really, she already had enough to deal with between her day job and raising her son alone. She much preferred ignoring Cratchett altogether and focusing her energy where it would be appreciated.

Her bedroom door opened and Leo came bounding in, wearing his superhero pajamas. "It's snowing!"

The thrill of winter hadn't worn off. She loved her son's enthusiasm, but they still needed to work on manners. "Leo, you're supposed to knock on the door before you come in. Remember?"

Leo frowned.

"Let's try it again."

He trudged out of the room as if he'd been told there was no Santa Claus and shut the door. Then knocked. "Can I come in?"

"Yes, you may," she called, and once more he raced into the room and dived onto the bed.

"It's snowing," he informed her, bouncing up and down on his knees.

"So you said." The stuff was beautiful and she understood her son's excitement. If only it would fall on just the lawns and leave the streets and sidewalks alone.

"Can I go out and play?"

"After breakfast. But first you need to get dressed. Your clothes are on your bed. Why don't you go put them on?" She laid out his clothes for him every night. Having to select a wardrobe for the day left him standing and staring at his dresser, paralyzed by indecision.

"Okay," he said cheerfully, then clambered off the bed and raced out of the room.

Seven thirty in the morning and they were up and running. There was no sleeping in for moms.

She showered and dressed and then stopped by Leo's room to make sure he was on track. He'd gotten as far as putting on his T-shirt and sweater—backward—and was sitting on the bed still in his pajama bottoms, picking at his toes.

Although she assured herself constantly that her son would be able to live a happy and productive life, there were times when dark moods settled over her, when she worried about what would happen to him after she was gone. Who would be his advocate? He had no siblings, only a cousin who would probably marry and move away.

The dark shadow hovered over her now, but she squirmed out from under it, reminding herself that even though her boy was slow, he was still teachable. He was mastering the basic life skills. He'd manage. Besides, it was many years before she had to worry about him being on his own. She didn't have to start today.

"How about you quit being a monkey and playing with your toes and get the pants on?" she suggested.

"I'm not a monkey," he said and laughed.

"No, you're not. Come on. Off with the jammies."

Another five minutes and Leo was racing down the stairs ahead of her. "I want pancakes!"

"Pancakes it is," she said.

"With peanut butter and bananas."

"With peanut butter and bananas. Yes, sir."

Leo became engrossed in the ritual of breakfast, setting the table with Mom supervising, stirring the pancake batter and watching as the pancakes rose on the griddle. He always wanted three pancakes, each one spread with peanut butter and sporting eyes made from banana slices and raisins lined up for a mouth. Leo never hurried through breakfast.

Or any other meal for that matter, and sometimes Sienna thought those other children who used the *R*-word could learn a thing or two from her son. Leo knew how to stay in the moment and savor it.

But finally, the savoring was done and the teeth were brushed and he was bundled up and ready to go outside. She sent him into the backyard to play, suggesting he try to make snow angels like she'd shown him earlier in the week. He lasted all of five minutes, then was back in the house.

"It's cold," he reported.

And he was bored all by himself out there. She knew his friend Jimmy was in Seattle with his family for the weekend, so there would be no playmate for Leo. Since snow was still such a novelty, she hated to have him stuck inside when he could be having fun in it.

Which meant she was going to have to put on her

snow pants. "I tell you what, I'll come out and play in the snow with you as soon as I get a couple of things done. Meanwhile, you can watch cartoons. Would you like that?"

Leo nodded eagerly. He loved cartoons and would happily sit in front of the TV like a turnip all morning if Sienna let him.

It was tempting, but after she'd cleaned up the kitchen and put in a load of laundry, she dug out her snow pants and parka. "Shall we make a big old snow-man for all the neighborhood to enjoy?" she suggested once she had him bundled up again.

"Yes!" Leo cried and blasted out the front door.

Sienna followed at a more leisurely pace. The snow had stopped but not before adding to the thick blanket covering their front yard. She walked partway across the lawn, pulled her cell phone from her jacket pocket and snapped a picture of her snowcapped house and sent it to her mom. Then she stood for a moment, enjoying the peace of a world wrapped in soft silence.

Until her son gave her a playful shove, catching her off balance and sending her toppling into the snow. "Oh, very funny," she said as she got back on her feet.

Leo thought so. "I got you," he chortled.

"Now I'm going to get you," she said.

He was off and running with a screech and she chased him around the yard until they were both breathless. Then she caught him and gave him a big, smacking kiss. "Are you my favorite boy?"

"I am!"

"Good. Now, favorite boy, should we make our snow-man?"

Leo nodded eagerly. "Yes!"

"Okay. Remember how I showed you." She bent and formed a snowball. "Let's roll this along until it gets really, really big."

Leo was all over that and she watched as he chased his growing snowball around the front yard. This was one of those moments to treasure. And record. Out came the phone again and she made a short movie.

She'd just put her cell away when she heard the crunch of tires on snow and saw Cratchett pulling up in his Cadillac. He aimed his remote at the garage door, which shuddered into action, then stopped halfway up.

Cratchett stopped his car in the driveway and got out, breaking the snowy silence with a string of words she hoped her son didn't hear. He slipped and slid his way over the latest covering of snow up to the door and tried to raise it manually. It didn't budge.

Sienna could almost feel a miniature Muriel Sterling-Wittman on her shoulder, whispering, *Kindness*.

Mr. Cratchett didn't look like he was in the mood for kindness. He gave up on the garage door, muttering and sliding his way back to his car. This was not the time to get neighborly. Anyway, she didn't know how to fix broken garage doors, and she doubted she'd be able to hoist up Cratchett's door any more than he could.

He opened the trunk and took out a large paper gro-cery sack, then started back to the house again, still muttering. He hit a slick patch and lost his balance. He did manage to stay upright, but the sack tumbled out of his hands, dropping onto the snow. Out fell a loaf of bread, some frozen dinners and two apples. A soup can dived into the snow on the yard.

Okay, she was going to have to help him before he fell and broke his neck. She hurried over. "Let me help you," she said and snagged the can.

"I don't need any help," he informed her as she tried to help him straighten up.

"Yeah, I can see that," she said and dropped the can into his bag. "It'd serve you right if you fell and broke your hip."

"Now you sound like my nephew," he said, his brows beetled. "I don't know why you don't mind your own business."

"I don't, either," she said irritably and marched back to her own yard. Kindness was so wasted on this man.

But not on you. Think of the pearl, whispered that imaginary Muriel.

Sienna told her to take a hike.

She refused. The pesky voice of Muriel Sterling, author extraordinaire, kept hounding Sienna as she helped her son put together his snowman. "Okay, fine," she finally muttered after they'd completed the snowman's face with the requisite carrot nose. "I get it."

"Get what?" Leo asked.

"Nothing. Why don't you see if you can build a baby snowman to keep this guy company?"

"Okay," Leo said eagerly.

Sienna got him started rolling his snowball around the yard, then fetched her snow shovel and went next door to take care of a certain undeserving man's slippery front walk. Leo didn't last long on his own in their yard. A few minutes later he was asking to help Sienna with her shoveling.

"Don't you want to work on your snowman?"

Leo shook his head. "I want to help you. Mrs. Brown says I'm a good helper."

It was in little moments like this that she knew she had a very special boy. "Yes, you are. All right, then," she said. "Go into the garage and get the other shovel. It's leaning on the wall right next to the door."

He nodded eagerly and bounded off, then returned a moment later dragging a shovel behind him. He mimicked her, digging in the shovel and pushing the snow with loud grunts. "This is fun!"

Fun. Right.

Shoveling was hot, sweaty work and halfway through, she took a break to lean on her shovel and catch her breath. She glanced in the direction of the house and caught sight of Cratchett peeking through the living room drapes. The curtains immediately twitched shut.

Her son might have had some mental challenges, but Cratchett was emotionally stunted, and if you asked Sienna, that was a far worse problem to have.

She was almost through with the job when Tim Richmond arrived. "What's this?" he greeted her.

"It's my good deed for the day."

"I'm helping," Leo added.

"I can see that. Good job, my man," Tim said.

She pointed to the grocery bag he was carrying. "You're a little late with that. Your uncle was already out getting groceries."

Tim stopped and frowned at the Cadillac in the driveway. "He flunked the vision test when he went to renew his license. He's not cleared to drive."

"That doesn't seem to be stopping him. He probably intended to hide the evidence but his garage door got stuck."

Tim shook his head. "This is going to make for an unpleasant conversation."

Sienna couldn't resist. "That should hardly come as a surprise since your uncle has a gift for unpleasant conversations."

"He does," Tim agreed. "So why are you being so nice to him?"

"He's my ugly-tree project."

Both Tim's eyebrows shot up. "Excuse me?"

Cratchett was on his front porch now, demanding to know if Tim was going to keep him waiting all day.

"I'm coming," Tim called back irritably. "I don't know why he has to do that," he muttered.

"He's not nice," Leo explained.

"Sometimes he's not," Tim agreed.

Sometimes?

"I'll finish shoveling the walk," Tim said to Sienna. "I'd say you've done enough."

Considering who she'd been doing it for, she couldn't have agreed more.

"You know, I'd like to hear more about this ugly-tree project of yours. How would it be if I came over when I'm done with my uncle?"

He was big and masculine and had a nice smile. He was the kind of man who showed up to help his family when he was needed. Unlike her ex, he appeared to be not only responsible but thoughtful. So why not?

Because Leo would get attached and be disappointed when it came to nothing.

And surely it would, since when it came to men, she couldn't seem to sort out the duds from the good ones. Tim seemed like a great guy, but she'd thought that about men before. She did not need to go barreling down Heartbreak Highway again.

She opened her mouth to tell him she was busy but before the words could come out, Leo said, "If you come to our house, my mama will make you hot chocolate."

"That sounds good," said Tim. He must have sensed her hesitation and, in order to avoid her canceling her son's invite, made a quick getaway. "See you both later."

And so it was a done deal. Tim Richmond was coming over for hot chocolate, and Sienna felt like she was sixteen again, getting asked out by the captain of the football team. *He's only coming over for hot chocolate*, she reminded herself. *Nothing's going to come of this.*

That didn't stop her from freshening up and putting on mascara and lip gloss and perfume.

By the time Tim walked through her front door, her hormones were heating up right along with the hot chocolate on the stove. The man just stirred her up with those broad shoulders and that deep, rumbling voice of his.

But as they settled at her kitchen table with hot chocolate spiced with cinnamon and some of Sienna's cookies, it was his smile and the kindness in his eyes that made her want to know more about him, got her wondering if, perhaps, just maybe this man was different from the losers who'd paraded through her life.

Leo was certainly taken with him, happy to show him his favorite Matchbox cars and his Lego creations. Tim appeared to have all the patience in the world, listening and nodding and agreeing that, yes, trucks were the best of all.

Finally, deciding that Tim had endured enough of the toy talk, Sienna relocated her son to the living room and put on *Cars* for him.

"He's a nice kid," Tim said when she returned to the kitchen.

"He's great," Sienna said. "He has his challenges," she added. Better to point out relationship land mines right off. Then Tim Richmond could run away and she and Leo wouldn't have to be disappointed down the road.

"Don't we all?" he said easily and took a sip of his cocoa. "This is good."

"Thanks." She almost wanted to add, *Did you understand what I just told you?*

"Is his dad in the picture?"

Sienna shook her head. "To his shame, he's not." And to her shame as well, since she'd chosen a weak man.

"Some guys can't handle challenges."

"And some guys are just plain selfish," Sienna said, not willing to let Leo's dad off the hook so easily.

"So, what's the deal with your boy?"

He had heard. "He's just a little slow."

"Yeah? How? He seems fine."

"On the surface, yes. But in school he's way behind other kids his age. He has trouble with simple chores.

It's not like he can't learn at all. It's just, well…" How to explain this? It was difficult.

"Have you always known?"

Sienna shook her head. "We thought he was fine when he was a baby, a little behind with his milestones, but nothing huge. Everyone kept telling me not to worry, that kids all develop at different rates. Of course, after a while it became obvious he had some problems. Once we had him tested…"

"Don't tell me. That's when the ex became the ex?"

"You guessed it," she said bitterly. "Leo has trouble paying attention and he struggles with a lot of reading and math concepts, but he's the sweetest boy you'll ever meet. He likes people and he can hit a baseball for miles."

"I heard about that," Tim said with a smile.

"That wasn't Leo," Sienna said hotly, "even though he got blamed for it."

"But you paid for it."

"It seemed like the right thing to do at the time."

"Tough being a single parent," Tim observed.

"It can be difficult," she agreed. "What about you? Do you have kids? An ex?"

"Yes to both. I see the girls most weekends, unless Erica has plans, which she did this weekend," he added, looking none too happy about it.

"You're pretty accommodating," Sienna observed.

He shrugged. "No point in fighting. I learned that early on." He sipped his hot chocolate. "So, tell me about this ugly-tree project."

Okay, change-the-subject time. Good idea. "Well, I was at this party." She went on to explain about Muriel's tree and the pact the women had made to try to see the best in those difficult people in their lives.

"There's something to be said for that," Tim said when she'd finished. "Although I can see how it would be hard in my uncle's case."

"Hard? How about impossible?"

"He wasn't always such a grumpy old bastard. I didn't see much of him when I was a kid. He was always too busy working. But I can remember a Christmas when I was little. He came to some big family gathering and cracked us up, showing us how to make a spoon stick to your nose." Sienna cocked an eyebrow and he demonstrated, balancing the spoon on the tip of his nose.

"Now, that's true talent," she mocked.

"We thought it was cool. And we all thought he was pretty cool. Of course, that didn't last…"

"What changed?"

"A lot of stuff. According to my mom, Uncle Bob was once a pretty nice guy. The family lived in West Virginia. They didn't have a lot of money growing up. He and Mom lost their mom early. And Grandpa, well, he was a coal miner. He didn't last long, either. Almost lived to see Mom graduate from high school, missed it by six months."

"Your poor mom."

Not having your parents in your life, what would that be like? Sienna didn't want to even try to imagine. Her parents had always been there for her, especially after things went sour with Carlos—helping her with legal expenses, watching Leo after school while she worked.

Even long-distance, they remained a big part of her life and her mom was her best friend.

"Mom had it rough," Tim said, "but not as rough as she'd have had it if Uncle Bob hadn't been there for her. He was ten years older than her, and he pretty much raised her after Grandma died."

"Wasn't there anyone else?"

"The other grandparents weren't much help. Grandpa Olsen had lung cancer and Grandma was busy trying to keep him alive and keep their two sons out of jail."

"Jail?"

"It wasn't a good environment. Who knows what Mom's life would have been if Uncle Bob hadn't moved them away."

"Amazing," Sienna said, still trying to match the Bob Cratchett she was hearing about with the one she knew. "What on earth happened to him?"

Tim shrugged. "Life."

"I guess," she said dubiously. "But he started out so…noble."

"And ambitious. Uncle Bob was determined not to be poor. I don't know how he managed it, but he somehow scraped together enough money to move himself and Mom out to the West Coast. He eventually bought into a small business with a friend making some kinds of widgets. After a few years they sold the company and he bought another. Built that company up and made a profit. And while he was doing all this, he managed to make sure his baby sister got an education. When Uncle Bob moved out to Washington, he brought Mom along with him. She met my dad and they got married, wound up here, had my sister and me. Uncle Bob stayed in Seattle and just kept working."

"So he never married."

"Oh, that's coming. He found a woman he loved. Her name was Gilda and he was crazy about her. But he was also addicted to making money and couldn't seem to find a balance between working and playing. I think he was so set on making sure he'd never be poor that he was afraid to let up on the throttle. Anyway, Gilda got tired of waiting for him to make time for her and found someone else, so he kept working and became less and less social. It frustrated Mom that he always had an excuse for why he couldn't come for Christmas or family weddings. You never saw the guy."

"Not too hard to figure out why," Sienna observed.

"Yeah, I'm sure he didn't want to hang around and watch families having fun or someone getting hitched when he'd blown his chance. He always sent a present, though."

So, once upon a time Bob Cratchett had been kind. "That's such a sad story."

"It gets sadder. Gilda's husband died twenty years later and she contacted him. They wound up getting married and it looked like he was going to get a second chance. They had a big bash in the Grand Ballroom at the Westin in Seattle, went off to the Caribbean for a honeymoon. The whole nine yards."

But Cratchett was alone now. "Did she leave him?"

Tim nodded. "Yeah, you could say that. She had lupus, but he was sure with all his money he could cure her. He spent a fortune, first on medical bills and procedures, then on trying to keep her happy—cruises, trips to Hawaii. You name it. Toward the end he moved her up here to the mountains, figuring the scenery and fresh air would be good for her. He was the first one to build on this street, as a matter of fact. He still owns those two empty lots in back of his place and one of the buildings downtown."

A regular Icicle Falls land baron.

"Aunt Gilda loved the house but she didn't live that long to enjoy it. She died of complications from the disease."

Sienna's resentment toward Cratchett melted. "That's awful."

"Yeah, it was. After she died, he became bitter. We tried to get him to come to family gatherings but he wouldn't. He didn't even come to my mom's funeral when she died last year," Tim added, and Sienna could hear the disappointment in his voice. "Sent a huge arrangement of flowers and donated money in her name to World Vision, but no personal appearance. Anyway, my sister and I promised my mom that we'd look after the old guy. Now with her gone and my sister in Idaho, it looks like I inherited Uncle Bob by default."

"Lucky you."

He gave a rueful smile. "Yeah, lucky me. I've got kids, an orchard to tend and an old coot to watch over. And yes, he is a pain in the neck. He's got no purpose, no one to care about. All he has is his money—what's left of it—a condo in Seattle and a time-share in Mexico, neither of which he ever uses. No one to enjoy any of it with."

"No wonder he's so grumpy," Sienna said.

"I've tried to convince him to move into a retirement home, but no go. So, I'm afraid you're stuck living next to him."

"It looks that way," Sienna agreed. "But maybe I'll be able to be a little more patient with him, knowing his past."

Tim shook his head. "Don't be too easy on the guy. Shit happens to everyone. It's no excuse for being rude."

"Hey, I'm trying to give him an out."

"He'd try the patience of a saint." Tim downed the rest of his hot chocolate. "I'd better get going. I've got some paperwork waiting for me."

She held up the plate of cookies. "One for the road?"

"Don't mind if I do." He took one and stood, grabbing his coat. "Thanks for being such a good neighbor to the old guy. I can't make any promises that he'll change, but I'll try to compensate for him. If you need anything fixed around here, I'm pretty good with my hands."

She wouldn't mind seeing just how good he was with his hands. Tim Richmond appeared to be a great guy.

But then, so had Carlos when she'd first met him. People often put up masks, hiding their real selves. A man didn't wind up divorced for no reason. Not even a Tim Richmond.

Muriel awoke to find she had more updates from Dot and Arnie waiting on her phone. Dot had sent a picture of the two of them seated at a table spread with fine china and crystal, enjoying their dinner. Dot was wearing a low-cut red dress that showed off what little cleavage—and wrinkled, at that—she had. Arnie sat next to her, wearing a blue sweater.

Talked Arnie into getting this sweater. I think he looks great.

He did look cute. And happy. He had his arm over the back of Dot's chair and their heads were tilted together as if they were a couple.

Muriel frowned at the picture. She texted back, I just got Arnie a blue sweater for Christmas.

Okay, she was being small. But a man can't have too many sweaters, she added.

He could certainly have too many female friends, though, and if you asked Muriel, Dot made one too many.

What a bad attitude. "Shame on you," she scolded herself. And really, to get irritated over something as silly as a sweater. Or a growing friendship.

Disgusted with herself, she went online and began to search for another gift she could give her old friend, something more unique than a sweater. At last she found it. Whiskey flasks were all the rage and the silver one she ordered for him was bound to be a hit. Not that Arnie was a big drinker but he did like his Jack Daniel's before dinner. She placed the order, then toasted a bagel for breakfast, feeling very pleased with herself.

Until her cell phone announced a new text. This time it was from Arnie and came complete with a picture of the whiskey flask Dot had bought him. *Nooo.*

I may have to start drinking more, he wrote.

At the rate things were going, Muriel would soon be drinking more herself.

Chapter Nine

When we decorate and bake, we're not just making something pretty or delicious, we're making memories.
—Muriel Sterling, *A Guide to Happy Holidays*

It seemed Tim had barely left before Leo began asking when they were going to get their tree. "You promised," he reminded Sienna.

"Yes, I said we'd get it this weekend." *Weekend* meant Sunday as well as Saturday, and if they waited until Sunday, they could get Tito to haul it in and set it up when he and Rita and the baby came over for dinner.

"Is it the weekend? I don't have school."

"Yes, it's the weekend. But we'll get our tree tomorrow."

"Why can't we get it today?"

"Because getting a tree is a lot of work."

"I'll help," Leo offered.

The sky was blue and the sun was out. The snowplow was grinding its way down the street, so she couldn't use the excuse of not wanting to drive in the snow, and Leo was looking at her eagerly. She didn't have any big plans for the rest of the day. Well, why not? It would be fun.

When they'd lived in LA, she'd had an artificial tree, but she'd left it behind, knowing that once they were living in Icicle Falls, she'd want a real one—a big, bushy tree that brought the fragrance of the great outdoors into her house. After all, what was the point of living in the mountains if you didn't have a real tree?

The point, she quickly realized, was that you didn't have to lug the monster home. Of course, once they were at the tree lot, Leo had picked a tree on steroids. She watched with trepidation as the tree lot attendants heaved it onto her car roof and secured it with ropes. She could almost hear the car groan. How was she going to manage to get this hernia maker off when they got back to the house? Meanwhile, speakers hovering over the lot blasted out a Christmas song telling her that she needed a little Christmas. Looking at what she'd just purchased, she began to suspect she'd gotten a little too much Christmas.

Taking the tree off the car once they were back in the driveway proved to be every bit as difficult as she'd imagined, the holiday version of going to the gym. No, going to the gym was easier. You had handheld weights you could control. This thing was uncontrollable. Had it grown another three feet between the car lot and her house? Paul Bunyan would have had a struggle with it.

Leo got whacked in the face with a branch while they were freeing the car and sent up a howl.

"You're all right," she assured him. "No blood."

"It hurt," he said, glaring at the tree.

"It's okay. Once we get it in the house and all decorated, it will be worth all the effort."

But how were they going to get it in? "If I pick up the trunk, can you lift its top?"

He scowled. "No."

"Well, let's try. Remember, you wanted a nice big tree."

Leo made a half-hearted effort to lift his end of the tree, then dropped it. "It's heavy."

This had been a mistake.

"Okay, stand back." She'd have to get in touch with her inner Hercules and drag the tree into the house.

Or they could wait until the next day when Tito would be around to help. "I tell you what," she said to Leo. "Let's wait until tomorrow when Tío Tito and Tía Rita can help us put up our tree."

"No, you said tonight," Leo protested.

"I said we'd go get the tree. We got it."

"Please, Mamacita," he begged. "Okay, I'll help." Reinvigorated, he grabbed a branch and gave a tug. Of course, the thing barely budged.

But he kept trying, so she had to reward his efforts. "Okay, you push and I'll pull. Let's see if, together, we can get it in."

Dragging the thing inside was like trying to wrestle a dragon through a keyhole. She grunted and groaned, sweated and strained, Leo joining in with exaggerated grunts of his own. Soon she was swearing under her breath. The tree did its best not to cooperate, moving inch by inch and shedding fir needles right and left. This was the tree equivalent of giving birth.

But, like giving birth, you couldn't stop halfway through the process. She gave a determined tug and the tree gave in and inched forward. Another mighty pull fueled by a grunt, and it burst through the door, pushing her off balance and sending her toppling backward. Not content to take her out, it also sent the vase from her hall table crashing to the floor.

"Mama?" Leo called from the other side of the door. The tree's fat butt hid him from sight, making him only a disembodied voice.

"I'm fine," she said, getting back up. *Having fun now. Having a real holly jolly Christmas.*

Getting the tree into the living room wasn't any easier. Not content with scratching and scraping her face, it also attacked the nativity set that had been on top of the bookshelf. With one sweep of its fat boughs, it took out the shepherds and decapitated a wise man. At least the holy family was all in one piece.

At last the stupid thing was finally in the living room, lying on the floor, ready to be set up. But before tackling that task, Sienna moved every breakable far from its reach.

"Okay, Leo, now you hold the tree stand while I put the tree in it. Can you do that?"

He nodded and assured her he could. Once more it was a wrestling match and for a moment, as she staggered about, trying to tame the thing into the tree stand, it looked as if the tree was going to win. But at last she succeeded. Their Christmas tree was up.

"We did it," she crowed.

The tree took a bow, then fell over, whacking her on the head.

This made her son laugh. "It hit you, too, Mama."

Oh, yes, what fun they were having. With a growl, she grabbed the thing again and set it back up. "Okay, you balance it. I'm going to make sure it's secure." The tree began to wobble. "Noooo." She dived under it, sticking one leg up to help keep it in place. Good thing nobody was around with a camera. This would have been one of those awful, embarrassing pictures that circulated all over Facebook and wound up on tacky greeting cards.

The tree finally gave in and cooperated, and after she'd filled the stand with water and gotten busy stringing lights, she vowed that she was going to buy a nice small artificial tree when they went on sale after Christmas. The real deal was more trouble than it was worth.

An hour later, after they'd strung it with lights and thrown tinsel on it and hung the treasured ornaments they'd brought with them, the tree was a thing of beauty. And the fragrance it shared sent a silent message: *Now, wasn't I worth it? There's nothing like the real deal.*

Yeah, well, she had plenty of the real deal outside her window. She really didn't need a real tree. Still, she couldn't help feeling pleased with herself.

"Tío Tito will be so impressed that we did this all by ourselves," she said, standing back to admire their handiwork.

Indeed he was when he and Rita and the baby and Mami Luci came over for dinner on Sunday. Sienna had made a casserole and a pan of gingerbread and splurged on a half gallon of eggnog so she could make eggnog lattes.

"It smells great in here," Rita said, shedding her coat.

The aroma from her kitchen swirled with the fragrance from the tree and the whole house smelled like they'd gotten more than a little Christmas.

"The tree is lovely," said Mami Luci.

"It's a beast," Tito said as Rita took off little Linda's snowsuit. "How'd you get it up?"

"Nothing to it," Sienna lied. "Right, Leo?"

"Right," Leo said with a nod. "The tree fell on Mama," he added. "And it broke our shepherds."

"You should have waited and let me help you," Tito said.

"She did fine on her own. A woman doesn't need a man to put up a Christmas tree," Rita informed him.

"I guess not," he said dubiously. "But there are plenty of things you do need us for, *mi corazón*."

Yes, there were. It would have been nice to have a man around, not only to help with the tree, but for company, also. Sienna would have enjoyed cuddling on the couch with someone and admiring the tree, would have liked to have had someone to talk with about the day's events.

There were times when she missed being married so much she could have cried. Not the bad years, but those early years when love had seemed indestructible, when laughter and caring words had been exchanged rather than heated accusations and recriminations.

Enjoying a meal with family diverted her from her

thoughts, but after Rita and the gang had left and it was just her and Leo and, God save her, yet another viewing of *Cars*, she became freshly aware of the fact that no matter how full she packed her life, there were empty places that refused to be filled.

Lots of women went through life alone, she reminded herself. Muriel wasn't married. Neither was her friend Dot. And Mrs. Zuckerman next door had been widowed for years. How did they cope?

She couldn't help asking when she took Leo over to Mrs. Zuckerman's for a playdate with Bandit.

"You simply accept what is," Mrs. Zuckerman said as they sat at her kitchen table with steaming mugs of tea while Leo and Bandit raced around the backyard. She added a packet of sugar to hers and stirred it. "I must admit, when I first lost my Alfred, I felt as if the world had come to an end. I didn't want to go on. But I had two young children. I had to." She gave Sienna a wistful smile. "You find the strength to do what you have to do."

Sienna nodded and gazed into her mug. No tea leaves to read, not with tea bags. Even if she could read the future, she wasn't sure she wanted to, wasn't sure she'd like what she saw.

"You're still young. You'll find someone," Mrs. Zuckerman assured her.

Tim Richmond sure looked like a find. But finding someone wasn't the same as finding the right someone. And then there was the matter of keeping him. "It would be nice," Sienna said wistfully.

"I know it's silly at this point in life, but I wish I could meet a nice man. It's no fun cooking for one."

"I wish I knew someone for you," Sienna said.

Actually, she did know someone. They both did. Could Bob Cratchett find love again with Mrs. Zuckerman? Maybe a good woman was all that was needed to transform that old, ugly tree. They could be like Beauty and the Beast, the senior version.

Except that was a fairy tale, and Sienna wouldn't wish Mr. Cratchett on her worst enemy, let alone a sweet woman like Mrs. Zuckerman. Still, maybe Mrs. Zuckerman could be the making of him.

Anything was possible. Could love change Robert Cratchett?

Nah.

The last of the weekend guests had checked out and Olivia's housekeeping staff had finished changing beds and cleaning bathrooms. Sheets and towels were still being washed in the laundry room, but James had promised to take care of folding them and putting them away so Olivia could get started on baking Christmas cookies for the following week.

Meadow had volunteered to help Olivia and Brooke and was excited to begin. The three women met in the kitchen, and as Olivia and Brooke began to assemble the baking tools, Meadow went to the fridge.

"Where's the dough?" she asked.

"We haven't made it yet," Olivia replied. "Bring the butter and eggs, will you?"

"Haven't made it?" Meadow walked back to the

workstation where Olivia was setting up her flour and sugar and set down the requested items. "You mean you don't buy the stuff in the package?"

"No," Olivia said, shocked. "I always make my cookies from scratch."

Now Meadow looked shocked. "Seriously? Why? Can't you just buy the dough and cut it up and you're done?"

"Cookies baked from scratch are so much better," Olivia said.

"I guess," Meadow said dubiously.

"You've never made cookies from scratch?" Brooke asked her. "That's like child abuse."

Meadow shrugged. "Mostly we bought them at the store already baked."

Olivia's recipe box bulged with cookie recipes that had been passed down to her from her mother and grandmother, as well as ones she'd collected over the years. She couldn't imagine not baking cookies at Christmas. Everyone baked cookies at Christmas. Or so she'd thought. Had the girl been raised by wolves?

"Well, of course, buying them is convenient," she said diplomatically, not wanting to insult the wolves.

"Mom always said baking was a waste of time."

"I guess we all like to spend our time in different ways," Olivia said. "Your mom was probably busy with other things."

Meadow gave a snort and Olivia decided not to go any further down that conversational road.

"I liked it when we did make cookies," Meadow continued. "I used to love to dump on the sprinkles."

"Then we'll put you in charge of sprinkle dumping," Olivia said.

That made her smile. The girl was so easily pleased. It was an admirable quality and probably one of the things that had attracted Brandon to her in the first place. Well, besides her looks.

"So, what are we making?" she asked, eager to begin.

Brooke already had the mixing bowl out and was measuring in the sugar and butter. "We're making several different kinds, starting with sugar cookies," she said and held up a tree-shaped cookie cutter.

"This was my mother's recipe," Olivia added. "A ton of butter and almond extract in the dough."

"Yum," Meadow said.

"While Brooke's getting the dough ready, you can make the layer cookies," Olivia said to Meadow and put her to work layering graham cracker crumbs, coconut, chocolate chips, chopped walnuts and sweetened condensed milk.

It was an easy recipe to make and Meadow was vastly pleased with herself after she'd gotten it assembled. "Okay, what next?" she asked eagerly.

"You can roll out the dough, if you want," Brooke said. "That way I can start on the lemon bars."

She pointed to the rolling pin and Meadow looked at it as if it were an alien artifact.

Olivia decided she'd better supervise. She sprinkled some flour on the counter. "You take about this much dough," she said, demonstrating, "set it on your floured surface. Put some flour on your rolling pin and then you roll it out, always rolling from the center. You want your dough about a quarter inch thick." With the dough flattened, she made several impressions with her Santa cookie cutter and transferred them to the cookie sheet. "Nothing to it."

"You sure do make it look easy," Meadow said.

"It is," Olivia said and smiled at her.

She was actually enjoying this time with Meadow. Perhaps the kitchen was the place where they could bond.

"Okay, I'm ready to go for it," Meadow said, and Olivia handed over the rolling pin.

Meadow's first attempt didn't go well, though. She neglected to put more flour on the counter and the dough stuck to it. "Crap."

"I always reflour my surface," Olivia said, scraping off the dough. "Try again. And put some more flour on the rolling pin, too. You'll get the hang of it."

Meadow didn't have much better luck the second time around.

"It takes a little practice," Olivia said, trying to be reassuring.

The third try was not the charm and now the air in the kitchen was turning a little blue as Meadow cursed the dough, the rolling pin and Christmas cookies in general. "This is a pain in the butt," she grumbled.

Easily pleased and easily frustrated. "Why don't you take a break?" Olivia said to her. "We'll put you to work later, when it's time to frost the cookies."

"I don't want to take a break," Meadow said with a frown. "If I do, I'll just go grab my vape and I'm trying to quit."

That was commendable. "Good for you," Olivia said, hoping to encourage her.

"That's not what your son says. He says I'm turning into a bitch."

Olivia didn't know how to respond to that. Happily, she was spared when Meadow's cell phone rang.

Except Meadow didn't appear to be in any hurry to answer it. "Go ahead and take your call," Olivia said.

"That's okay. It's just my mom."

"I'm sure she'd like to talk to you. We can spare you for a few minutes."

"I can call her later."

"Oh, go ahead. We're fine. Really." And the work would go a lot smoother if Meadow was occupied with something else.

Meadow took the call with a reluctant hello and Olivia suddenly remembered what Brandon had said about her not having the best relationship with her mom.

"I'm kind of busy right now," she said, turning her back to Olivia. "I'm baking cookies...No, not that kind. We're making the dough ourselves...Yeah, they really do that up here...No, I like it." There was a pause on her end of the conversation and she began to pace as she listened to her mother. Olivia caught sight of a frown. "Yeah, I got your text. I've been busy, okay?...No, I'm staying up here." She lowered her voice and started out of the kitchen, but Olivia still heard what she was saying. "That's not gonna work. They're all booked for Christmas."

Hmm. So, Meadow's mom wanted to come up and see her daughter for Christmas. They could make room for one more.

But what would that one more be like? Was she the Meadow prototype?

Maybe not. Perhaps she and her daughter didn't get along because Meadow was the black sheep of the family. Olivia could envision a middle-aged nonsmoker, frustrated with her daughter's choices.

Meadow was in the kitchen again, her phone back in her jeans pocket. "Is your mom hoping to see you at Christmas?" Olivia asked.

"Yeah, but I know Brandon wants to be here. And so do I," Meadow added.

"And of course we want to have you," Olivia said. Sort of. Almost. Well, one of them, anyway. *Be nice. Invite her mother.* "If you'd like to invite your mom to come up…"

"I don't think that would work out," Meadow said.

Brandon entered the kitchen in search of treats. "What wouldn't work out?"

The timer went off on the layered cookies and Olivia took them out of the double oven.

"Nothing," Meadow said.

"We did have a room cancellation," Olivia told her. "If your mom would like to come up Christmas Eve and spend the night, she's more than welcome." *There, see what a good mother-in-law she was being?* She hoped Brandon appreciated her efforts.

Meadow didn't appear to. She shook her head. "Not a good idea."

"I think it is," Brandon said. "She can come up and bring your sister."

Meadow had a sister? A Meadow the Second. Oh, trepidation.

The girl shook her head again, this time vehemently.

"Babe," Brandon pushed, "I have to meet your mom sometime."

"You haven't met her mother?" Olivia asked. She'd assumed he had.

"Or her sister."

This was most peculiar.

"They've been busy," Meadow said.

"Well, now they're not. Call 'em back and invite them to come on up," Brandon said.

Meadow chewed her lip.

"We'll make sure they have a good time," put in Brooke.

"Want me to call them?" Brandon pressed.

"No, I'll do it," she said shortly, then marched out of the room, pushing the swinging door open with a shove.

"What on earth is that about?" Olivia asked her son. More to the point, what had she gotten them all into?

Brandon shrugged. "I told you. She and her mom don't get along very well. She says her mom's a pain."

Which meant there were sure to be fireworks. A pain for Christmas, just what Olivia always wanted. She should have kept her big mouth shut.

Oh, well, she already had one pain. What difference would two more make? Anyway, Meadow's mom couldn't be that bad.

Meadow was back in the kitchen now. "Okay, she's coming," she said to Brandon. "You happy now?"

He grinned at her and pulled her into a hug. "Yeah, as a matter of fact, I am."

"Yeah? Well, don't say I didn't warn you. Now, get lost," she said, giving him a playful smile. "We're busy making cookies here."

"Okay, I'm going," he said. "After I get a sample." He cut into the bar cookies and lifted out a generous piece. "Oh, yeah. Good stuff, Mom."

"I made those," Meadow informed him.

"You did? They're as good as Mom's. You told me you didn't know how to bake."

"I do now," Meadow said proudly. "Thanks to her."

The acknowledgment was touching. "I think Meadow's going to become a good baker," Olivia told her son. At least she had the interest and that was half the battle.

"I knew it was a good idea to come back home," he said.

"It sure was. I just wish we didn't have to spoil it all by having my mom show up," Meadow added with a scowl.

"Don't worry. Everything will be fine," Brandon said easily. He gave Meadow a kiss, threatened to return later for more cookies and then exited.

"Only for him," she said, shaking her head.

For once Olivia could identify with her daughter-in-law. She'd felt the same way when her son had asked her to make Meadow feel welcome.

The first batch of the sugar cookies was out of the oven now and cooling on racks. "I think we're ready to start frosting," Brooke said.

"All right. I can do that. Piece of cake," Meadow said. She sobered. "I bet you don't use the frosting in a can."

"I bet you're right," Brooke replied with a grin. "Mom makes the best frosting."

"Yeah?" Meadow looked intrigued.

"With vanilla extract for the trees," Olivia said as she mixed the powdered sugar, cream and butter, "and rose water for the Santas. It's how my mother did it when I was a girl."

"That's awesome," Meadow said and peered over Olivia's shoulder.

"So, the frosting goes into two different bowls. We do green for the trees and pink for the Santas." Olivia dropped in food coloring and the extracts and nudged a bowl toward Meadow to stir. Once the frosting was finished, she demonstrated with a small spreader, painting a Santa's pants pink and then dabbing pink frosting on his hat. The tip of the hat received a silver dragée. So did the tip of each Christmas tree after it had been frosted and decorated with a tasteful amount of colored sprinkles. "Remember, sometimes less is more," Olivia said as she demonstrated.

"They look almost too good to eat," Meadow said, eyeing her first try.

"But they're not," Brooke said and helped herself to one.

"Can I have one?" Meadow asked Olivia.

"Of course! That's one of the perks of baking, isn't it, Brooke?"

"Absolutely," Brooke said and rubbed her lower back.

"Are you getting tired, dear?" Olivia asked her.

"A little," Brooke admitted.

"Go ahead and sit down. I can help Olivia finish," Meadow told her.

"Meadow's right. Why don't you make yourself a cup of tea and take a break?" Olivia suggested.

"Okay, if you're sure."

"Yes. We can handle it," Olivia said.

"This is nice," Meadow observed after Brooke had brewed her tea and gone out to the dining room with a cookie.

"Baking cookies?"

"Baking cookies with you."

The comment surprised Olivia. "Me? What's so special about me?"

"You do stuff with people," Meadow said with a shrug. "You care." She didn't look Olivia in the eye. Instead, she focused on swirling green frosting on a tree.

Olivia suddenly found she had to keep her eyes on the Santa she was frosting. Were her cheeks as pink as the frosting on Santa's cap? She didn't deserve that praise, not with the attitude she'd had.

"My mom never did stuff like this with us."

"That's too bad." Olivia loved her sons, but she'd always wanted a daughter. She'd envisioned them shopping for special dresses for Christmas and Easter together, having little tea parties, had longed to be able to pass on favorite family recipes.

Not that she hadn't taught her sons to cook—they both could manage in the kitchen. But neither of them really enjoyed it. Anyway, there was something both time-honored and bonding about a mother and daughter working together, whether it was in the kitchen or enjoying a shared hobby.

Olivia and her mother had been close and had spent many enjoyable hours together in the kitchen. It didn't sound like Meadow's mother had spent much time doing anything special with her, in the kitchen or otherwise. Daughters were wasted on some women.

Meadow topped her tree with green sprinkles, then carefully set a dragée on its top. "I wish I'd had...someone like you for a mom."

It was a painful tug on the heartstrings. What had happened between this girl and her mother? Where had things gone wrong between them?

She longed to ask, but really, she and Meadow still barely knew each other and it didn't seem appropriate. Besides, every story had two sides. If Meadow's mother were here, perhaps she'd paint a very different picture of their life together, maybe one of a rebellious daughter who didn't want to spend time with her mother.

"Brandon says you were the best mom ever."

"Oh, I don't know about that." She'd loved her boys with all her heart and hardly ever yelled at them. She'd probably spoiled them too much, but what little boy didn't benefit from some spoiling, especially one who had lost his father?

"He says you read them bedtime stories every night."

"I did. Brandon's favorites were the Little Bear stories." Olivia could still feel the weight of her little boy curled up against her, hanging on to every word as she read to him about the bear cub's adventures. He was so proud of himself when he got old enough to sound out the words for himself. It was a cherished memory, but not extraordinary. "Of course, all mothers do that."

"Not mine."

No bedtime stories? Didn't women tell their children bedtime stories anymore?

"What was he like as a kid?" Meadow asked.

"He was the sweetest little boy—always happy, always laughing, even as a baby. I'd go to get him up from his nap when he was a baby and there he'd be, walking along the crib railing with a smile on his face, ready for the next adventure. He was a mischief, though."

"Did he pull a lot of crap?"

"Well, he got into his share of trouble."

Olivia went on to tell tales of her son, recounting the time he'd broken one of her figurines and tried to hide the evidence by gluing it back together. "Then there was the year he and his brother played barbershop, cutting each other's hair. Right before it was time for school pictures, mind you," Olivia said. "One year he tried to match me up with one of our guests. His brother was furious with him because by then Eric considered himself the man of the house and he didn't want any competition." Not that anyone could have competed with George. The memory of her first husband brought a wistful smile.

"They were pretty young when your husband died, weren't they?" Meadow prompted. "That had to be hard."

"It was, but we got through it somehow. Even though I wouldn't want to relive those years, I think they made the three of us closer."

And was that a big part of why she was having so much trouble letting Meadow into her heart? Was the real problem that she didn't want to share her baby boy?

Surely not. She'd had no trouble sharing Eric. But then, the girl Eric had married had been a match made in heaven.

A mini-me.

Dot's words came back to taunt her. Surely she wasn't so selfish that she'd resent Meadow for simply not being like her?

No, it went deeper than that. She'd been upset because Brandon had rushed into marriage so quickly without confiding in her. And to top it off, he'd chosen someone she'd been sure wouldn't make him happy.

But so far he seemed perfectly happy. So was Meadow. So was the rest of the family. The only one not happy was Olivia, and what did that say about her?

"And life's good now, right?" Meadow asked. "With James?"

"Oh, yes."

She'd never thought she'd find someone she could love as much as she had her first husband. She'd been wrong. Now she was beginning to wonder if she'd been wrong about this second daughter-in-law who'd come into her life.

"I guess stuff has a way of working out," Meadow said. "It did for me."

It had, indeed. Being at the lodge was obviously filling a void in Meadow's life. She was like a fairy-tale heroine who'd married the prince and wound up living at the castle. So, if Brandon was the prince and the lodge was the castle, did that make Olivia the queen? And was she a good queen or an evil one, who'd as soon give the newcomer a poisoned apple?

This last question was not a comfortable one to ponder, and she was relieved when the cookie baking was over and she could return to her throne, er, apartment.

Sienna didn't sleep well Sunday night. She'd gotten into the Sweet Dreams chocolate truffles she'd purchased at the grocery store—impulse buying, one of her weaknesses—and while the sugar and chocolate had made her taste buds merry, they hadn't done much to help her sleep when she'd finally trundled off to bed.

The next morning she inspected her reflection in the mirror. "You look old," she said in disgust. She felt old, too.

But she'd feel better once she got to work. Her love affair with her job was still going strong, and being at the bookstore made her happy.

"You look tired," Pat greeted her.

"I am. It took me a while to get to sleep last night."

"Too much to do?"

"More like too much to eat. I got into the chocolate."

Pat chuckled. "Did the chocolate happen to come from our local chocolatier?"

"It did."

"Then I bet it was worth every lost wink."

"It was," Sienna admitted. "But I need to stop. I've gained six pounds since I moved here."

"Where?" Pat scoffed.

"Everywhere."

"Well, you look great, so maybe you needed to gain a couple of pounds."

"Not really, and I sure don't need to gain any more."

"Good luck with that. It's hard to keep up the will-power when you live in a town that has its very own chocolate factory."

"It's a curse," Sienna said, deadpan.

Their conversation was interrupted by a shriek, and one of Pat's regular customers, who'd asked to use the employee restroom, burst out of the back room. "Pat, your toilet's overflowing!"

Pat, who was normally calm and cheerful, looked ready to commit murder. She rushed to the back room and Sienna could hear her apologizing. The woman, who was mortified, didn't linger to buy any books.

"Dick!" Pat called, and her lazy part-timer, Dick Belcher, popped his head around the corner of a book-case. "The toilet's overflowed. Can you get in there and deal with it?"

Dick looked far from eager to oblige. "Kind of busy here," he called back.

Pat went over to where he was trying to look busy. "Kind of need you there. Now."

"Okay, okay."

Dick was in his sixties. He was overweight and undermotivated, not a lover of books. A former foot-ball player, his tastes ran more toward ESPN than PBS, but Pat had hired him a couple of months back as a favor to his wife, who was desperate to get him out of the house a couple of days a week. At the rate he was going, his wife was probably going to have him home again come the New Year.

"I don't know why Sienna couldn't take care of it," he muttered as he slouched past his boss.

"Because I have other things for her to do," Pat snapped. "Anyway, I'm sexist. You're the man here, so man up."

"Sexual discrimination," he grumbled.

"That's for sure," Pat said as he disappeared into the back room. "I discriminated against several hard-working women when I hired you."

She grabbed the phone and called the landlord. "Harvey, you need to get over here and replace that toilet now. No more stalling. We just had another incident."

Sienna was sure she could see Pat's blood pressure rising as she listened to whatever Harvey's latest excuse was.

"I don't care if you've got pneumonia. I don't care if you're dying. I want this taken care of before lunch or I'm not paying my rent."

"Maybe he does have pneumonia," Sienna said after Pat had ended the call.

"And maybe I'm Mrs. Claus." Pat shook her head. "Some ugly trees just can't be fixed."

She took a deep, restorative breath. "Okay, onward and upward. We got in more copies of Susan Wiggs's latest that need to be shelved and a ton of signed copies of Muriel's book that have to get mailed out today. The post office will be a zoo."

Pat had been right. The post office was, indeed, a zoo. It seemed as if half the residents of Icicle Falls had come to mail off their presents, and a few were grumbling about government inefficiency, but for the most part, everyone was genial. It probably had something to do with the woman manning the window.

"Don't worry, folks," called Marge Johnson, everyone's favorite postal worker. "We'll get to you. And I have candy canes up here to keep you all sweet."

Only in a small town, Sienna thought as the line inched forward.

She was just reading a text from the ex: Money on the way—yay!—when someone called her name.

"Sienna, hi!" She turned to see Bailey Black heading toward the line, carrying two boxes. "I haven't seen you since Mom's party. How are you doing?"

"Great." For the most part she was. Yes, she still got upset every time Leo came home in a funk because he'd been teased. And she wished she'd see Tim Richmond again. And she wasn't happy about that extra six pounds. Other than that, what did she have to complain about?

"How are things going with your neighbor?" Bailey asked, stopping beside Sienna.

Oh, yeah. There was that.

"The line ends back here," said an irritated middle-aged woman.

"I know. Don't worry," Bailey said sweetly. "So, are you making any progress?" she asked Sienna.

"Define *progress*."

Bailey nodded. "Uh-huh. That about says it all. Hey, come on over to the tea shop one day on your lunch break. You can try the new bread pudding we're serving."

"I'm already getting fat on your family's chocolate, thank you very much."

Bailey grinned. "That's addicting. But hey, it's the holidays. We suck all the calories out until January. Seriously, come on by. I'll give you a cup of Christmas tea, our own special blend."

The few friends Sienna had when she'd lived in the city had been so busy working it seemed like she'd never seen any of them. People were busy here, too, but somehow they still managed to make time for each other.

It had been a smart move coming up here. You couldn't beat the scenery—trees cloaked in snow, mountains all around, watching over a town lit up for the holidays like a jewel box. And even though most of her family was still in California, she felt a sense of community in this place that she hadn't found living in the city. She missed her family but she knew she belonged in Icicle Falls. She was meant to be an Icicle.

But by the time she and Leo made their way home at the end of the day, Sienna was a melted icicle. Her shift had gotten busier as the afternoon raced on, and the bookstore had been filled with customers, all anxious to finish their shopping, not to mention a number of crying toddlers who'd been kept out well past nap time. All she wanted to do was get home, put a couple of frozen potpies in the oven and then flop on the couch.

At least there had been no new snow since the snowplows last came through. The streets were clear.

Except for the dog darting in front of the car. *Ack!*

Chapter Ten

We may celebrate love on Valentine's Day, but it blooms at Christmas.

   —Muriel Sterling, *A Guide to Happy Holidays*

"**D**on't hit Bandit!" Leo cried as Sienna swerved to avoid the dog.

Bandit bolted out of the way and ran off down the street, and Sienna pulled into her driveway with her heart racing faster than the dog would ever be able to run.

"He's running away," Leo reported as they got out of the car.

"He'll come back," Sienna assured him.

Mrs. Zuckerman didn't look all that assured. She came hurrying down the street, bundled in a blue parka, calling after the dog. "He doesn't know the neighborhood. He's going to get lost," she fretted.

"I'll get him," Leo said and ran off in the direction of the dog.

Sienna was sure Bandit could find his way home, but she wasn't so sure about her son. "Leo, wait!" she commanded and took off after him.

"Wait for your mommy," Mrs. Zuckerman added and followed Sienna.

The sun was about to retire for the day and temperatures were dropping. Sienna was still used to the warmer climates farther south, but there was nothing like chasing after a puppy and a boy on the loose to warm a woman up. Plus, she was more than a little steaming over the fact that her son appeared to have developed a hearing problem.

"Leo, you need to listen when I ask you to wait," she scolded when she caught up to him, halting him in his tracks.

"But Bandit's running away," he protested, ready to take off again.

Sienna kept a firm hold on his arm. "You still need to listen. And don't worry, we'll get him." The dog was now three houses down, sniffing bushes and leaving his doggy calling card.

Mrs. Zuckerman came up beside them. She was out of breath and red in the face. "Honestly, I don't know what I'm going to do with that dog. Every time I open the door, he bolts right out. Come here, Bandit," she called.

"Come on, Bandit!" Leo echoed.

Bandit raised his head, looked their direction and wagged his tail, then trotted off to another yard.

"All right, let's try the pincer move," Sienna said. "Leo, you and I will circle around that way. Mrs. Zuckerman, you be ready to catch him from the other end. And, Leo, don't go into the street."

Mrs. Zuckerman got herself in position and Sienna

and Leo made their way to where Bandit now had his nose to the snowy ground in yet another yard.

"Come on, Bandit," Sienna called, slapping her thighs in the time-honored dog-calling gesture.

Bandit barked and happily bounded toward her. Then, as she reached out to grab him, he darted away. Out of reach, he stopped, barked and wagged his tail.

"Okay, we're done playing," she informed him. "Come here." She lunged for him.

A big mistake, because he took off again. At least this time he was heading in the right direction.

"Oh, no," groaned Mrs. Zuckerman after he'd dodged her and raced past.

"Don't worry, we'll get him," Sienna said. "Come on, Leo." And off they went, running back down the street, Mrs. Zuckerman following at a more sedate pace.

They were almost to Cratchett's yard when they finally snagged him. "Gotcha," Sienna said, picking up the wriggling pup.

Bandit was perfectly happy to have been gotten. He yapped and licked her face.

"You're cute, but you're a pain," she informed the dog.

Cratchett had come out and was sprinkling rock salt on his driveway when they walked past. "So you don't have a dog, huh?" he mocked.

Excited to see a new person, Bandit began to wriggle and lick her face. "No, I don't. This is Mrs. Zuckerman's dog. Leo, go inside," she commanded her son. It was all she could do to hold on to the dog and give Leo the house key. He took it and dashed off, happy to avoid a conversation with Cratchett.

Bandit jumped out of Sienna's arms and trotted up to Mr. Cratchett, tail wagging. Great. Cratchett would probably drop-kick him clear across the lawn. Sienna hurried up the walk to rescue the dog.

To her surprise, Cratchett bent down and petted him. "You're a rascal. We need to talk to your owner about keeping you in your own yard, don't we?" Bandit licked Cratchett's hand and the man smiled. Actually smiled.

Robert Cratchett smiling? Sienna had to be seeing things.

Now Mrs. Zuckerman had joined them. Here was a chance to introduce Beauty to the Beast and see if she could have any luck turning him into a human being.

"Mr. Cratchett caught Bandit for you," she greeted her friend.

His face suddenly looked as red as Santa's suit. "Well…"

"Mr. Cratchett, have you met Mrs. Zuckerman?"

"Pleasure," he said, the word coming out stiffly.

"Thank you so much," said Mrs. Zuckerman. She picked up her dog and smiled at Cratchett. "Let me bake you some cookies as a thank-you."

"You'll have to be careful what you make for him," Sienna taunted, bringing back his habitual frown.

"Do you have a favorite cookie?" Mrs. Zuckerman asked.

"My wife used to make chocolate chip cookies," he said. Memory softened his expression. "Right out of the oven, they were something else."

"I love chocolate chip cookies," said Mrs. Zuckerman. "I'll bake you some. Maybe you'd like to come over and have lunch, as well."

"That's really nice of you," Cratchett said, not committing to anything.

"Wonderful," said Mrs. Zuckerman as if they actually had a date. "Thanks again for helping with Bandit. I'm eternally grateful."

Once more his cheeks turned red and he waved away her praise. "Happy to help," he said and—shock!—for the second time in five minutes, smiled. Then he caught sight of Sienna staring at him. He dropped the smile and got busy with the rock salt.

"You must have the magic touch," Sienna said to Mrs. Zuckerman as they walked away. "I've never seen Mr. Cratchett smile."

"Perhaps he's needed something to smile about," Mrs. Zuckerman said. "Like chocolate chip cookies?"

"Or a pretty woman," Sienna suggested, and now Mrs. Zuckerman was blushing. "Still, I'll die of shock if you ever get him out of his house."

"You never know," Mrs. Zuckerman said.

The guy had smiled. So, yes, you never knew. But Sienna wasn't holding her breath.

Olivia and James had gotten in the habit of having dinner with Eric and Brooke on Monday evenings when life at the lodge was relatively quiet. With Brandon back home, he and Meadow were automatically included in the family dinner invite.

This night everyone was squeezed into Olivia's little

apartment, seated around her table with slices of pizza from Bavarian Alps and a tossed salad Olivia had put together. After discussing business—how many guests were registered for the upcoming weekend, what needed to be repaired around the place and who was going to do it—talk turned to the anticipated birth of Eric and Brooke's baby.

"Have you two decided on a name yet?" James asked. "You're running out of time."

"I think we finally have," said Brooke. "William George if it's a boy."

James's middle name coupled with Olivia's first husband's name. "Your father would be so pleased," she said, beaming.

"I know I am," James said.

"And Olivia Joy if it's a girl," Brooke continued. "After the two best moms ever," she said, smiling at Olivia.

It was James's turn to beam. "I can't think of two better names. Or two better women," he added, squeezing Olivia's hand.

She dabbed at her eyes, which were suddenly teary. "That is so sweet. But don't you want to put your own mother's name first?" she asked Brooke.

"Olivia Joy sounds better," Brooke said. "And I know Mom wouldn't have minded."

"Anyway, we need to always have an Olivia here at the lodge," Eric said.

"If she'll stay," Olivia cautioned.

"She will," he said confidently. "This is the best place in the whole country to live."

"I couldn't agree more," Olivia said, "but children do get married and leave."

"Yeah, but they eventually come back," Eric said. "Even little brothers," he added.

"What can I say?" Brandon shot back. "There's no place like home, even if you do have to put up with your pain-in-the-butt bro."

"Speaking of kids...I've got an announcement," Meadow said with a smile for Brandon. "Guess what, babe? We're pregnant!"

"No way," he said. "For sure?" She nodded and he grabbed her and hugged her. "That's great."

"Good news, indeed," said James. "Two grandkids in one year."

"Congrats, bro," Eric said.

"No wonder you've been acting so, uh..." Brandon stopped himself, obviously coming to his senses before he could say anything to get in trouble with his wife.

"Bitchy?" she supplied.

"Well, yeah."

"Hey, I've felt like crap, so bite me," she said, and he chuckled and gave her a kiss.

Of course, morning sickness. So those excuses for not helping with breakfast weren't excuses at all. Olivia should have figured that out.

"And I've been trying to quit smoking," Meadow added.

"I'm proud of you, babe," Brandon said and took her hand.

"I can hardly wait," she said. "I hope we have a girl. Baby-girl clothes are so cute."

"But boys are wonderful, too," Olivia said. Hers were.

"Oh, man, I don't know anything about boys. I never had a brother."

"We're pretty easy," Eric told her. "Feed us cookies, keep us in sports and try to keep us from beating the crap out of each other. Right, Mom?"

"Something like that," Olivia said.

"I don't care what we have," said Brandon, "just so long as it's healthy."

"For sure," Meadow agreed. She turned to Brooke. "Our kids can grow up together. How cool is that?"

"Very," Brooke said.

"I always wanted kids." Meadow's brow furrowed. "I hope I don't screw up."

"You'll be a great mom," Brandon assured her.

Olivia hoped so. Meadow a mother, heaven help them.

Muriel used to enjoy Facebook. Lately, though, not so much. Both Arnie and Dot showed up on her feed on a regular basis and it seemed like daily—no, hourly— there was a new post from one or the other of them, raving about their trip. There they were in Bamberg, posed in front of an ancient castle. Or at an open-air market, surrounded by booths of colorful merchandise. There were pictures of their boat all decked out with lights and ornaments, shots as they went through various canal locks, enough pictures of food to fill an entire cookbook.

Muriel shut down Facebook and opened an empty document marked Book Ideas and typed *How to Stay*

Friends When You're Not Feeling Friendly. Now, that could make an interesting book.

Except she'd have to find someone to write it for her. At the moment, she had little enough advice for herself, let alone anyone else.

She should write about something different. The joys of grandparenting? How to stay on a diet when you owned a chocolate company? How to fall off your diet when you owned a chocolate company? Ugh.

She sighed and shut her laptop. Maybe she should quit writing and find something else to do with her time. Maybe she'd said all she had to say.

Her phone told her she had a message. It was from Dot.

I think I'm in love. Oh, gotta go. We're leaving for Rothenburg.

Muriel's dream town. She'd seen pictures of the medieval town—surrounded by thick walls, crisscrossed with cobblestone streets and abounding in flowers in the spring and summer, glistening in white snow in the winter—and been charmed. One day, she'd promised herself, she'd go there.

She could have. She should have. And now Dot was there. And in love. In love with whom? The answer to that was obvious.

Dot in love with Arnie, Dot and Arnie a couple. Muriel tossed aside her phone without answering the text. She had work to do.

Her laptop mocked her. *On me? You're kidding, right? You're out of good ideas.*

She had other work to do. She needed to clean her house. And she'd promised to watch Cecily's children later that afternoon for her while Cecily put in some extra hours at Sweet Dreams. She got busy scrubbing her bathroom. The woman in the mirror didn't look happy and no amount of glass cleaner or positive self-talk did anything to change her.

Even time with the grandchildren didn't help, and staying for dinner proved awkward. Cecily had a sort of sixth sense when it came to people's feelings.

"What's wrong, Mom?" she asked as they loaded the dishwasher together.

"Nothing. Why do you ask?"

"You seem a little down," Cecily observed.

"No, I'm tired. That's all."

"You looked really tired when I asked how Dot and Arnie were enjoying their cruise."

"Cecily," Muriel said sternly.

"They're not a match, Mom. Don't worry."

"I'm not worried, and I don't care if they are." *Liar, liar, panty hose on fire.* "Anyway, it's none of my business."

"I guess. When do they come back?"

"Next week." Not soon enough. Dot and Arnie had enjoyed quite enough time together.

Muriel left after she'd helped her daughter with cleanup. "You need time with your family, and you and Luke definitely need a few moments alone." She remembered how it had been when the girls were lit-

tle. That small window of time she and Stephen had together once they were in bed had been more precious
than gold.

She'd had no idea back then how quickly their time
would come to an end. The same thing had happened
with Waldo. It seemed that one minute they'd been together and the next he'd been gone. Life went by so
fast when you were with someone you loved. The days
spun away, leaving you wishing you'd hung on tighter.

Except time was the one thing you couldn't hold. It
was an antsy visitor, unable to sit still and taking with
it both people and opportunities when it left. And now
it had struck again, washing past her and moving Arnie
and Dot into new territory where there was really only
room for two.

"You have no one to blame for this situation but yourself," she muttered as she made her way home. That
didn't make her feel any better.

Back in her little cottage, she started a fire in her
fireplace, put on a CD of Christmas music and grabbed
the book she'd been reading.

"I never thought I'd find love again," Jocelyn said
with a sigh as she nestled into Gregory's arms.
"Me, either," he said. "But how are we going
to tell Amelia? She's your best friend."

Muriel slammed the book shut. Why was she reading this ridiculous novel, anyway? She shut off the CD
player, turned on the TV and searched for a movie on
Netflix. Ah, yes, *A Christmas Carol*. Perfect.

Except it wasn't. Watching Ebenezer Scrooge make his foolish choices irritated her and she was in no mood to stick with him to the end of the movie.

At last she gave up and went to bed, hoping to drift into a dreamless sleep. But Muriel was a dreamer and there was no drifting tonight. Instead, she found herself on a long ship all decked out with holiday lights, standing at the railing and watching a picturesque European town float by.

She was enjoying the moment until Dot Morrison joined her. This was a new and improved Dot. She'd had a face-lift, and she'd filled out. She had cleavage now and it was spilling over the top of a slinky red sequined evening gown.

"What are you doing here?" Muriel demanded.

"Me? What are you doing here? You weren't invited."

"I certainly was."

"Well, no one wants you here now."

"Arnie wants me," Muriel insisted.

Dot patted her blond curls. Since when had she become a blonde? "Not anymore he doesn't, cupcake. You had your chance."

"Arnie's always loved me."

"I don't know why. You've ignored the poor man for years. You know what your problem is, Muriel? You're a poor sport."

"I am not!"

"Oh, yes, you are. And a fake. All those wise words, always so kind to everyone…except when you're crossed."

"I *am* kind," Muriel insisted.

Dot leaned over, getting in Muriel's face. "Deep down, you're just like all the rest of us. A conceited, selfish little—"

Muriel didn't let her finish. With a growl, she gave Dot a push, sending her over the railing. *Not so kind after all.*

Dot went into the icy water with hardly a squeak. "Bon voyage," Muriel called after her and chuckled.

"That wasn't nice," said a deep voice.

She whirled around and saw two figures standing in the shadows. When they emerged, she saw that one was Santa Claus. His companion was a giant nutcracker complete with the big black Hessian hat and a face that looked just like…

"Arnie?"

Nutcracker Arnie didn't say anything.

But Santa did. "Do you know what happens to naughty girls?" Santa asked with a jolly smile.

"No Christmas stocking?"

"No. They have to leave the party." The jolly smile disappeared and his eyes narrowed. "Get rid of her."

"Arnie, you love me," she protested as the nutcracker made his stiff way to her.

"Not anymore," said Nutcracker Arnie.

He picked her up in his hard wooden arms and heaved her overboard.

Nooo.

She awoke right before she landed in the icy river, which was a good thing, since she'd always heard that if you didn't wake up in time, you'd die in real life, too.

Of course, no one had ever come back from the dead to confirm this but she didn't want to test the theory.

She put a hand to her chest where her heart was pounding as if she'd just run up Sleeping Lady Mountain, and her hair was as tangled as her blankets. What an awful dream. She didn't feel that angry toward Dot.

At least, not consciously.

She looked at the clock on her nightstand. Good grief, it was only 5:00 a.m. She never got up this early. She was up now, though. No way did she want to go back to sleep and encounter Santa and the heartless Nutcracker Arnie, so she turned on the light, sat up in bed and grabbed her favorite devotional book.

The day's devotional was on showing love at the holidays. *Love is not jealous*, it reminded her.

Love also didn't dream about throwing friends overboard. Was there some symbolism in that dream? Would she want to dump Dot as a friend if she and Arnie became a couple? She hoped not. She hoped she was bigger than that.

She sighed and slipped farther back into her pillows. She wanted what was best for her friends. She'd be happy for them. She loved them both. Well, Arnie more than Dot—Dot often had a gift for irritating her— but that was beside the point. They were friends. They were…

Her eyes drifted closed and her subconscious came after her again. This time she was paddling around in frigid water, and there went the longboat she'd been on, cruising off down the river. She could faintly hear a choir singing "Joy to the World."

"Help!" she cried.

"Ah, so you've joined me, have you?"

Dot appeared like Aphrodite rising out of the water. Only she was no Aphrodite. She loomed above Muriel, gaining stature like some kind of Disney villain, her hair wild and her eye makeup running. "I knew you never really liked me, you fake. Well, guess what? I never liked you, either. And now I'm going to get rid of you once and for all and Arnie will be mine at last."

With that, the evil Dot laid both hands on Muriel's head and pushed her down under.

Muriel woke up with a gasp. It was definitely time to get out of bed.

Her horrible dreams dogged her all morning long, and getting a text from Arnie when she was at Safeway with yet another picture of him and Dot enjoying themselves didn't improve her mood.

It was a selfie. They were in the ship's lounge, beaming happily. Dot was wearing a silver metallic top, a Santa hat and a big grin.

It looks like you're having a wonderful time, Muriel texted. I'm so glad.

Yes, she was. She was not going to stoop to being jealous. She was bigger than that.

Silver was not a good color for Dot.

Muriel frowned. She was also not going to be petty!

Resolving to have a good attitude and actually having a good attitude were not always the same thing, and her noble self and her less noble self battled as she made her way up and down the various aisles.

She had to stop this—that was all there was to it. Dot

and Arnie deserved to be happy and they also deserved to have their friends be happy for them.

It was wrong to be jealous, she told herself as she drove home from the grocery store. She'd had a great life, and if she'd only take the time to count her blessings, she'd feel so much better. She'd had two wonderful husbands, her daughters were all lovely and accomplished, she had adorable grandchildren, she had enough money to live on, she had...

A patrol car following her.

And not only was it following her, it was flashing its you're-in-trouble light at her.

Muriel hadn't had a ticket since she was thirty. What could she possibly have done wrong? At first she wasn't sure. Then she remembered. There'd been that stop sign on the corner. She'd been so busy counting her blessings she'd failed to notice it.

The driver's side of the patrol car opened and out stepped Dot's daughter, Tilda, the toughest cop in Icicle Falls. Grown men got stopped by Tilda and whimpered.

But Muriel had known Tilda since she was a girl. Surely that counted for something.

She let down her window and smiled up at her. "Hello, Tilda."

Tilda did not smile back. "Mrs. Sterling-Wittman, did you know you ran a stop sign back there?"

"I just realized that. I'm so sorry. I'm afraid I..." Wasn't paying attention? That didn't sound right. Muriel found herself at a loss for a proper explanation. She could hardly say that she was busy trying to adjust her attitude about Tilda's mom.

"Can I have your license and registration?" The request was both polite and intimidating.

Muriel fished her license out of her purse and grabbed her registration from her glove compartment. "I'm so embarrassed," she confessed as she handed them over. It was no lie. She was. How mortifying.

Tilda said nothing to that, just nodded and returned to her patrol car, where she sat for about a million years.

Muriel's heart began to race again. She passed a hand over her damp forehead. Getting stopped by the police was awful. And if someone she knew came by and saw her, she was going to be mortified. She'd had such a good driving record.

At last Tilda returned and gave her back her license and registration. "Please pay attention, Mrs. Wittman. You didn't even slow down back there. Someone could have been crossing the street."

Muriel hung her head. "You're right."

"I'm going to let you off with a warning. It is Christmas, after all," Tilda added with a smile that flooded Muriel with relief. "But please drive more carefully in the future," she added sternly.

"I will," Muriel assured her. "By the way, it looks like your mother's having a lovely time on her cruise."

"She is."

And I really wouldn't throw her overboard.

Muriel wisely kept that random thought securely locked behind tightly closed lips.

Tilda gave her a quick nod. "Have a nice day."

Nice. Right.

Chapter Eleven

Encouragement and support are gifts that everyone appreciates.
—Muriel Sterling, *A Guide to Happy Holidays*

Brandon was excited over the prospect of being a father. It was all he'd talked about since Meadow had made her announcement, and Olivia was determined to be supportive.

Now, before the baby came, was the time to cement her relationship with Meadow into something positive, so Tuesday, when Meadow finally made an appearance in the kitchen, she said, "I'd like to knit a blanket for the baby."

Meadow's face lit up like the giant tree in town square during the holiday tree-lighting ceremony. "Really?"

"Would you like to go yarn shopping with me today and pick out the color you'd like?"

"Oh, yeah. That would be awesome. When can we go?"

"Whenever you want."

"I'll get my coat," Meadow said and dashed out the swinging door.

Her excitement was convicting, making Olivia freshly aware of her bad attitude about her new daughter-in-law. It was also touching. To Olivia, knitting a blanket wasn't that big of a deal. She liked to knit, and anytime there was a baby shower for someone's daughter, she always made a blanket. But Meadow had drunk up the gesture like a thirsty plant. Once more Olivia found herself wondering what Meadow's life had been like growing up. Whatever her past, here in the present she was desperate to fit in at the lodge. As the matriarch of the family, it was up to Olivia to help her do it.

She wants to be part of the family, Olivia reminded herself as she went to get her coat. *That says a lot.* Some daughters-in-law didn't like their husbands' moms and wanted nothing to do with them. That didn't appear to be the case here. Although heaven knew, if Meadow could have read Olivia's mind these past few weeks, she wouldn't have been feeling so cordial.

She'd barely gotten into her apartment when Meadow was knocking at the door. "I'm ready. I can drive."

Olivia agreed but soon came to regret that decision. The girl drove like they were going to a fire and Olivia found herself gripping the handle on the passenger door. "There's no hurry. The Yarn Barn is open all day."

"Oh." Meadow eased up on the gas and Olivia let her breath out. "Sorry. I guess I'm just excited. Nobody's ever done something like this for me."

"You've never been pregnant before," Olivia pointed out.

Meadow's smile fell and Olivia remembered the

story of the lost baby. So, it had been true. She'd misjudged the girl.

"I'm sorry," she said. "I didn't think."

Meadow shrugged. "It's okay. I guess that first one wasn't meant to be. I like to think of him up in heaven, though, like an angel. Maybe he'll watch over his little brother or sister."

"I'm sure he will."

"Did you ever lose a baby?" Meadow asked in a small voice.

"No, I never had to go through that."

"It sucks. I don't want to ever go through it again," Meadow said and bit her lip.

The poor girl. "It'll be fine this time," Olivia assured her.

"I hope so. Brandon really wants kids. And so do I. I just hope I can be a good mom."

"You will be." What else could a mother-in-law say?

"You think so?"

She hoped so. "Wanting to be a good mom is half the battle." And it was. She had to give Meadow credit for such good intentions.

"Even if I screw up, at least the kid will have a good grandma."

The words, said so casually, weren't flattery. They were a statement of fact, a vote of confidence. And possibly even a bridge to an improved relationship.

It seemed that so far Meadow was doing most of the bridge building. Well, today Olivia would do her part to help with that bridge.

Once inside the yarn shop, Meadow was dazzled

by the array of yarns and the rainbow of colors available. In addition to acrylics, polyesters and microfibers, Etta Johansen featured a wide variety of yarns in her shop, wools from Scandinavia and Britain, as well as locally sourced wools. The walls of the shop were lined with bins that overflowed with skeins of yarn, tables sported more yarns, and mannequins modeled inspiring examples of knitters' artistry, wearing everything from vests and sweaters to scarves and shawls. Knitting books, knitting needles, knitting bags—Meadow took it all in with hungry eyes.

She was like a tourist in a foreign country, eager to experience everything. Olivia couldn't help but be touched by her enthusiasm.

"Olivia, nice to see you," Etta said as Olivia and Meadow walked in. "And is this your new daughter-in-law?"

"This is Meadow," Olivia said.

"Meadow, what a great name. Welcome to Icicle Falls."

"Thanks," Meadow said.

"Are you a knitter?" Etta asked.

"Me? No way," Meadow said as if Etta had asked her if she did brain surgery in her spare time.

"We're here to pick out something for a baby blanket."

"A baby blanket?" Etta smiled at Meadow. "Well, congratulations."

"Thanks," Meadow said and grinned.

"Do you know what you're having?"

"Not yet. I just did the pee-on-the-stick thing Sunday."

TMI, Olivia thought. But that was the younger generation. Thanks to Facebook and Twitter, everyone told everyone everything.

"Oh, uh, well, you two look around and see what you like," Etta said and scurried back to the shelves.

Meadow gnawed her bottom lip. "I think I just screwed up."

"Well, usually you don't talk about peeing to strangers," Olivia said.

Meadow's cheeks turned pink. "But that's how everyone does it."

"I know. And that's exactly why you don't need to offer all those details."

"Oh," Meadow said, again, this time more thoughtful. "Okay, got it. I won't do that again."

"It wasn't a cardinal sin," Olivia said, not wanting her to feel bad.

"Yeah, but I guess it wasn't very classy."

There was that. "Don't worry about it," Olivia said. Meadow was open to suggestions. She wanted to improve her social skills. All commendable. This was a little like working with Eliza Doolittle, the urchin in the musical *My Fair Lady*. Olivia hoped she could be more patient than Henry Higgins. And more understanding!

Meadow wandered over to a table piled with skeins of yarn and fingered one. "They're all so pretty."

"Do you have a color in mind?" Olivia asked.

"I don't know. It's hard to decide."

"I could do the blanket in something neutral since you don't know what you're having yet."

"Good idea," Meadow approved.

"Do you have a favorite color?"

"Yellow. But I like green, too."

Olivia found a multicolored acrylic yarn. "What about this?"

"Oh, yeah, that's perfect," Meadow said. "I always thought it would be kind of cool to learn how to knit. I knew this girl in high school. Her mom taught her how to knit and she made these really awesome scarves."

She sounded so wistful. "It's not that hard to knit a scarf. Would you like me to teach you?"

"Would you?"

It could be a real bonding experience, and Brandon would be pleased. "Of course," Olivia said and found that she herself was pleased. Here was a chance to develop a common interest and forge a bond with her daughter-in-law.

"All right." Meadow picked up the skein. "I'll knit a scarf for Brandon for Christmas."

It was a sweet thought. Olivia smiled at her. "I think that's a great idea."

"Can we start today?"

"Sure," Olivia said, pleased by her eagerness.

She did begin to wonder what she'd gotten into once they got back to the lodge and had settled on her sofa. Meadow was all thumbs with the needles, struggling with even the simple task of casting on.

Olivia reminded herself she, too, had been all thumbs when her mother had first taught her as a girl. Manipulating those needles had felt like trying to wield a broadsword.

Another couple of tries and Meadow did master casting on. Moving from that to the knit stitch had her chewing her lip in concentration and swearing like a sailor when she screwed up. "This is hard," she complained.

"You'll get it," Olivia said. "Learning a new skill takes time."

"Learning a new skill is a pain in the butt," Meadow grumbled, but she kept on. Once it looked like she was getting the hang of things, Olivia started on the baby blanket, and they fell into a companionable silence. "My mom always said it's stupid to knit when you can just buy a sweater," she said after a while, "but I think it's awesome to be able to make something you can wear. It's almost like…art."

"It is an art," Olivia said. "A time-honored one that a lot of women have been rediscovering."

Meadow held up her first four rows. "This is cool. I love watching Brandon's scarf grow."

"You'll be surprised how fast it does," Olivia told her.

As they sat side by side, all was happiness and contentment in Olivia's little living room. Until Meadow got a dozen rows done only to realize she'd dropped a stitch and would have to take out six. "This sucks," she declared after several muttered curses.

"It happens sometimes," Olivia soothed. "We can fix it. Let me help you."

Meadow handed over the yarn. "I don't think I'm meant to do this," she said as she watched Olivia put her messed-up row back together.

"You might surprise yourself." Olivia handed the scarf in progress back to her.

She took it with a scowl. "I doubt it. Okay, I'm gonna go watch *Dr. Phil*. I need a break," Meadow declared.

So did Olivia. Meadow's mercurial temperament was exhausting.

But, as Muriel would say, there was potential—both in the girl and in their relationship. With a baby on the way, giving up was not an option. With knitting, you grew something one stitch, one row at a time. It was the same with relationships. A dropped stitch here and there? You picked them up and started again. And that was what Olivia was going to keep doing.

Most of us like surprises, Sienna had read in Muriel's book.

Think back to when you were a child and you rushed to the Christmas tree on Christmas morning to see what Santa had brought or when you explored the contents of your Christmas stocking. Think of how much fun it is to receive an unexpected flower delivery or a greeting card from a friend who was thinking about you. Don't you love it when the person in line ahead of you at the coffee shop pays for your drink? Surprises are treats for our hearts.

Who can you surprise this holiday season? How about picking someone unlikely? Perhaps you know an older relative who's been overlooked or a lonely neighbor. Everyone loves a secret Santa.

The words followed Sienna around at work all day like a lost puppy. She wished she could think of someone as unlikely as Cratchett to surprise. Unfortunately, he was the only one who came to mind. Was it worth wasting Muriel's good advice on him? Nothing Sienna had tried so far had worked. Probably the best way to have a happy holiday was to avoid him altogether. Let Mrs. Zuckerman deal with the ugly tree.

Except he had actually smiled the day before. She'd seen it with her own eyes. Maybe there was hope. Well, she'd think about it.

That afternoon when she picked up Leo, she learned that he'd had a particularly bad day. Some kids had teased him on the playground and he'd gotten in trouble for being a distraction in class. Sienna suspected there was a strong connection between the two. She'd email his teacher later that night and see what could be done. These days bullying was not tolerated at school, and she was determined to make sure it ended.

"I hate Tommy Haskel," Leo grumbled as they walked through the parking lot to the car.

"We'll get it sorted out," she promised him. "Meanwhile, remember that he's the one with the problem. He can't see so well."

"Yes, he can," Leo argued. "He doesn't wear glasses like Alan Wills."

"No, but he has a worse kind of seeing problem. He can't see what's good in other people. He doesn't understand what a special boy you are."

"I'm not special," Leo muttered. "I'm stupid."

"No, you're special," Sienna said firmly. "You're special to me, Leo, and you're even more special to God. We all are."

Leo found it hard to believe that any of his tormentors could make God's A-list, especially Tommy Haskel, the king of them all.

"That's because we don't see him as God does. Think of the Grinch and how rotten he was. But it was because he was unhappy and his heart was too small. I think maybe this boy Tommy is a grinch."

"Will he be nice like the Grinch someday?" Leo asked.

"Maybe. Or maybe not." More like probably not. "But we're not going to worry about that, are we?"

Leo frowned.

"We're going to keep on being good people no matter what. And we're going to keep being kind to others no matter what. Because we don't want to turn into grinches."

"Are we going to keep being kind to Mr. Cratchett?"

Once more the words from Muriel's book drifted back into the picture, the Ghost of Christmas Kindness. "Yes, him, too," Sienna said reluctantly.

"I don't like Mr. Cratchett. He's always mad."

"Maybe he's mad because he's sad and feels left out, like the Grinch." And maybe she needed to be a little more empathetic. She'd conveniently forgotten what Tim had shared about his uncle. What if the man wasn't so bad at heart? She'd heard his story from Tim and she'd gotten a glimmer of the kinder Cratchett when he was talking with Mrs. Zuckerman. If he truly was simply a man who had allowed disappointment to sour him, kindness had to be the antidote for that.

"So, what could we do to help make him happy?" she prompted. Here was the perfect opportunity to implement the suggestion in Muriel's book and be a good example to her son.

Leo shrugged.

"If you were mad, what would make you happy?"

"A Twinkie!"

Somehow Sienna didn't see that as the kind of surprise that would warm Cratchett's heart. "I don't think Mr. Cratchett likes Twinkies."

"A deep-fried Twinkie," Leo suggested, still going with his favorite snack food.

"Even when they're deep-fried."

"Suckers! Let's get Mr. Cratchett a sucker."

"Let's get Mr. Cratchett something," Sienna said and turned the car in the direction of the Sweet Dreams Chocolate Company sweets shop.

Heidi Schwartz was at the counter and she greeted Sienna with a hello and gave Leo a chance to select a complimentary piece of chocolate from the bin of seconds. "What can I help you with today?" she asked Sienna.

"We have to get something for Mr. Cratchett," Leo informed her. "He's a grinch."

"Leo," Sienna chided.

"A grinch, huh?"

"We have a neighbor who could use some holiday cheer," Sienna told Heidi, glossing over the whole grinch analogy. "What would you recommend?"

"How much did you want to spend?"

Not much. It was the thought that counted, after all.

Sienna tossed out a budget-friendly figure and Heidi nodded and picked up a small box wrapped in thick red paper and tied with a gold ribbon.

"Our mixed truffles are always a big hit."

"Perfect." Hopefully, they'd be a hit with Mr. Cratchett.

Back home, they sneaked over to Cratchett's place, stumbling up the porch steps in the late-afternoon dark. "Okay, Leo," Sienna said, setting the little box in front of the door, "ring the doorbell and then we'll run around the corner of the house and hide in front of the garage."

"Okay," Leo said with an excited giggle. He rang the doorbell and they hurried down the steps and around the corner of the house, Leo laughing wildly as they went. They stood for a moment in breathless silence, waiting for the door to open.

Nothing happened.

"Why isn't he coming?" Leo asked.

He had to be home. He hardly ever left his house.

Sienna poked her nose around the side in time to see Cratchett standing in the doorway, looking suspiciously around. Their gazes locked for a moment, hers embarrassed, his awkward. Then she pulled back around the corner and pressed herself against the garage door.

Was that a chuckle she'd just heard? Well, well. She peered around the corner again and saw the door shut. The chocolates were gone. The grinch had been fed.

She smiled and held out her hand to her son. "Let's go home."

"Did Mr. Cratchett like the candy?" Leo asked.

"I think he did."

It was a simple little act of kindness, but the harvest of happiness that she got from it was huge and she feasted on it all evening long. Muriel Sterling-Wittman was surely onto something.

The happy texts and pictures from Dot and Arnie kept on coming. Muriel sat on her couch with her morning coffee and scowled at the latest batch of pictures. One was of Arnie and Dot seated at a dining table with six other people, all with glasses of champagne, toasting whoever was manning the camera.

How nice Arnie looked in his new blue sweater. He'd put on a little weight from all those German pastries he'd been enjoying, and the blue in the sweater brought out the blue in his eyes.

To her surprise, Muriel felt a flutter in her chest looking at him.

He looked downright jaunty in the green German Alpine hat he was wearing in another picture, and there went the unexpected flutter again. He stood in front of a booth filled with candles and luminarias, many of which Muriel would have happily purchased. If she'd had the good sense to go on the trip.

When we got back to the ship tonight, the crew greeted us with hot chocolate, Dot said in one of her texts.

Never mind the hot chocolate. When was Dot going to follow up on that earlier text and spill who she was falling in love with? It didn't *have* to be Arnie. There had to be other single men on that boat. It couldn't be Arnie.

But here came a new picture, proof that it could, indeed, be Arnie. Someone had captured him and Dot in action on the dance floor. She was wearing that flashy red sequined dress and Arnie was in a tux. They were waltzing like a pair of contestants on *Dancing with the Stars* and looking oh, so happy with each other.

Showing off our new steps, Arnie explained. There's a couple on the ship who teach ballroom dancing and they gave us some pointers. Dot's a natural.

Dot's a natural. Yes, Muriel had seen Dot in action before at the annual Fourth of July street dance and she had the moves. But since when did Arnie like to dance? Since he started hanging out with Dot, apparently. Perhaps Dot wasn't the only one falling in love.

Muriel studied the picture, trying to analyze the smiles on her friends' faces. Were those the smiles of two people who had stumbled into love or were they simply the smiles of two friends enjoying themselves on the dance floor?

You two look great, she texted Dot.

Okay, supportive response done. Now she needed info. So, who are you having a shipboard romance with? Did you fall for the captain? she added. There, a light, teasing little question. Then she couldn't help adding, Has Arnie met anyone?

Dot didn't say. In fact, she didn't say anything. Muriel got no reply to her text. What did that mean? Were they being coy? Were they waiting to make a big announcement when they got home? Was Arnie worried about hurting her?

Except for Arnie to be worried about hurting her he'd have to know she cared. And how could he have known when she hadn't even known?

Oh, what stupid timing on her part! Why couldn't she have realized how much she cared two weeks ago?

She went through the rest of her day under a gray cloud. By evening it had descended, wrapping her in a thick fog of misery. She wanted nothing more than to stay home and pretend she was a hermit. But her calendar decreed otherwise. That night she had a speaking engagement.

She made her way to the Icicle Falls Public Library, wishing all the way that she'd never agreed to give a talk. Discover the Joys of the Holidays with Author Muriel Sterling, the poster hanging in the entryway promised. In her present frame of mind, she'd be much better at helping everyone explore how to be cranky. Temperatures were supposed to drop. Maybe nobody would want to come out on a wintry weeknight and she could turn around and go home, snuggle under a blanket on the couch, eat chocolate and feel sorry for herself.

No such luck. The library parking lot was packed. She got out of her car and made her way into the library. Millie, the librarian, had been watching for her and greeted her enthusiastically. In honor of the evening's festivities, Millie had donned a red dress and was wearing dangly earrings shaped like Christmas packages. Muriel was dressed in black. Maybe Millie should give the talk.

"We've got a full house," she informed Muriel. "Everyone's anxiously waiting to hear what you have to say."

Muriel managed a smile. "I hope I won't disappoint them."

"Of course you won't. Everyone loves you."

All except for a certain someone, who had defected and was now roaming Germany with Dot. Muriel murmured her thanks and let Millie lead her into the room reserved for events.

It was, indeed, a full house. In addition to several new faces, she saw a lot of familiar ones. Stacy Thomas and the members of her book club were present. One of the members, Jen Armstrong, pregnant with her second baby, waved enthusiastically at Muriel. Jen claimed that Muriel's book *Simplicity* changed her life, and she never missed a book signing or an opportunity to hear Muriel speak. Missy Truman, who now ran Sleeping Lady Salon, was clutching Muriel's book as if it were a first-edition classic. Vance Fish, who owned a bookstore in Seattle where Muriel had made many appearances, gave her a nod and a wink. Pat was present, along with Sienna, and they would be selling *A Guide to Happy Holidays* to anyone who hadn't yet gotten a copy. Beth Mallow was there, and so was Olivia, along with her two daughters-in-law. Stefanie Stahl was seated next to Cass Masters and her husband and clutching a copy of the book, and Janice Lind and her circle of friends were present, as well. And, of course, Muriel's daughters had all come to offer their support.

"I'm sure our guest speaker needs no introduction," Millie began, once the crowd had settled down. "Many of us have known Muriel all our lives, and I'm sure everyone here has gotten a chocolate fix at Sweet Dreams many times." This sent a ripple of chuckles through the crowd. "Muriel has been both a good friend and an inspiration to so many of us over the years."

An inspiration? She didn't feel very inspiring tonight. She sure talked a good talk, but these days that was as far as it went.

"And since she's started writing, she's expanded her circle of influence and touched many more hearts and lives," Millie continued. "We're so lucky she consented to spend some time with us tonight and share her insights on how to have a happy holiday. Please welcome Muriel Sterling."

The fraud. How on earth was she supposed to talk about making the holidays happy when she was anything but?

Practice what you preach and start focusing on what's good in your life! It was easy to do when she looked out at her three beautiful daughters, smiling encouragingly at her, not to mention all the friends who were present.

Except...two are missing. Off together, falling in love.

She reined in her wandering thoughts and pulled out her notes. "Thank you all for coming. I see so many familiar faces and I can't help but be grateful that God has put so many wonderful people in my life. And that brings me to my first point. Attitude is everything. To really appreciate the joys of this season I think it's important to go into it with a grateful heart."

Yes, grateful that Arnie and Dot are having fun without you.

Muriel frowned and consulted her notes. Where was she? Oh, yes, grateful. "Sometimes we focus on the wrong things."

Like Arnie and Dot.

"And that can make us lose sight of the good things." She went on to talk about her ugly tree and how she and some of her friends had decided to try to see the best in other people. Olivia wiped at a corner of her eye and Pat nodded in agreement.

"That's your foundation. If your attitude is right, then the other aspects of the holiday begin to fall into place."

Remember that!

She moved on from the philosophical to the practical, sharing tips from her book for cutting down on stress and busyness, such as marking off days on the calendar for a "silent night," which meant not scheduling anything but to stay home and enjoy a holiday movie or a soak in the tub with a good book.

"Like yours," called out Cass, and once more everyone chuckled.

Smiles, nods, happy faces. Muriel felt her own cranky attitude melting. All right. Even she was beginning to believe what she had to say.

She finished her talk and Millie opened the floor for questions.

"Muriel, most of us know you've gone through some hard times. How have you managed to keep your good attitude?" asked Cass.

She had gone through some hard times. She'd lost two wonderful husbands and nearly lost the family business. She still remembered how, after her second husband, Waldo, died, she'd almost given up on living herself. All she'd wanted to do was sleep and hide from the world while Sweet Dreams crumbled and her daughter Samantha had to scramble to save it. Not her finest hour. But, somehow, she'd pulled out of that tailspin. And eventually, she'd come to realize that she had something to say.

"I'm not the only woman here who's faced hard times and loss," she said, looking to Pat and then Olivia, "but I think one of the ways you carry on is to find something good to do with your life. Find the purpose God put you here for. Focus on that and you'll feel so much better."

And her purpose was to be an encouragement to others, which she was doing here tonight. There, now she felt better.

Another hand shot up, this time from a thirty-something woman Muriel didn't recognize. "You have so much good advice in your book on how to deal with difficult people this time of year. I'm wondering, do you have any difficult people in your life? And do you follow your own advice when dealing with them? What do you do when people make you mad?"

I push them overboard in my dreams.

Suddenly, Muriel was feeling a little less positive. "Well, we all know difficult people."

Several people in the crowd leaned forward, waiting for more words of wisdom from Muriel, the author. But Muriel, the author, seemed to have retired for the night, leaving in her place Muriel, the betrayed friend. Make that Muriel, the exaggerator.

She cleared her throat, making way for those words of wisdom. None came. Finally, she shrugged. "All I can do is try to follow my own advice." *And remember that I brought this whole mess with Dot and Arnie on myself, so there's no point in being unhappy with either of them. Especially Dot.* If Dot had found love, good for her. If only what was good for her didn't also happen to be not so good for Muriel.

"So, what *do* you do?" her eager questioner persisted.

"I do the best I can."

Her answer wasn't exactly profound but it was the best she could do. And now she was done. She needed to go home and reread her own books. She looked pleadingly at Millie. *End my torture, please.*

Millie, God bless her, got the message. "Well," she said, "I think that does it for tonight. I know Muriel will be happy to sign copies of her book. We also have several copies of her other books available for checkout. Muriel, we're all so glad you could spend the evening with us."

The applause was followed by a line of people, all wanting to talk to her, tell her how much they'd enjoyed her talk and to get their books signed. She smiled and nodded and wished everyone would hurry up and leave so she could take her fraudulent self home.

"That was really good," Olivia's new daughter-in-law, Meadow, told her. "Except the part about difficult people." She shook her head. "You haven't met my mom. Even you'd have a hard time with her."

What to say to that? "Well, at least you have a wonderful mother-in-law to balance the scales."

It had been the right thing to say. Meadow smiled. "Yeah, I do."

Olivia had come up in time to hear her words, and her face suddenly matched the red sweater she was wearing. "It was a good talk," she said and hugged Muriel.

Finally, the crowd dispersed. Muriel could drop the happy ruse and head home at last.

"Ready to go to Herman's for hot-fudge sundaes?" Samantha asked her.

She'd forgotten she'd promised to go out with the girls. "I don't know. I'm a little tired."

"Too tired to hang out with us?" Bailey asked, shocked.

Okay, it looked like she was going out for ice cream.

But even the company of her daughters coupled with one of her favorite chocolate treats couldn't lift her spirits. She set aside the last half of her sundae.

Samantha pointed to the unfinished treat. "Mom, you're not finishing your sundae?"

"I'm not very hungry."

"What's hunger got to do with it?" Bailey said. "I'll finish it," she added and pulled the bowl over to her.

Her other two daughters exchanged worried looks.

"Don't look like that. I'm fine," she assured them. She would be. Eventually.

Chapter Twelve

Never underestimate the power of mistletoe.
—Muriel Sterling, *A Guide to Happy Holidays*

Sienna popped next door to Mrs. Zuckerman's after work to borrow a cup of brown sugar. It was a manufactured need based on a sudden desire to bake cookies, which was based on the real desire to find out how things were going between her and Cratchett.

"Did you make him cookies?"

"I did. He came over today to collect them and stayed for lunch," Mrs. Zuckerman said as she spooned sugar into Sienna's measuring cup. "And he brought me a box of Sweet Dreams chocolates. Wasn't that thoughtful?"

More like cheap. It wasn't hard to figure out where he'd gotten the chocolates.

"He told me about his wife. Such a sad story. The poor man has been lonely all these years."

"That tends to happen when you're a hermit."

"I think he's been at a loss for what to do with himself," Mrs. Zuckerman said. "You know, men don't do as well as we women when they're left on their own.

We have our friends, which gives us a bit of a safety net. Most men don't have that group of tight friends who will be there for them when something bad happens. I think that makes life so much harder for them. Anyway, Robert and I had a good time together."

"I'm glad," Sienna told her. Not to mention surprised. Even knowing that, once, he'd been a very different man, she found it difficult to envision Cranky Cratchett having a good time with anyone.

"We discovered we have quite a few things in common. We're both big readers. And can you believe it? He watches the Hallmark Channel."

Right. Someone was giving Mrs. Zuckerman a snow job.

"I'm going over to his house tonight. We're going to watch *Miracle on 34th Street*."

Miracle on Alpine Drive—Bob Cratchett was becoming human. Who knew? Maybe there was hope for cranky Mr. Cratchett. But if you asked Sienna, Mrs. Zuckerman had her work cut out for her.

"That sounds like fun," she said, then couldn't help cautioning, "But don't go rushing into anything."

Mrs. Zuckerman chuckled. "At my age you don't have a lot of time to waste. And when you find a good man, trust me, you count that as a gift and take him with a heartfelt thank-you."

"There's gifts and there's white elephants," Sienna pointed out.

Mrs. Zuckerman handed back the cup of sugar. "You're sweet to worry, but there's no need. I know the difference."

Sienna hoped so. As she went back home to start on her own cookies, she couldn't help worrying that, contrary to all her talk about girlfriends and safety nets, Mrs. Zuckerman was lonely. Loneliness tended to blind people.

She had finished her baking binge and was starting dinner when her doorbell rang.

"I'll get it," Leo called and raced for the door.

A moment later she heard a deep male voice in her hallway. The only man who ever stopped by was Rita's husband, Tito, but this wasn't him. She came out of the kitchen to see what stranger her son had let in and was surprised to find Leo towing Tim Richmond down the hall like an energetic little tugboat.

Tim seemed to fill the hallway with his presence and she could smell the faintest whiff of spicy cologne. He looked good, he smelled good, and his smile was great.

And here she was, with her makeup worn off and her hair pulled back in a sloppy bun. Her ratty sweatshirt, jeans and Uggs. Ugh.

"Tim." There was a brilliant conversation starter. "Hi." *Oh, brother.* "What are you doing here?" Okay, she gave up.

"I was just at Uncle Bob's," he said, pointing next door. "I was going to take him out for dinner but it looks like he's got a hot date with Mrs. Zuckerman. What's that about?"

"I guess love's blooming here on Alpine Drive," Sienna said.

And if it could bloom for a sour old guy like Cratchett,

could it bloom for her? What was Tim Richmond doing for dinner? Maybe she should invite him to stay.

"So, uh, I was in the neighborhood..."

Yes, she should. "Since you're in the neighborhood, would you like to stay for dinner?"

"We're having enchiladas," Leo informed him.

"Enchiladas? Wow."

"I guess that's a yes?"

"For sure that's a yes."

She found herself feeling ridiculously pleased that he'd accepted her offer. *It's only dinner*, she told herself.

Leo pulled on his arm. "Come on, Tim. I've got Legos."

"Leo, it's Mr. Richmond to you."

"Naw, Tim's fine."

"And maybe our guest doesn't want to play Legos." Although when you dropped in on a woman with a son, you took your chances.

"Legos rock," Tim said and let Leo tow him into the living room.

"Would you like some wine?" she called after him.

"Got any beer?"

She hated beer but she always kept some on hand for Tito when he came by. "Sure."

"Can I have some beer?" Leo asked.

"You know you can't."

"Beer's kind of nasty," Tim told him.

"But you're drinking it."

"Good point. What do you think I should drink?"

"Chocolate milk," Leo said, jumping up and down.

"Well, then chocolate milk," he said.

"Me, too!"

"In the kitchen," Sienna said to her son.

Now Leo looked torn. Chocolate milk in the kitchen or playing Legos?

"I tell you what," Tim said to him. "Let's play Legos right now and then we'll have chocolate milk at dinner. How does that sound?"

Leo nodded eagerly. "Okay."

Sienna left them to it and went back into the kitchen to put together a salad and heat some corn. This felt good. It was nice to have another adult in the house, nice for Leo to have someone kind to look up to.

It would be nice to have someone to help her get Leo ready for bed at night, to help tuck him in. To tuck her in, too. That big chest of Tim's—her hands itched to touch it. Yes, it would be nice to have sex again. She missed sex. She missed intimacy.

Don't get your hopes up, she cautioned herself as she got busy shredding lettuce. She'd been down this road before. Things didn't work out with men. There was no reason to think they should with this man, either.

It didn't stop her from hoping.

Dinner together felt so natural. Leo kept up a steady stream of chatter, talking about the Lego monster Tim had made for him. "It ate my foot," he announced and took a large gulp of his chocolate milk. "I like chocolate milk. It's better than beer. Aren't you glad you've got chocolate milk, Tim?"

"Oh, yeah. It's way better," Tim agreed and took a drink of his milk.

"You are a sport," Sienna told him.

He shrugged. "I like milk. It's good for your bones, makes you strong. Right, Leo?"

"Right," Leo said.

"These enchiladas are great, by the way," Tim added.

"I like Mama's enchiladas," Leo informed him.

"Me, too," Tim said and smiled at her.

His smile was like a hug for her heart.

"You can come for dinner tomorrow," Leo told him, and Sienna felt herself blushing.

"Mr. Richmond has a family of his own," she told Leo. *Other obligations, so don't get your hopes up.*

"But they're not with me all the time and I get lonely," Tim said and scraped the last of his enchiladas off his plate.

"My daddy doesn't live with us," Leo said. He frowned at his plate. "He doesn't like us."

What to say to that? She could hardly contradict her son. They never heard from Señor Poop. If it weren't for the obligatory child support payments she had to pry out of him by court order, she'd think Carlos were a figment of her imagination. Sadly, he was still real to Leo, and the fact that he made no effort to keep in contact hurt her son. It made her wish she'd kept a picture of him. That way she could have thrown darts at it.

Tim spoke before she could. "Well, your daddy is missing out. Legos, chocolate milk, a nice kid and a pretty mom—what's not to like?"

Sienna felt her cheeks warming. She looked across the table at her son, who was beaming up at Tim. *Don't fall*, she warned herself.

Too late. She wasn't sure which of them was farther over the cliff and plummeting, her son or herself. "We're fine on our own. Aren't we, Leo?"

Leo shrugged and poked at his half-eaten enchiladas. Awkwardness descended.

Tim cleared his throat. "I could manage some more of those enchiladas."

"Of course," Sienna said, eager to get past the unpleasant moment.

Not only did he manage more enchiladas, he also managed a second helping of flan. "Best meal I've had in a long time," he told Sienna when he finally pushed away his bowl. "Thanks."

"Mi gusto," she replied, making him smile.

"It sure beats spending the evening with my uncle and listening to him gripe about everything and anything."

She could only imagine. "It's nice for us to have company." Especially when that company was big and testosterone packed with a deep voice and a kind smile. *Yep, plummeting.*

"We like company," put in Leo.

"I bet you like everyone," Tim said to him.

"I don't like Tommy Haskel," Leo said with a frown. "He calls me names."

"He does? Well, that's not nice."

"But we don't let mean people ruin our day," Sienna said lightly, conveniently overlooking the many times Cratchett had put her in a bad mood. "Now, let's show Tim how great you are at clearing the table. Leo is a good helper," she added.

"I'll bet he is," Tim said, and Leo's smile reappeared.

Tim helped with clearing the table and loading the dishes. "I guess I should get going," he said once they were finished.

"Don't go, Tim," Leo begged. "Come play Legos."

"We need to work on your math," Sienna said to him.

Leo's brows dipped and his jaw jutted out. "No. I hate math."

"I know, but you need to learn it."

"I don't want to." Leo's voice began to rise in volume.

"Think how proud your teacher will be if you learn your subtraction tables."

"No, I don't want to." Leo began a hasty retreat from the kitchen.

"Math can be more fun than Legos," Tim said.

Leo stopped in the doorway. "No, it can't."

"I'll prove it to you," Tim said. He turned to Sienna. "Got any M&M's?"

It was her favorite candy and she never dared to bring the things into the house. "No."

"How about…those little marshmallows?"

Those she did keep on hand for hot chocolate. She nodded.

"Marshmallows!" Leo hooted.

"Want to do marshmallow math?" Tim asked him.

Leo nodded eagerly.

"Think your mom will let us have some marshmallows?"

"Mama, can we have marshmallows?"

Anything was worth a try. "Sure," Sienna said and

fetched a bag of miniature marshmallows from the cup-board.

A few minutes later Tim and Leo were settled at the kitchen table with them. "Now, we're not going to do a lot of marshmallow math, because you'll probably get all buzzed and bounce off the walls. But we'll do some."

He reached into the bag and pulled out one marshmallow. "This guy looks lonely. Do you think he needs a friend?"

"Marshmallows can't have friends," Leo said with a giggle.

"Sure they can, if they're doing marshmallow math. He's all by himself, so let's name him Mr. One."

"Mr. One," Leo repeated.

"Let's give Mr. One a friend." He pulled another marshmallow from the bag and walked it over to the first. "Hi, Mr. One. Would you like a friend?" he said in a falsetto voice. "Yes, I would," he said, lowering his voice and jiggling the first marshmallow. "What's your name?

"I'm Miss Two," he continued, falsetto. He lowered his voice and bounced the original marshmallow up and down. "Let's be friends, Miss Two. If we add one and one, that gives us…"

"Two," Leo said easily.

"Right. But they still want more friends. Let's add another." Another marshmallow joined the first two. "How many do we have now?"

"Three!"

Two more marshmallows came out. "How many now?"

Leo counted them out. "Five!"

"Oh, no. These two don't want to play anymore." He gave one to Leo and popped one in his mouth. "Two went away. How many are left?"

"Three."

"Very good. So, we had five marshmallows and we took away two. If you take two from five, you have?"

"Three!"

The marshmallow math went on for another few minutes, moving up to higher numbers, with marshmallows going into mouths and over to visit Sienna, who had decided to make some hot chocolate to go with all those marshmallows. There were a few times when Leo bit his lip and strained to concentrate, but Tim was patient and encouraging and had no problem backtracking, moving marshmallows around the table, hiding them in his shirt pocket and pretending to pull one from behind Leo's ear. Instead of tears and tantrums, the kitchen was filled with giggles.

Tim finally gave the bag back to her. "We'd better stop with the marshmallows before he gets a sugar overload," he said, then turned his attention back to Leo. "Okay, now let's think about our marshmallow friends. How many did we have when we first started?"

The drill went on for another few minutes as they enjoyed their hot chocolate and, amazingly, Leo enjoyed it.

"Good job, my man," Tim said when they were done. "Knuckle bump."

He made a fist and held it out to Leo, who fisted his small hand and bumped it against Tim's.

"Let's play Legos," Leo said, jumping up from the table.

Poor Tim. Sienna was ready to rescue him but he said, "Good idea," and went back into the living room with Leo. Sienna followed, settling on the couch and watching. Tim Richmond was great with kids.

After half an hour Sienna decided it was time to set Tim free. "Okay," she said to her son. "Time to get ready for bed."

"Aww, Mama."

Tim got up from the floor and stretched out his tall frame. "Thanks for showing me your Legos," he said to Leo.

Leo grinned. "You're fun, Tim."

Yes, he was. And patient. And looking more perfect all the time. "Let's run your bath," Sienna said and held out a hand to her son.

"Okay," he said, resigned to his fate. "Bye, Tim."

"Bye, Leo."

"I'll be right back," Sienna said.

"Take your time," he told her and sat down on the couch like a man who meant to stay.

"Can Tim come back tomorrow?" Leo asked as she ran his bathwater.

"Probably not tomorrow," she said. Although it would have been fine with her if he did. And the tomorrow after that, too. Oh, she was falling hard.

"I like Tim," Leo informed her when she finally tucked him in.

"So do I." But it was crazy to get her hopes up.

"Sorry to keep you waiting so long," she said when she finally joined Tim in the living room. "You probably need to get going."

"I'm in no hurry," he said. He rested an ankle on one knee and slung an arm over the back of the couch, looking very much at home.

"It takes a while to get Leo settled."

"He's a nice kid. How old is he?"

"Nine." Nine and still trying to master basic addition and subtraction, while other children his age were adding and subtracting four-digit numbers and learning their times tables. Sometimes she got discouraged on her son's behalf. "It was nice of you to help him like that."

Tim shrugged. "No big deal."

"It was to me."

"He's a good kid, easy to like. You are, too," Tim added with a look that got Sienna's hormones singing "Joy to the World."

"Thanks," she said. Tim was so easy to like it scared her.

"Too bad his dad's a lightweight."

Like the other men who had come along since. "Yes, it is. But we don't need someone like that in our lives. If someone can't see Leo's worth, he's not worth being with." May as well let this someone know that right up front.

"Everyone has value," Tim said simply, and she could have kissed him.

Actually, she could have kissed him, anyway. This man was perfect.

Except there was no such thing.

Conversation moved into new territory. Tim wanted to know how long Sienna had been in Icicle Falls and where she'd lived before moving to the mountains. Then he wanted to know why she'd moved.

"A new start. Sometimes you just need to get away."

"Sometimes you can make a new start right where you are," he said.

"Is that what you did?"

He nodded.

"Tell me more about your orchard," she prompted. "How long have you owned it?"

"Ten years," he said, "although it was in my family long before I took it over. I like tending the trees, watching the apples grow. I guess it's kind of a simple life. But what can I say? I like to keep life simple. Well, as simple as you can with an ex in the picture."

Sienna wished her ex were in the picture. But he wasn't, and her life wasn't simple. At some point that would sink in and Tim would be gone, back to his apple trees.

But for the moment he was in no hurry. He stayed on, talking about his own kids and how involved he was in their lives.

"Amelia's seven and Amy's eleven going on sixteen. God help me when she gets old enough to date. She's a regular fashionista and wants to design clothes when she grows up. Amelia's decided she's going to be a princess. Her mom says she's well on her way since I spoil her and get her everything she wants."

"Well, she is a princess."

"There you have it," he said with a grin. "They're both great kids."

With such a nice man for a father, that was hardly surprising.

"Between them and the ex and the uncle, they all keep me hopping," he finished.

Leo all by himself was enough to keep anyone hopping. Did Tim have room in his life for anyone else, really?

Finally, he said, "I'd better get going. You probably have stuff to do."

No, nothing. I have no life. He was already standing, so she stood, too.

"Thanks for dinner. It was great."

"Thanks for helping my son." *You're great.*

For a moment he stood there smiling at her. Then his gaze fell on her lips and she found herself holding her breath. *Kiss me.*

He didn't. "Well." He motioned toward the front hall. "Like I said."

"I know. I need to let you go."

Another moment and he was gone and the house, which she'd so loved when she moved in, suddenly felt like it was missing something.

More like someone. She sighed. It was stupid to even start anything with this man. It was stupid to start anything with any man.

She said as much to her cousin the next day when she came to the house to pick up Leo.

"Tim, Tim, Tim, that's all Leo's been talking about ever since he got here," Rita said. "You'd be crazy not to see where this goes."

"I know where it's going to go," Sienna said. "The

same place every other relationship I start goes. Nowhere."

"I don't know. This guy seems different."

"They all seem different. In the end they're not."

Although heaven knew she wanted this man to be different. But once he spent more time with Leo and her, once he saw more of what their life was like...

Why take a chance on a man again and wind up disappointed? No, she was beyond simple disappointment already. Tim Richmond had the potential to break her heart into more pieces than any other man she'd known.

"I'm not going to encourage him," she said to Rita. "It's not worth it."

Except she didn't discourage him when he called and suggested stopping by on Friday night with pizza. She would, though. She'd wait and discourage him in person.

"Oh, yeah," Rita said when she reported this new development. "It's so much easier to discourage someone in person."

"Well, I didn't want to be rude."

"No, of course not. And you'd better be polite if he kisses you, too."

She should call him right back and tell him she couldn't see him.

But he was probably busy. She'd stick with her plan and discourage him come Friday. She had to stop him before this snowball rolled along any further.

When he showed up bearing a box of pizza from Bavarian Alps as well as a movie he'd picked up at Redbox, microwave popcorn and Milk Duds, her resolution dwindled. He was such a nice man, and just looking at him got her heated in all the right places. Things could work out...

"Hi, Tim!" Leo cried, bouncing up and down as if Santa himself were standing in their front hall. "Is that pizza?"

"It is. Are you hungry?"

"Yes!" Leo hooted and raced down the hall to the kitchen.

"I hope you don't mind me inviting myself over," Tim said to Sienna as they followed him. "I don't get the girls till tomorrow and it seemed wrong to sit home alone on a Friday night."

So, she and Leo were the second string. He probably wouldn't have called her if he'd had his kids. "Don't you have your girls every weekend?"

"Pretty much." He frowned. "I make a handy baby-sitter for the ex and the new boyfriend."

Drama with exes—did she want to get pulled into that? Between her own ex and the disastrous boyfriends who had followed, she'd had enough drama. This was a mistake.

Still, watching how easily Tim interacted with her son, it was hard not to wish they'd met earlier in their lives. Too bad she hadn't moved to Icicle Falls years ago. Maybe life would have been different for both of them.

With so many thoughts rolling around in her head she didn't say much at dinner, but Leo kept up a steady chatter. He had much to tell Tim since he'd seen the man last. His teacher had been impressed with his improved math skills and he'd shared with her about Mr. One and Miss Two.

"You're smart," Leo finished. "I want to be smart like you."

"You just be yourself, Leo, and you'll be fine," Tim said. It was the perfect reply.

After dinner Leo hauled Tim back to play with his Legos and they topped off their playtime with some good-natured roughhousing. Leo was starting to get tired, the tips of his ears turning pink, but in spite of that he wasn't ready for the fun to end and pouted when Sienna informed him it was time to get ready for bed.

"We can play Legos again another time," Tim said to him.

There shouldn't be another time. Leo was getting too attached. So was Sienna.

She finally got Leo settled and went downstairs to end the evening.

But Tim had picked up a romantic comedy she'd been dying to see. What would a couple more hours hurt?

When he sat next to her on the couch and she felt the electric charge as his thigh brushed hers, she knew what a couple more hours would hurt. And yet she let the movie play on, right along with dreams of what life could be like with this man.

The story moved from laughter to that moment of doubt when it looked like the relationship was doomed and then on to the requisite happy ending with the couple kissing under the mistletoe. *Sigh.*

"That's what you're missing," Tim said.

A man? "What?"

"Mistletoe. I haven't seen any hanging around here?"

"There hasn't exactly been much need."

"There is now," he murmured, and her heart seized. *Don't let him kiss you. Don't let him kiss you.*

Too late. She did.

With his lips on hers and his fingers slipping through her hair, nerve endings that had settled down for a long winter's nap awakened. *Merry Christmas, happy New Year and hallelujah.*

What do you think you're doing? demanded her sensible half.

She was enjoying herself—that was what she was doing. But her sensible half was right. She pulled her hand away from his chest and put some distance between them. "This isn't a good idea."

He looked surprised. "It's not?"

"No, it's really not."

His arms fell to his sides. "Okay, tell me why."

"You have kids."

"Well, yeah. So do you."

"And mine needs a lot of attention. It's just..."

His brows pulled together. "Are you worried I can't handle adding another kid to the mix?"

"Leo takes a lot of time and energy."

"I think I've got enough of both."

Sienna shook her head. "I don't know."

"Look, I don't know, either. I don't have a crystal ball, so I can't tell you what the future might hold. But this much I can tell you. I think you're great and I'm crazy about you. I like your kid a lot and I want to spend more time with you guys. I want to see where this goes because I think it could go someplace good."

"I've tried before. It's never lasted and that's been hard on Leo." It had been hard on her, too. "I don't want to get his hopes up."

Tim nodded slowly. "I get that. I understand you wanting to play it safe. But not much happens when you play it safe. You don't exactly score a lot of points."

"Life isn't always about scoring," she said stiffly.

"It's not about sitting on the sidelines, either. Do you really want to sit on the sidelines, Sienna? Do you want to keep your kid there?"

She bit her lip. "I don't know."

"Think about it," he said. He caught her hand and kissed it, starting everything sparking all over again. "And if you decide you want to get in the game, I'll be taking the girls to the tree-lighting ceremony tomorrow. Let me know if you want to join us."

With that he retrieved his movie, got his coat and slipped out of the house, leaving Sienna to deal with her disappointed nerve endings as best she could.

Chapter Thirteen

Keep your smile no matter what and you'll find
that little trick helps you also keep your joy.
—Muriel Sterling, *A Guide to Happy Holidays*

After much tossing and turning Friday night, Sienna
finally came to a decision. She wasn't ready to give up
and sit on the sidelines. So the next day, she and Leo
bundled up and joined the throng of holiday revelers
in the town square.

With its Alpine village theme and beautiful scenery,
the town of Icicle Falls had become a popular tourist
destination. It was especially popular at Christmas, with
people coming to town from all over the state of Washington and beyond to enjoy the shopping, the restaurants and the party atmosphere. The tree lighting had
become an integral part of that party. In addition to
arts-and-crafts booths and vendors selling roasted nuts
and candies, people looked forward to gathering to see
the giant tree in the center of town come to life with its
hundreds of colored lights. The rest of the downtown lit

up also, with millions more lights, turning itself into a magical snow globe scene.

And there, right in the middle in the snow globe beside her and Leo, were Tim and his daughters, Amy and Amelia. The girls were beautiful. Both had long blond hair and blue eyes, pert little noses and lovely smiles. Amy, the fashionista, was sporting lip gloss, the shine accentuating perfect little lips. They both looked ready for a fashion magazine photo shoot, dressed in pastel-colored parkas, fancy earmuffs and trendy boots worn over their leggings.

Leo was enthralled. They seemed to take to him, also, and were happy to share their roasted chestnuts and sugared almonds and skate with him around the town's skating rink.

"They're being awfully nice to him," Sienna said later as she and Tim strolled along behind them on the way to the stage and gazebo where Santa was soon to put in his appearance.

"Why shouldn't they be? He's a nice kid."

And Tim was a nice man. Maybe things could work out between them. Maybe she'd finally gotten it right in the love department. He took her gloved hand in his big one and smiled down at her, giving her a glimpse into her possible Christmas future and making her heart flip. Oh, yes, she could get used to this.

"I'm glad you called me," he said.

"Me, too."

The crowd gathered for the tree-lighting ceremony was monstrous—couples visiting for a holiday weekend, holding hands and snacking on gingerbread boys from Gingerbread Haus and Sweet Dreams chocolates, young families with babies in strollers or young ones perched on daddies' shoulders, senior citizens looking on fondly as their grandchildren danced around them in excitement.

"How many people do you think are here?" Sienna asked Tim.

"There's gotta be several hundred," he said, looking around.

She believed it. The town square was jammed, everyone jostling for a better view.

One of the families looking for a good spot was Bailey Black and her husband, who was carrying the baby. "I thought you'd be at the tearoom," Sienna greeted her.

"No point in being open now," Bailey said. "Everyone wants to be here for the tree lighting, me included. I've been coming since I was a little girl. It's kind of corny, but it's tradition. Nobody misses a tree lighting."

It sure looked that way. Sienna doubted she'd be able to find her cousin in the crowd without texting her.

And yet, with so many people, some of the mean kids still managed to find Leo. "Look, it's the retard," one said.

Okay, that was it. Christmas or no Christmas, Sienna was going to commit murder. She'd emailed Leo's teacher and talked to the school principal. Had no one been listening? Hadn't these little brats' parents been contacted and told to turn their children into decent human beings?

She was about to push through the crowd and teach this kid a lesson herself when she saw Amy come to

Leo's defense. She pointed scornfully at the offender and said, "Gosh, what an ugly boy. And look at that big zit on his nose. Do you know him, Leo?"

Leo scowled. "He's mean."

"What a mouth-breather," Amy said haughtily.

"Yeah, what a mouth-breather," Amelia parroted and linked her arm through Leo's.

The boy's face turned redder than Santa's suit. He tried to mask his embarrassment with a sneer and turned away. The boy with him laughed at his humiliation and he shouldered his way off through the crowd.

The girls' support cleared away the thunderclouds from Leo's face and brought back his sunny smile.

"Amazing," Sienna murmured, taking it all in.

"Never underestimate the power of a cute girl," Tim said.

"I guess," she replied, astonished.

"Hey there!" called Rita, then excused herself past people to get to Sienna and Tim. Tito followed, carrying little Linda, who was ready for her tree-lighting experience in a pink snowsuit.

"It's freezing out here," she said when she finally reached them. "Why do we do this every year?"

"You're the one who told me I needed to come," Sienna reminded her. Although it had really been Tim's invitation that had brought her out.

"Well, it is tradition," Rita said. She looked at Tim speculatively. "Hi there. I'm Sienna's cousin Rita."

"Tim Richmond," Tim said, giving her a nod and shaking hands with Tito.

Once introductions were made, Rita began happily

grilling Tim like a steak on a barbecue. "How did you meet Sienna?" As if she didn't know.

"She lives next door to my uncle, poor woman," he said with a smile.

"I don't think I've ever seen you in Zelda's." She might as well have added, *With someone.*

"I've usually got my girls on the weekends," he said.

"So, how long have you been divorced?"

"My wife," Tito joked. "She's nosy."

Too nosy. Sienna pulled her aside. "Stop already. Give the man a break."

Rita looked at her, wide-eyed. "Just being friendly."

Fortunately for Tim, there was no more time for talking—the event had begun and a parade of Christmas characters were making their way to the gazebo. Nutcracker soldiers marched alongside a twirling Sugar Plum Fairy, elves and snowmen frolicking in their wake as the brass band played "Santa Claus Is Coming to Town."

"Look, there's Santa," Leo cried, pointing to the red-suited figure and his plump wife.

Santa took the stage with the requisite "Ho, ho, ho" and asked if all the boys and girls present had been good.

"I have!" Amelia called.

"I have!" Leo chimed in.

Amy, who obviously knew the truth about Santa, simply smiled.

The mayor welcomed everyone and brought out the high school music teacher to lead the crowd in some Christmas carols. Santa returned and reminded all the kids to be on their best behavior, and then one of the local pastors said a prayer. After that it was time for the countdown to the big moment.

Leo had trouble counting forward. Backward was impossible. But he bounced up and down and clapped his hands, excited to see the big tree come to life.

"Three, two, one," roared the crowd.

And then magic happened. The tree blazed with a multitude of colors and every other tree on Center Street turned into a galaxy of light. Every building sparkled against the dark with gold and blue and green and red. Golden lights contrasted with the red plastic ribbon and greens trimming the gazebo, and the band began to play "We Wish You a Merry Christmas."

"Wow," Sienna breathed.

"Told you it was awesome," Rita said with a smile.

It was, indeed. She pulled out her phone and took a picture. Then, seeing Tim's girls taking a selfie of themselves and Leo, she took a picture of that, too, capturing the smiles on their faces and Leo's happy grin and sending it off to her mom.

"Would you and the girls like to come over for hot chocolate?" she asked Tim as the crowd began to disperse.

"Oh, yeah."

Hot chocolate and cookies, laughter as the girls played Candy Land with Leo and admiring looks from Tim were like frosting on red velvet cake, making Sienna's day perfect.

Until the kids' conversation turned to their parents. She was frying quesadillas, while Tim stood at the counter, chopping vegetables for a tossed salad.

"Where's your mama?" Leo asked Amelia.

"She lives at a different house."

"Doesn't she like you?" Leo asked.

"She doesn't like our daddy," Amelia explained.

Sienna sneaked a look at Tim. He froze for a moment; then the chopping resumed, more vigorous than before.

"Amelia," Amy said sharply.

"My daddy doesn't live with us," Leo offered. "He doesn't like me."

Sienna felt her heart crack. If only she could say it wasn't true. But it was. "Your daddy loves you in his own way, sweetie." Lame. But then, so was Carlos.

"That's okay, Leo," Amy said. "We like you. Don't we, Amelia?"

Amelia nodded vigorously. "My daddy has an orchard," she offered. "And he has a big tree in his yard. You can climb it." She turned to Tim. "Can Leo come over and play tomorrow?"

"I like to climb trees," Leo said eagerly.

"This isn't exactly tree-climbing weather," Sienna told her son, not wanting to put the man on the spot. Still, no matter the weather, she wanted to come over and play, too.

"I have to take you back to your mom's tomorrow. Remember?" Tim said to his daughter.

"Before we go?" begged Amelia. "We have games," she told Leo.

"I want to play a game," Leo said.

"How about it?" Tim said to Sienna. "I don't have to take the girls back until three."

"I'd like to see your orchard," she said. And his house. And more of him. "Okay."

"Want to come for brunch? I make a mean pancake."

"I like pancakes," Leo offered.

"Well, then, that settles it," he said, and they set a time.

Yep, no more sitting on the sidelines. She was truly in the game now.

After the meal, they put on a movie for the kids and then settled at the kitchen table with cups of coffee and talked. She got him to talk more about his orchard and then his life growing up. It sounded idyllic, living in the country, riding horses and tending trees. It turned out he'd taken over the orchard completely when his mom learned she had cancer.

"I bought Dad out after Mom died. He needed the money and he had to get away. He's in Arizona now. I keep hoping he'll change his mind and come back. He knows he's always got a home here."

"He's lucky to have you."

"I'm lucky I could keep the place. I like what I'm doing and where I am. It's a good life, and keeping their grandparents' house provides extra stability for the girls. They love coming over on weekends, and I get them for a big chunk of the summer. Every Christmas they put up all the decorations that were my mom's."

"Is that hard?" Sienna didn't even want to think about losing her mother someday. Surely putting out treasured family decorations had to be painful.

"It was hard the first year," Tim admitted. "But we did it, anyway. I do it with the girls now because I think it's important to keep her memory alive for them. They were really little when she died."

Tim Richmond had had his share of loss, just like his uncle. What a difference in how the two men had dealt with the hard things in their lives.

"We've got everything from Santas to the ceramic nativity set she made when I was a kid," he said. "Between that and doing the tree, it takes the whole day."

"I love decorating for the holidays," Sienna said. "Especially Christmas."

"Not my thing," he said, "but I love watching the girls in action, and seeing all the stuff go up brings back good memories."

"So, worst Christmas ever," she said. "Mine was when I got into trouble for sneaking into my presents early. That wasn't the worst part, though. The worst part was getting nothing but clothes while my best friend scored a Barbie Dream House."

"Tough times," he teased.

"They were, indeed. My parents were on a pretty tight budget back then. Of course, once I hit twelve, I was thrilled to get clothes. I got lip gloss and nail polish from my aunt and there was no complaining that year, let me tell you. How about you?"

Tim's smile vanished. "The one when Erica told me she wanted a divorce."

Okay, big blunder. Sienna couldn't have known about that, but all the same she felt guilty for introducing a painful topic. "I'm sorry."

"Oh, well. I've had plenty of good ones. And, you know, in some ways finally splitting was a relief. It seemed like all we were doing was fighting. She was going through this second adolescence, wanting to go out with her girlfriends all the time. And then, after a while, even that wasn't enough."

"What was that all about?"

He shrugged. "Who knows? She lost a bunch of weight, got fit, got some new clothes. Not that I minded the clothes," he hurried to add. "It was just the new attitude that bugged me. Anyway, it seemed she wanted to try out the new chassis, because she went from new clothes to new men. I guess I wasn't giving her enough attention."

Really? His wife had cheated on him and he was blaming himself? "Or maybe she was shallow."

"Whatever. Anyway, I got past the anger and we're okay now. I almost wish she'd marry this clown she's with now so he could be her handyman and not me. But, oh, well. At least I get to see the girls a lot."

"I wish my ex wanted to see Leo," Sienna said.

Tim covered her hand with his. "Hey, his loss."

The small gesture of support warmed her. "You're a good man, Tim Richmond."

He shrugged off the praise. "I'm trying to be."

The kids burst into the kitchen, announcing the end of the movie. "What are we going to do now?" Amelia asked.

"We're going home," Tim said. "It's getting late."

"No," both girls groaned. "Do we have to?" Amelia whined.

"Yeah, it's time. So, we'll see you tomorrow?" he said to Sienna as everyone moved into the front hall.

"We'll be there."

He nodded. "Richmond Orchard. It's right off the main drag. You'll see the sign for it."

"Goodbye, Leo," Amy said. "See you tomorrow."

"Bye, Leo," Amelia said and kissed him on the cheek, making him blush and take a sudden interest in his stocking feet.

"Thanks for joining us," Tim said as the girls trooped off the porch. He leaned down and gave Sienna a quick kiss, leaving her as flushed as her son and hungry for more kisses.

"What are we going to do now?" Leo asked as she shut the door, bringing her back to the moment at hand.

"We are going to start getting you ready for bed."

"I don't want to go to bed," he protested.

"I know. Let's get your bath and get you in your jammies and then we can read a story. How does that sound?"

Anything sounded better than being banished to bed. "All right!"

Leo was in no hurry to settle down, and Sienna understood why. They had enjoyed a Hallmark-movie kind of day, a veritable ice-cream sundae of fun, their two families blending perfectly. The cherry on top had been seeing Leo's archenemy get a dose of the humiliation he'd been doling out. Ah, yes, a very satisfying day.

Rita called after Leo was in bed. "So, did you guys hang out after the tree lighting?"

"We did."

"Good. It looks like maybe this relationship is going somewhere."

"Maybe. It's too soon to know for sure." Although that kiss…

"Are you kidding? Anyone with eyes can see you two are crazy about each other."

But they were in that early phase of a relationship where everything about the other person looked perfect, where flaws played hide-and-seek.

Still, when she pulled up in front of Tim's house, she couldn't help feeling that she'd somehow come home, that her house, which she'd considered her forever home, had been only a warm-up act for this.

It was a Craftsman-style farmhouse, painted red. It had a big porch with an old-fashioned porch swing that begged visitors to come sit for a while and enjoy themselves. His truck sat in the driveway along with an older compact car. There was the big tree in the yard, with a snow-covered wooden picnic table under it. This was a house that had been meant for a family.

The girls had been watching, and they came racing down the porch steps to greet Leo as he and Sienna came up the walk. Tim stood in the doorway, a large, welcoming figure. *Yes, I come with the place.*

"Want to see my doll collection?" Amelia asked, grabbing Leo's hand and towing him inside.

"Hi, Sienna," Amy said shyly.

"Thanks for having us," Sienna said to her as Tim took her coat.

"We made blackberry syrup for the pancakes," she said.

"I've never made syrup. Maybe someday you can show me how."

Amy gave her a quick smile and a nod, then raced off down the hall after the other two.

"They're sweet kids," Sienna said to Tim.

"Yeah, they are. They like you."

"I'm not…a threat? Or an intruder? I mean, they already have a mom."

"Sort of. She's not bad," he amended. "She's there for the big stuff, but I think a lot of times the girls come in second after the boyfriend. Anyway, the girls and I already had a talk," he added with a grin. "They gave their old man permission to date. They figure if Mom can have a boyfriend, I should be able to have a girlfriend."

"That's generous of them." Not to mention mature.

"I thought so. Know anyone who might want to apply?"

"I might."

He chuckled. "That will be a relief to Amy. She's my little worrier. She doesn't want me to be alone in my old age. She's already volunteered to take care of me if I can't get it together and find someone."

"Very noble," Sienna said with a smile. As if Tim Richmond would have trouble finding anyone.

"I told her not to worry. I could handle it." He reached out and drew Sienna to him. "How am I doing so far?"

"So far, so good," she told him, and he kissed her. Every time he touched her, she felt the jolt. The electricity between them was addicting.

Oh, yes, so far, very good.

Sharing a meal with Tim and his girls felt natural, as if they'd all been together for years. "Your syrup is really good," she said to Amy, and the child flushed with pleasure.

"We picked those berries last summer, didn't we, girls?" Tim said.

Amelia nodded. "Daddy freezes them so we can make syrup when we come over."

Whatever Tim Richmond's hidden flaws were, they weren't in the parenting department.

After they'd finished, the girls took Leo outside to make a snowman and Tim and Sienna strolled to the orchard for a closer look. The trees were nothing more than twisted skeletons edged in white, reaching toward a weak winter sun.

"If you saw it in spring when this is all in bloom, you'd fall in love with it," Tim said.

She was already well on her way, even with the trees taking their bleak winter slumber. "I can imagine." She could also imagine being here permanently, watching the orchard go through the seasons. "You know, in California a lot of people have orange or lemon trees right in their yards. I always thought that was so cool, picking your fruit right off the tree instead of out of a bin in the store."

"I don't have any orange trees but you can pick an apple off one of my trees anytime. In fact, I hope you will," he added and put an arm around her.

"Thanks," she said and smiled up at him. She loved the feel of that big arm hugging her. It felt so right. He felt so right. "Tim Richmond, do you have any faults at all? I can't seem to find a single one."

"Oh, I've got 'em," he said. "I love to tinker on cars and get all greasy. I lose track of time and tend to run late. I'm a wimp when it comes to disciplining my girls—I hate to say no to them. I snore."

"Terrible flaws," she said, shaking her head.

"I can find more if you need me to," he joked.

"These will do for starters," she joked back.

They had just gotten back to the front yard when a car roared up the drive. It was a new model and made quite the contrast to its older cousin parked next to Tim's truck. The driver was a woman, somewhere in her late thirties with long blond, perfectly highlighted hair. It wasn't hard to figure out who it was.

"Shit," Tim muttered and made his way over to the car.

Sienna hung back as the woman let down her window, but she could still hear the conversation from where she stood. "You weren't answering your cell," the woman complained. She shot a speculative look in Sienna's direction. "I thought you were going to have the girls back by two."

"You said three, Erica."

"Mom's party starts at three. Now we're going to be late," she said irritably.

"Hey, don't blame me because you got your wires crossed. The party will still be going when you get there. Girls," he called. "Your mom's here."

"Come on, girls, hurry!" she added.

The girls made their way toward the car slowly. Leo followed them. "Where are you going?" he asked.

"We have to go to our grandma's," Amelia said.

"You get to go to your grandma's," her mother corrected. "Oh, Tim, look at them. They're all sweaty," she said in disgust. "Now we'll have to go back to the house and clean up."

"Kids play. They get sweaty."

"They wouldn't have if you'd brought them back when you were supposed to."

"Hey, lighten up," he growled. "Or next time you need a midweek babysitter so you and the moron can run off to Vegas for a so-called convention, I may be too busy to help out."

"You're an asshole," she informed him. "Get in the car, girls," she ordered.

"Bye, Leo," Amelia said, her disappointment at having to leave behind her new friend evident.

"Bye," Leo said, equally despondent.

Then Erica, the ex, turned the car around and roared off.

Amy leaned her head out the back window and called, "Bye, Daddy! See you at Christmas!"

Tim waved, smiling for his daughter. As soon as the car had reached the end of the drive, he dropped both his hand and his smile. He turned to Sienna. "Well, now you've met the ex."

"You have my condolences," she said, trying to lighten the moment.

He shrugged. "She's not that bad, really. She is kind of a drama queen, though," he added.

"A little bit," Sienna agreed. She'd seen the way the queen had looked at her. She may have divorced Tim but she still expected to reign supreme in his life.

Sienna was wondering if she could live with that when he asked, "So, what are you doing Christmas

Day? Want company? I've only got the girls Christmas Eve."

He wasn't married to the queen anymore. She'd had her chance with Tim. The old queen was gone. Long live the new queen.

"You don't want to be alone on Christmas Day," she said. Neither did she.

"I sure don't. Normally I go over to Uncle Bob's, but it looks like he's been invited out to Christmas dinner."

"Don't tell me—let me guess. Mrs. Zuckerman?"

"Her kids are coming up and she wants him to meet the family."

"Wow, that's moving right along."

"He tells me he's not getting any younger and he doesn't have any time to waste," Tim said with a smile. "I know how he feels. I don't want to waste time, either."

That made two of them. It looked like this Christmas was going to be one of the best ever.

Chapter Fourteen

Friendship is one of the best gifts you'll ever receive. Every friend we have brings something special into our lives.

—Muriel Sterling, *A Guide to Happy Holidays*

Dot and Arnie returned from their trip on Saturday. Muriel had expected to hear from him, had been sure he'd come over Sunday after church or at least call. Instead, it was Dot who called.

"Hey, I'm back."

"Welcome home," Muriel said dutifully.

"Come on over this evening," Dot said. "I've got prezzies for all you girls."

There was only one present Muriel wanted, and that was to go back in time and put herself on the cruise with Arnie, but she promised to show up for Dot's postcruise party. Maybe Arnie would be there.

He wasn't. It was only the girls, the members of the original LAMs—Life After Men. A lot had changed since the four women first formed their widows' support group. Both Pat and Olivia had gotten remarried. And now it was looking like even Dot would no longer be a LAM. Everyone was now a LWM. Except Muriel. She had to force herself to smile as she sat down in Dot's living room.

It was a cozy room, with a vintage floral couch, a matching chair and a rocking chair. Pictures of Dot's daughter, Tilda, were everywhere, hung on the walls and in silver frames on end tables, marking the milestones of her life, from her school athlete days to her graduation from the police academy.

Dot had lived vicariously through her daughter for years. Now she was finally living for herself. Muriel knew she needed to be happy about that. *Okay, happiness elves, get busy and mix up some happiness for me.*

The elves were obviously on strike for more candy canes, because Muriel was finding it hard to find the requisite happiness. And that made her even more miserable. What a rotten friend she was.

Especially in light of how generous Dot was being. In addition to making them all *rouladen*, she'd brought back presents for everyone—Christmas decorations she'd purchased at the various Christmas markets. Pat received a nutcracker to add to her collection. For Olivia, Dot had found a miniature cuckoo clock tree ornament to hang on the tree in the lobby of the lodge. She'd brought Muriel a set of three small glass votive candleholders painted with holiday scenes.

"They're really pretty when you have the candle lit in them," she said. "I thought they'd look nice on your mantel."

"Thank you," Muriel murmured and felt like even

more of a heel for her bad attitude. The gift was truly beautiful.

"I think Ed and I are going to have to take this cruise next year," Pat said. "Sounds like you two had a great time."

"We had the time of our lives," Dot said. "The food, the people, the scenery—all those gorgeous old towns."

"Which one was your favorite?" Pat asked.

"Rothenburg, hands down. It's a walled town on the Neckar—cobbled streets, gorgeous old buildings. It looks like something out of a storybook. And, of course, it was all lit up for the holidays, and they had snow. Well, you saw the pictures."

"They were all gorgeous," Olivia said. "So, how did all those towns compare to Icicle Falls?"

"Well, the fact that they really are German towns gives them all a head start," Dot said with a chuckle. "But we're not doing so bad. Still, there's nothing like the real thing. I loved Germany—loved the Christmas markets, loved the food, loved the scenery and the people. I'd go back in a heartbeat. And let me tell you, I'm hooked on cruising. Especially with Arnie. He's the best."

Yes, he was. And up until now he'd been Muriel's. She'd seen the potential in that stupid tree she'd bought. Why hadn't she been able to see the potential in a closer relationship with Arnie?

"What's wrong, Muriel?" Dot asked.

Muriel pulled herself out of her unpleasant reverie. "Hmm? Oh, nothing. I'm great."

"Are you sure? You're not your normal sweet, syrupy self."

"I am not syrupy," Muriel snapped.

Dot's eyes widened. "Sorry. I was only teasing. But you don't look happy."

"Well, I am," Muriel said with a scowl. "And I'm glad you had such a nice time." *So there.*

"All right, spill," Olivia said later as she and Muriel drove away. "What's the matter? Dot was right. You're not yourself."

"I don't know," Muriel said. "I'm happy Arnie and Dot had a chance to get away." At least, she was trying to be.

"But?"

Muriel sighed. "But, if I have to be honest, I'm jealous. Dot and Arnie..." She sighed again. "I shouldn't be. They're both my friends. And poor Arnie. I've never given him any reason to hope. Do you think there's something going on between them?"

"I don't know. They obviously had a good time."

"Of course, it would be impossible not to have a good time when you're on a cruise. With a friend."

"True."

Muriel gnawed on her lip. "Dot texted me that she thought she was in love. Do you think it could be with Arnie?"

"Well, she did disappear into the kitchen when he called." Olivia gave Muriel a sympathetic look. "There's only one reason you disappear to take a call. Love talk."

Love talk. Now Muriel was even more unhappy.

Arnie was in love, but not with her. She could have had him so many times, if only she hadn't been such a man snob.

Man snob—that brought back memories. Suddenly, it was the fall of her sophomore year in high school again. A new boy had moved to town and every girl had been eyeing him.

Bill Bernard was a junior, an older man. He was a football player and he had the husky build to prove it. He was rugged and sexy, and with his blue eyes and blond hair, Muriel and her best friend, Pat, had dubbed him the Viking. Half the girls in school had crushes on him, including Muriel.

"So he plays football," Arnie said as he walked home with her and Pat and Olivia. "Big deal."

"It is around here," Pat said. "We need good players. Our team stinks."

"I don't get why everybody likes football," Arnie said in response. "It's just a bunch of fat guys knocking each other over. Neanderthals. And you know what happened to the Neanderthals? They died out. It was the smart guys who survived."

"You would have survived," Muriel said, wanting to make him feel better.

Arnie wasn't big enough for football. He'd made the track team, but sadly for him, that didn't have the same sex appeal as football. Anyway, Arnie's smarts were his claim to fame. His friends already had him pegged for valedictorian when it came time for their class to graduate.

"I sure would have," Arnie said and smiled at her.

As usual, his smile was filled with adoration, and she found herself wishing she hadn't complimented him. He had been trying to get her to go on a date with him all summer. She'd managed to put him off, always with excuses about doing something with her girlfriends or having to work in the Sweet Dreams candy shop, but it was getting increasingly hard to hold him at arm's length. Arnie was a nice boy, but she thought of him only as a friend.

"I saw Bill talking to you in the hall today," Olivia said to Muriel and gave her a playful nudge. "Were you flirting with him?"

"No. We were just talking about our classes."

"Uh-huh. And maybe about homecoming? Did he ask you to the dance?"

Muriel was aware of Arnie walking next to her, anxious to hear her answer.

"Well," Muriel hedged. She wished she could say he had. She'd been hoping he'd ask. They'd been running into each other in the hall a lot lately, and only the other day he'd asked her if she had a boyfriend. That had been after he'd seen her and Arnie leaving English class together, laughing about… What had they been laughing about? She couldn't remember.

"He probably will," Olivia said. She shook her head. "Honestly, Muriel, you get all the cute guys after you."

"That's because she's cute," Arnie said.

"Well, all the best guys can't have you. You should share," Olivia said.

"Whoever goes out with Bill is going to have to share," Pat predicted. "He's a huge flirt."

"I wish he'd flirt with me," Olivia said. "Who are you going to the dance with?" she asked Pat.

"Gary, if he ever gets around to asking me. Sometimes it just doesn't seem right that we always have to wait for the guys to ask us."

"Except for Tolo," Olivia reminded her. "But that's not until February. By then everyone will be all matched up."

"Not all of us," Arnie said, bitterness bleeding into his voice.

"Well, if we're not matched up by then, let's go together," Olivia said to him. "Okay?"

Muriel could feel his gaze on her. "Okay," he said reluctantly. "But don't worry, Olivia, I'm sure you'll have a boyfriend by Valentine's Day." That was Arnie, always gallant.

They got to Olivia's house first and said goodbye to her. Then Muriel, Pat and Arnie continued on, and Arnie brought up the subject of the dance again. "You never said. Did Bill ask you to the dance?"

She hated being put on the spot. "Not yet."

"I suppose you're waiting for him to," Arnie said, looking none too pleased.

"There's not a girl in the whole school who isn't hoping," she said.

"I saw him walking Cindy Clark to biology," Arnie reported.

Cindy was a cheerleader. Cheerleaders and football players went together like cookies and milk. Still… "That doesn't mean anything," Muriel said. At least, she hoped it didn't. She really wanted Bill to ask her to the homecoming dance.

"You shouldn't wait for him to ask you," Arnie continued. "You should go with someone who really wants to take you—someone who's wanted to ask you all along."

Oh, dear. She knew where this conversation was headed. Now they were at Pat's house. If she let Pat go in, it would be just her and Arnie and he'd ask her for sure. She didn't want to have to hurt his feelings. Stalling was her best option. She'd stall until Bill asked her to the dance. Then she'd have a perfect excuse for turning Arnie down when he invited her.

Pat started to turn in at her front walk and Muriel grabbed her by her jacket sleeve. "You're coming over to my house. Remember?"

Pat looked puzzled. "I thought you had to work at the store this afternoon."

"No, that's tomorrow," Muriel lied. She turned her head so Arnie couldn't see and gave her friend a pleading look.

"Oh. Oh, yeah. I forgot."

There. Girlfriend armor safely in place. Surely Arnie would be too self-conscious to ask her in front of Pat. She sneaked a look his direction. He wasn't happy. She hoped he hadn't figured out what she was up to, but given how smart he was, it was a distinct possibility. If only he'd fall for Olivia.

Once they'd said goodbye to Arnie and gotten inside Muriel's house, Pat said, "You do have to work today, don't you?"

"Yes," Muriel admitted. "But you know Arnie was going to ask me to homecoming."

"He still is. You can't stall him forever."

"I don't need to stall him forever, just until after Bill asks me."

"And what if he doesn't? Will you go with Arnie?"

Muriel shook her head. "It wouldn't be fair."

"You know, Arnie's an awful nice guy."

Muriel shrugged. "He is. But he's no Bill."

"A guy doesn't have to be a gorgeous football player to be a good catch, you know," said Pat.

Muriel blushed. "I know."

Pat cocked an eyebrow.

"What?" Muriel demanded.

"It's just that… Oh, never mind."

"No, what?"

"Muriel, Arnie's one of the nicest boys in school. Plus, he's smart, he's thoughtful. He's friendly. Everyone likes him."

"Of course they do. What's your point?"

"Just that he's a really great guy. And there are plenty of girls who'd be happy to go out with him. Like Olivia."

"She can have him. I'm not trying to hog him."

"I know, but he's hooked on you, anyway."

"That's not my fault. You know I never encourage him."

"I know. But maybe you should. Look, I'm not saying you have to like him just because he likes you. But you're always going after cute football players who can barely hold up a conversation. Or who wouldn't even open up a door for you, never mind do any of the sweet things Arnie does for you. These guys you date, they never end up being much of a match for you. And they've never treated you the way Arnie does. But you're so distracted by their looks that you don't really see Arnie."

"I do see him," Muriel insisted, though she knew Pat wasn't far from the truth. Still, she was young and just wanted to have fun and enjoy high school. These boys she was attracted to—they were fun! Maybe they weren't the smartest or the most thoughtful, but what did it matter, anyway? It wasn't like she was looking for a husband. "We're just friends. Arnie just doesn't make my heart race."

Pat nodded. "Obviously," she said in a superior tone.

"Oh, look who's talking. You've had your share of crushes on cute boys," Muriel said in her own defense.

"And I've gone out with boys who aren't so cute. And I'd take Arnie in a heartbeat. He's going to make something of himself, you wait and see."

"And I'll be happy for him when he does. But I'll bet Bill's going to make something of himself, too. And he's *really* cute."

Pat shook her head. "You know what your problem is, Muriel? You're a man snob."

"A what?"

"A man snob. A guy has to look like a movie star for you to be interested."

"That's not true!" Muriel protested.

Pat cocked an eyebrow. "Oh?"

"Are you honestly going to make me feel guilty because I want to go to homecoming with Bill?"

"Only if you ditch Arnie to do it. You know, most everybody has already asked someone. How do you know Bill hasn't?"

"I'd have heard. Everyone would have heard."

"Well, I wouldn't be holding my breath if I were you," Pat said. "Go with Arnie. He really cares."

"Bill cares," Muriel insisted. He was interested in her, she was sure of it.

"I'm betting all Bill cares about is how many girls he can make fall in love with him. Arnie's worth ten of him."

"I can't help it if I'm not interested in Arnie," Muriel said.

"No, I guess you can't," Pat agreed. "Poor Arnie."

But the next day it was more like poor Muriel. By third period her hope of being asked to the homecoming dance by Bill Bernard was crushed under the news that he'd asked not Cindy Clark, the cheerleader, but her best friend, Ellie, who was also on the cheer squad. Ellie and Cindy currently weren't speaking.

"I told you he's a flirt," Pat said when they all sat together at lunch.

"He's a Neanderthal," Arnie muttered.

"Oh, well," Muriel said with a shrug. "I can live without going to the dance."

"If you want to go, I'll still be happy to take you," Arnie said. "Just as friends," he quickly added. "There's no sense sitting home, right?"

"Just as friends?" Muriel repeated.

He nodded. "Sure."

Arnie was right. She didn't want to sit home and miss the dance. She said yes.

And so Muriel went to the dance with Arnie, but her gaze kept sneaking in Bill's direction.

As she and Arnie stood at the punch bowl, she watched Bill say something to his date that made her giggle. Ellie was cute, with red hair and freckles. But Muriel didn't think Ellie was any better looking than her. Why had he asked Ellie? Maybe because he'd seen Muriel and Arnie together and assumed, in spite of what she'd said, that they were a couple. Darn it all, that was what she got for being nice to Arnie.

But Arnie actually cared. He had been willing to make sure she got to the dance and had a good time.

The only problem was, she wasn't exactly having a good time.

"Are you okay?" he asked. She turned to see him looking at her, concern on his face.

He really was a sweet guy, and he'd brought her to the dance even though he knew she wanted to be there with someone else. Surely the least she could do was pay attention to him and try to have fun instead of peeking at Bill all the time.

"I'm fine," she said.

"Sorry I'm not a football player." Coming from any other guy that comment would have been bitter and sarcastic. But this was Arnie and she knew he was genuinely apologizing.

And she felt instantly ashamed of how she was neglecting him. "Oh, Arnie, you're great the way you are."

His rueful expression made it plain that he knew she meant great for anyone but her.

The band started playing a fast song. She grabbed his hand. "Come on. Let's dance."

"May as well," he said and managed a smile.

Arnie may not have been a football player, but he was a good dancer.

It wasn't the most romantic date Muriel had ever had and it certainly wasn't the date of his dreams, but they did have a good time. They ended the evening at Herman's Hamburgers, enjoying burgers and fries and chocolate shakes, and she let Arnie brag about the latest test he'd aced. Then he took her home and told her she'd been the prettiest girl at the dance. And she rewarded him with a kiss on the cheek.

And as she slipped into the house, she couldn't help wishing it had been Bill Bernard she'd kissed. Except him she wouldn't have kissed on the cheek.

And so it had been all through high school—Muriel always dating the best-looking, most testosterone-loaded boys; and Arnie, the one who'd been the perfect match all along, looking on. He'd continued to look on as she'd fallen for and married two other men.

Funny, now who was looking on? It served her right.

Back home her little tree mocked her. *Not very bright, are you?*

No, she wasn't.

Her daughters came over Monday evening to wrap presents and enjoy a potluck meal, and Muriel greeted them, determined to enjoy their time together. Samantha had made a pot of soup, Cecily had concocted a winter salad using squash and pomegranates, and Bailey had, of course, baked, contributing white-chocolate-peppermint cupcakes.

"I just felt three pounds plaster themselves onto my

thighs," Samantha said as she pushed away her empty dessert plate. "I'm going to have to do a million laps around Mom's ugly tree to work this off."

Bailey grinned. "Have another."

"Oh, no. One was enough of a killer," Samantha said, moving away from the table. "I'm going to start wrapping presents."

She moved into the living room and Bailey followed her. Cecily remained at the table with Muriel, pouring them both more chocolate-mint tea. "Is Arnie back?"

"Yes." Muriel helped herself to another cupcake.

"You never have seconds," Cecily observed.

"It's Christmas."

"Have you seen him?"

"Who?"

Muriel could hear the frown in her daughter's voice. "Mom."

"Oh, Arnie. No, not yet." He was probably too busy with Dot.

The problem with having a daughter who had a gift for matchmaking was that she was also a mind reader. "They're not a match."

But she wasn't always prescient. "I think you could be wrong this time, dear."

"Call him and tell him how you feel," Cecily urged.

She could, of course, deny how she felt. But what was the point? She shook her head. "That wouldn't be fair to Dot. Anyway, I had my chance. I took the poor man for granted for years."

"Maybe you weren't ready."

"Maybe I just couldn't see. Either way, it's too late."

"I still think you should call him, Mom."

"No. I'm going to let Arnie finally have a life of his own."

It was a noble vow, but not an easy one to make. She hoped she could keep it.

"Cec, come see what I got for Serena," Samantha called.

"Come on, Mom," Cecily said and left the table.

Muriel took the last bite of her second cupcake and joined the girls in the living room. She'd eat another later. Maybe she'd eat all the rest of them.

"You haven't turned on the extra lights on your tree," Bailey said and plugged in the pinecone lights Muriel had pulled out specially for her little tree. "There, that's better. It sure turned out pretty."

"Speaking of ugly trees, we have news," Samantha said. "Cec matched up Prissy. She had her first date with one of our sales reps and it went well. She came into the shop all smiles and actually bought a box of candy. Boom. From ugly tree to human being. Shocking, huh?"

"Not so much," Muriel said. "There's always more to people than we realize." The only problem was that some of "us" realized it too late.

"I guess it just goes to show you it's never too late for someone to change," Bailey said. "Look what you started, Mom."

Yes, look what she'd started.

She almost didn't answer her phone when Dot called her later. But her curiosity got the better of her.

"Can you come by the restaurant tomorrow morning? I have a present I forgot to give you."

It would be nice if Dot would give her back Arnie. "More presents? You shouldn't have."

"I know, but this was pretty and it's right up your alley."

Muriel was still recovering from Sunday. "I'm a little busy tomorrow. The book," she added. It was a poor excuse, but it was the best she could do on short notice.

"You've got to eat," Dot argued. "Come by around ten after the breakfast crowd has cleared. That way we can have a nice long yak."

Muriel had yakked about as much with Dot as she cared to for a while but she agreed, and the next morning found her walking into Pancake Haus. She met Beth Mallow, who was just coming out and was happy to stop and visit.

So was Muriel. Anything to postpone having to hear more about Dot's fabulous time with Arnie. "Are you all ready for Christmas?" she asked.

"Just about. We're going to have a houseful this year. Colin and Mia and the baby and Dylan's girlfriend and her daughter and grandson will be joining us, too."

Dylan had been seeing the new owner of Lupine Floral and it looked like things were getting serious.

Beth confirmed it when she added, "I suspect he's going to propose, if not on Christmas Eve, then for sure on Valentine's Day. I caught him at Mountain Jewels scoping out rings the other day."

"I'm glad. He deserves to be happy."

"Yes, he does. It seems like everyone has mistletoe

fever these days." Beth nodded toward the back of the restaurant. "Looks like something's brewing between Dot and our old pal Arnie. They've got their heads together and are laughing like a couple of teenagers."

Arnie was here, too? Muriel didn't know whether to be happy or miserable.

"I'd better get going," Beth said. "I've got a ton of baking to do."

Muriel was tempted to turn around and leave with her, but she made her way to the booth where Dot and Arnie sat side by side with their phones. Beth had been right. They were acting like teenagers. They were probably texting each other.

"Hi, you two," she said and slipped in across from them.

Arnie looked up and beamed at her. "Hi, Muriel. You look—" he gave a grunt, a sure sign he'd just been kicked under the table "—uh, festive."

Barely a couple and Dot was already acting possessive. Poor Arnie couldn't even compliment another woman without getting in trouble.

He was looking good himself, wearing his blue sweater over a shirt casually unbuttoned at the neck. And he was in jeans. Arnie never used to wear jeans.

"Thank you," she murmured. "What are you two doing?"

"Looking at our pictures from the cruise," Dot said. "Talk about a once-in-a-lifetime trip. Huh, Arnie?"

"Oh, yeah," he confirmed.

"I'm ready to do another cruise," Dot went on. "How about you?"

"Definitely," he said.

"Together?" Muriel couldn't help asking.

"Why not? We both got some onboard credit for the next one," Dot said. "We'd be crazy not to use it." She flagged down one of her waitresses. "Bring Muriel her usual omelet, will you?"

The girl nodded and departed.

"I see you two didn't wait for me," Muriel said, pointing to the plates of half-consumed pancakes.

"I guess we should have," Arnie said.

But they hadn't. Why had Dot invited her to come for breakfast if she wasn't even going to wait for her? To torture her, obviously. The present had just been an excuse for Dot to rub her new relationship with Arnie in Muriel's face.

"So, here's your other present," she said, sliding a wrapped package over to Muriel.

Arnie didn't say anything about a present. So much for bringing her back something from Germany. Not that she'd needed anything. It was the thought that counted. Obviously, he'd stopped thinking about her once he and Dot got together.

Muriel took the gift with a frown. Unwrapping it, she found a handcrafted leather-bound journal with superfine paper. It had probably cost Dot a pretty penny.

Too bad Muriel didn't have a pretty attitude to match. "Thank you," she said stiffly.

"Don't you like it?" Dot asked.

"Of course I like it. It's lovely. It was very thoughtful of you," Muriel added, trying to infuse more gratitude into her voice.

Dot's brows drew together and she cocked her head. "Are you okay?"

Why did Dot have to keep asking her how she was? "Of course I'm okay," Muriel insisted. A little more forcefully than necessary. All right, a lot more forcefully than necessary.

Dot cocked an eyebrow at Arnie. Cute. Now they were developing their own special communication. That observation cemented the scowl on Muriel's face.

She was being a brat—she knew it. But everyone should be allowed an ugly-tree moment once in a while. "You know, I forgot I have an appointment." Surely she had an appointment somewhere. "I need to run."

"You haven't even had your breakfast," Arnie protested. Surprising he even noticed, considering how taken he was with Dot.

"Sorry. I'm not very hungry." She scooted out of the booth. "Thank you again for the journal, Dot." After she'd gotten control of herself, she'd write something nice in it.

"I'll come by later this week," Arnie called after her.

If you can spare the time. She kept the catty remark penned inside her mouth and managed a polite wave.

Once outside, she left her car parked at the curb, determined to walk off her bad attitude, and hurried down the street, oblivious to the snow that had started falling, barely responding as people called hello. Her cell phone summoned her. She left it in her purse.

What was she going to do? How was she going to cope with this? She had to find a way. She was a mature adult, not a spoiled child. These were her friends.

She had just passed the bookstore when Pat called to her. She pretended not to hear and kept walking, picking up her pace. The last thing she and her bad attitude needed was to talk to her old friend, who would be too perceptive for Muriel's comfort. And if one more person asked her if she was okay, she was going to scream.

Feigned deafness didn't work, which was probably a good thing since Pat caught up to her and grabbed her arm just before she stepped off the curb and into the path of a turning SUV. "Muriel! What are you doing? You almost got hit."

Muriel put a hand to her heart, which was now in overdrive. Amazing how fast a broken heart could still beat.

"Didn't you hear me calling you?"

"Were you?" Muriel hedged.

"Yes. I just tried to get you on your phone, too. I got in some more orders for your book and they need to go out today. Can you sign them? It'll just take a minute."

"Of course," Muriel said and turned back with her. She'd sign the books. Then she'd get her latte. After that she'd go home and eat the leftover peppermint cupcakes, all four of them.

"Are you all right?" Pat asked.

Don't scream right here in the middle of town. "Yes, I'm fine," Muriel said between gritted teeth.

"Where were you earlier? Why weren't you answering your cell?"

"I was at Pancake Haus with Dot and Arnie." She couldn't resist asking, "Do you think they're a couple now?"

"I don't know. Maybe. Does the idea of them being together bother you?"

"No. Of course not."

Pat gave her a knowing look. "Muriel Sterling-Wittman, we've been friends for too many years for you to be able to lie to me."

Muriel kept her mouth shut.

"You had your chance with Arnie, many times over."

"I know." Did she have to rub it in?

"The man waited a lifetime for you. The least you could do is to let him enjoy his last few years with someone who'll appreciate him."

"I am." Well, she was working on it and that had to count for something. "I want Arnie to be happy. I really do."

"And Dot. Think how long she's been widowed."

"You're right, I know. It's just taking me a little while to get used to this new development. I do want them both to be happy, really."

If only there could have been a way for them to be happy and not together. How was it she'd been able to see so much potential in a stupid tree and yet miss Arnie's potential? She didn't deserve him.

Once inside the bookstore, Sienna cornered her, anxious to tell her the many ways she'd been bringing joy into her life—everything from tea at Bailey's tearoom to giving herself permission to splurge on a pink glass cake platter at Timeless Treasures. "And my cousin and I gave each other manis and pedis," she concluded, showing off her red nails tipped with tiny snowflakes.

"I'm glad you're getting so much out of the book," Muriel said as she signed her last copy. She should go home and read it herself before she turned into a grinch. Oh, wait. She already had.

She left the store and went to Bavarian Brews to self-medicate with an eggnog latte. The latte helped not at all, but seeing poor Hildy Johnson coming into the coffee shop in a cast, her eyes still black-and-blue, was a good reminder that her own life wasn't so bad.

"How are you doing?" she asked Hildy.

"As well as can be expected," Hildy replied. "A car accident right before Christmas, just what I always needed."

"You're lucky you're alive," Muriel told her.

"So's the drunk who hit me," Hildy said with a frown. "He walked away without a scratch."

"At least you're still here," Muriel said.

"Yes, there's always something to be grateful for," Hildy said.

Muriel bought Hildy a latte, then mulled over her words as she made her way back to her car. Yes, there was always something to be grateful for. In her case, much. Her children all lived nearby, she'd seen several books published and she had encouraged many people. She'd been loved by two wonderful men. She didn't need to be greedy. And really, it wasn't as if Arnie would be disappearing from her life. He and Dot would still remain her friends.

If she stopped acting like she was twelve.

Mountain Jewels was coming into sight. She loved jewelry.

She reminded herself that she was trying to stay on a budget and she had plenty of jewelry, anyway. Still, it was always fun to window-shop. She stopped in front of the window.

There at the ring counter stood Arnie.

Chapter Fifteen

Christmas is a perfect time to tell that someone special how you feel.
—Muriel Sterling, *A Guide to Happy Holidays*

Muriel practically galloped down Center Street, but no matter how fast she moved, she couldn't lose the image that was now embedded in her brain of Arnie looking at diamond rings. *I think I'm in love*, Dot had texted. Obviously, so was Arnie. This was...

No, not terrible. This was wonderful for both of them.

Keep your smile no matter what, she told herself. Who was the idiot who'd said that?

Her. Well, what did she know?

She got in her car and started off down the street. Okay, she was going to have to bring out her better self. She'd host a celebratory dinner party for the happy couple.

And poison Dot.

No, no, no! Where did these awful thoughts come from? This was not like her.

But maybe it was.

That thought was more upsetting than all the others that had preceded it. She'd always thought of herself as a kind and generous person. It looked like she'd thought wrong. She was…a bitch.

She needed to get home and have a good cry. She stepped on the gas.

Why wait to start the pity party? She began to sob.

"Stop," she commanded herself. "You're bigger than this." Yes, she was. Okay, back to the dinner party. She'd invite Pat and Ed, and Olivia and James, Tilda, of course, and her husband.

Oh, no. Speaking of Tilda, here she was again in her patrol car, flashing her lights. Honestly, did she have nothing better to do than follow people around? Was there no real crime in Icicle Falls?

The answer to that, of course, was no. Other than mailbox baseball and the occasional brawl at The Man Cave or graffiti adventure at the high school, the town was a quiet one.

Muriel put the brakes on the sobs, gave a final sniff and pulled over. By the time Tilda came to the window, she'd wiped her eyes and already had her driver's license and registration ready.

"Mrs. Sterling-Wittman, do you know how fast you were going?" Tilda asked, her expression stern.

"No, Tilda, I'm afraid I don't."

Tilda went from stern to scary. "This is a school zone."

All the children were presently in the school but Muriel wisely kept that observation to herself.

As if reading her mind, Tilda continued, "I know all the kids are in school, but if one of them happened to come out, happened to walk out on the street, would you have seen that kid?"

It was a sobering thought. She went from feeling sorry for herself to feeling ill. Thank God there had been no children around. "You're right. I was driving irresponsibly."

"You were," Tilda agreed. She took the driver's license and registration and walked back to her patrol car to write up the ticket she'd threatened on their last encounter.

"You've got to be more careful," Tilda said when she returned.

"Yes, I do," Muriel agreed. "I'm afraid I was upset and not paying attention." She seemed to be very good at not paying attention. She certainly hadn't paid proper attention to Arnie all these years.

"Then don't drive when you're upset." Tilda gave her a curt nod, then returned to her patrol car.

"Better yet, don't get upset," Muriel told herself and put the car in gear. If she didn't know better, she'd think the whole family were out to get her.

The Icicle Creek Lodge had only a few guests—the lull before the next weekend storm, when they'd be back to no vacancy—and there wasn't much happening, but someone still had to mind the reception desk. Today that someone was Meadow, and she was multitasking, trying to finish the scarf she'd started for Brandon.

"I gotta get this done today so I can start one for my mom," she told Olivia when she stopped by to see how everything was going. She held it up. "Look. No more dropped stitches."

"Very good," Olivia said.

"I think it's long enough now. Right?"

More than long enough. A giraffe would have tripped over it. "Yes, it is. I think you can finish it off now."

"How do I do that?"

Olivia came around the desk and showed her how to cast off.

"Shit," she muttered as she attempted to mimic what she'd just seen.

"You'll get it." Olivia demonstrated again.

This time Meadow caught on. "This is awesome," she said happily. "My first scarf done. I hope Brandon will like it."

He'd certainly appreciate the thought behind it. Meadow had worked hard to master this skill. "I'm sure he will," Olivia told her. "I'll get some scissors to cut the yarn."

At that moment Brooke came up. "I'm on my way to Safeway. Is there anything either of you need?"

"Eggnog," said Meadow. "I'm dying for eggnog."

"Cravings, huh?" Brooke said.

"I guess," Meadow said and smiled.

"How about you, Mom?" Brooke asked.

"I think I'm fine. Oh, wait, on second thought, I could use some more coconut oil. I've run out and my poor fingernails are getting brittle."

"Oh, your scarf's done," Brooke said, catching sight of the giraffe scarf.

"Yep. I just finished it," Meadow said proudly.

"And I need to get those scissors," Olivia said. "I can get some money for you while I'm at it," she told Brooke.

"Don't worry about it," Brooke said with a wave of her hand.

"I have to duck into the apartment anyway, dear. I'll just be a minute."

She hadn't quite shut the door that led to her little apartment in back of the reception desk when she heard Meadow say, "I wish she'd call me *dear*."

Dear. The word came so naturally when she was with Brooke. She wanted it to do the same with Meadow. She didn't want to play favorites.

Once she was back with the scissors and Brooke had left on her errand, it was just her and her new daughter-in-law again. The scarf was finished. "You did a lovely job," she said to Meadow. "Would you like me to help you start another one?" *Dear. Say it.*

She couldn't. Meadow would know she'd overheard and the word would be meaningless.

How did one work one's way to that point in a relationship where an endearment came easily? She needed to figure it out for Meadow's sake.

Who was she kidding? She needed to figure it out for her own sake.

Arnie stopped by Muriel's house on Saturday evening unannounced. She'd been parked on the couch in yoga pants and a ratty sweater, trying to get into a mystery novel that she'd checked out from the library. Sadly, she simply didn't care who'd bumped off the spoiled, rich heiress.

"Arnie," she said in surprise when she opened the door and found him standing on her front porch. Why hadn't she bothered to put on makeup?

"I should have called," he said, stepping inside. "Were you busy?"

"No, not really. Come on in. Would you like some huckleberry liqueur? I'm afraid I don't have anything good to eat in the house."

She'd consumed all the leftover cupcakes and gained two pounds in the process. There would be no baking for her until Christmas Eve, when she'd make the requisite red velvet cake for the family gathering at her house. Although she was longing to self-medicate with a hit of sugar and carbs.

"That sounds good. I love that stuff." He held out a wrapped box. "I brought you back something from Germany."

"Oh, how sweet. I'll just put it under the tree."

"Open it now," he urged.

"All right." She fetched him his drink and then they both settled on the couch. "It was awfully sweet of you to think of me," she said.

"I'm always thinking of you," he replied gallantly.

Not so much lately. She opened her present to discover a box of hand-painted glass ornaments. "'Baumschmuck,'" she said, reading the package.

"Tree jewelry," he translated.

"They're lovely," she said and gave him a hug. "Thank you." Then she screwed up her courage and casually asked, "Speaking of jewelry, did I see you in Mountain Jewels the other day?"

His face flushed. "I was just looking around."

"Were you looking for something in particular? For someone in particular?"

He studied her. "Why do you ask?"

The flush seemed to have migrated from Arnie's face to hers. She could feel her cheeks heating. "I just wondered. I mean, you and Dot…" How to finish this sentence? She didn't.

"Dot and I?" he prompted.

Her face was on fire now. "Well, you seemed to have a wonderful time on that cruise."

"We did," he agreed and took a drink of the liqueur. "This is really good. I hope you've saved out a bottle to give me for Christmas."

She made the liqueur every fall and always saved out a bottle for Arnie. "I suppose now you'll be sharing it with Dot." She sounded like the world's sorest loser.

But so what if she did? Losing at cards or bingo or in a raffle drawing was one thing. Losing in love was quite another. She could feel his assessing gaze on her.

"What?" Now she sounded petulant. Well, she was.

"Muriel, if I didn't know better, I'd swear you were jealous."

Sweet Muriel disappeared and bitchy Muriel surfaced to take her place. "All right. Maybe I am. You and I have been friends since junior high, and here Dot comes to the party later and all of a sudden she's… Well, what is she, Arnie? Do I need to be offering you congratulations? If so, then congratulations."

"You don't sound very happy."

Very perceptive. "If you want me to be honest—"

"I'd appreciate it."

"I guess I don't really want to share you." There, it was out.

"What does it matter if you and I are just friends?"

"Arnie, I…" No, she couldn't do it. She couldn't step in and take him away from Dot. "If Dot makes you happy, then I'm glad for you."

"Dot does make me happy."

So there it was. Dot would probably have a diamond ring by New Year's. Muriel blinked back unbecoming tears of self-pity and nodded.

Arnie set his glass on the coffee table. "But you're not smiling."

One of those pesky tears made its escape, and she swiped at her eye. "It's going to take me a while to get used to, is all."

"Muriel, you've always made it perfectly clear that you never wanted to be anything more than friends," he reminded her.

"I never really appreciated you, did I?" she said in a small voice. "I took you for granted all these years. But, Arnie, you're a wonderful man, and Dot—"

"Is just a friend."

"Just a friend?" Was she hearing right? "Really?" Arnie hadn't abandoned his love for her?

"If she was more, if Dot and I had fallen in love, what would you have done?"

"I would have been supportive," she said. "It wouldn't have been easy. Actually, it hasn't been easy, thinking…" She sighed. "I would always be your friend."

"I don't want to be friends anymore. I'm tired of only

being your friend. And if you can't give me anything more than friendship, now's the time to let me know, because one thing I did learn on this cruise, Muriel, is that there are women out there who would like to be with me."

"*I* want to be with you," she insisted, and for the first time in all the years she'd known him, she grabbed Arnie Amundsen and kissed him.

And Arnie kissed her right back. Who knew Arnie could kiss like that?

"Do you know how many years I've waited for this moment?" he asked after he'd finished thoroughly kissing her.

Too many. More than any man in his right mind would have.

"Never mind," he said before she could answer. "It was worth the wait."

She snuggled up against him, happy for the first time in weeks. "I thought for sure I was losing you."

"You thought wrong," he said and kissed the top of her head.

"You certainly did a good job of convincing me."

"Now, let me convince you how wrong you were," he said and kissed her again. Yes, she could get used to this.

"So who was Dot falling in love with on the cruise if it wasn't you?" she asked when they finally came up for air.

"I'll leave that to her to tell. Suffice it to say it wasn't me."

"You could have fooled me. You two sure seemed pretty chummy."

Arnie grinned. "Dot makes a good coconspirator."

Muriel pulled back and frowned at him. "What do you mean by that?"

"Well, when it appeared you were getting a little…"

"Jealous," she supplied.

"…jealous," he said with a smile. "We hatched a plan. Dot thought perhaps you needed to realize—" there came the flush again "—what a good catch I am. She thought if it looked like you might lose me to another woman, it might, uh, bring you to your senses. Those were her words," he hastily added.

Well, well. So Dot *was* being sneaky and keeping secrets, but they were all to help Muriel, in the end. She shook her head. "You both did a good job of convincing me you were falling in love." All those terrible thoughts she'd had about her friend! She owed Dot chocolate for life.

"We did have a good time together, I won't deny that. I only wish you'd been along to share it."

"Me, too," she said with a sigh.

"A new year is right around the corner," he said. "I'll take you anywhere you want to go."

"Oh, Arnie, you are a dear."

"You've said that for years. I don't want to be a dear anymore. I want to be your dear."

"You are, and I'm so happy I don't have to share you," she added. "Now I don't have to poison Dot after all."

He chuckled, pulled her close and kissed her again. This was going to be a very merry Christmas.

Chapter Sixteen

You never know who you may meet at a holiday
gathering. Be open to new friendships.
  —Muriel Sterling, *A Guide to Happy Holidays*

Almost everyone was checked into the Icicle Creek
Lodge by four in the afternoon on Christmas Eve.
Parents and children played outside on the huge front
lawn, taking advantage of the remaining light to make
snowmen and throw snowballs. Some guests had gone
into town to shop. Others relaxed in the lobby, sipping
hot apple cider and cocoa and listening while a pianist
entertained them with Christmas songs. Everything
looked festive and elegant and all was contentment and
congeniality.

Until the final guests arrived. Olivia was passing out
a platter of cookies to the guests when they made their
appearance, the dubious fragrance of cheap perfume
mingled with cigarette smoke preceding them.

She turned her head and saw a woman probably in
her late forties dressed in high boots and an even higher
leather skirt under a short jacket with faux-fur trim that

was ready for retirement. Her hair was long and colored the same brassy blond as Meadow's and she wore it up in a thick ponytail. She had multiple piercings in her ears and was holding on to a designer purse. Her gloves with no fingertips displayed maroon fingernails, a poor match for her bright red lipstick. Her eye makeup would have been perfect for the stage because Muriel was sure you could see it from a hundred feet away. She was looking around the place, taking everything in with an eager and assessing gaze.

The girl with her wore ripped jeans and a leather jacket decorated with metal studs. Her hair had been buzzed nearly to the top of her head, where a black thatch reigned supreme. The style showed off the stake sticking out of her nose and the holes in her earlobes. She was a pretty girl with luminous brown eyes and delicate features, but the features didn't make as big of an impression as the expression on her face, which was as black as the polish on her fingernails. This had to be Meadow's mother and sister. Oh, boy.

The woman banged on the service bell at the reception desk and then leaned against it, surveying the scene. "Looks like your sister did okay. This place probably rakes in the bucks," Olivia heard her say as she approached.

"Good for her," the girl said sourly.

"Good for all of us," the woman said.

It wasn't hard to see why Meadow hadn't wanted her mother and sister to come up for Christmas. Olivia heartily seconded that sentiment. Maybe she could pretend they were all full.

The woman gave Olivia a condescending once-over, then said, "My daughter and I have a room booked here. My daughter owns the place."

Since when? "Actually, I own the place," Olivia said, forcing a smile. "And you are?"

"No kidding. Really? You're Brandon's mom?" The way the woman was looking at Olivia, she might as well have added, *You're nothing special.*

"I'm Olivia Claussen," Olivia said stiffly.

"Hi there. I'm Tawny Anderson, Meadow's mom. And this is my other kid, Arielle."

"Hello, Arielle," Olivia said.

"Hi," Arielle grunted.

Olivia searched for something nice to say. "That's such a pretty name."

"Thanks," the girl muttered. The sour expression remained in place as she took in her surroundings.

"Meadow's in the dining room helping set up for dinner," Olivia said to Tawny. "I'll let her know you're here. She can take you to your room."

"Great. I haven't seen that kid in months," said Tawny. "This is gonna be fun."

Fun.

Olivia put in a call to the kitchen phone and got Meadow herself. "Your mom and sister are here. Would you like to come take them to their room?"

"I'll be right there," Meadow said, sounding like a woman on death row about to get the needle. Olivia could see why.

"So, how long have you had this place?" Tawny asked, removing her gloves.

"Years," Olivia said. "My husband and I built it."

Tawny nodded, taking that in. "Bet it's a real money-maker."

"We manage." Next thing, Tawny would want to know how much they made a year.

"So, how much do you make off a place like this?" she asked and Olivia cringed.

"Enough to live on." Thank God, here came Meadow. "Here's your daughter." Olivia handed over an envelope with their room cards. "She'll see you to your room."

Tawny turned on her stiletto-heeled boots and made a dash for Meadow. "Hey there, brat," she said, hugging her.

"Mom, you're squishing me," Meadow protested and pulled away.

"Well, excuse me," Tawny said. She took in Meadow's dirndl. "What the hell are you wearing?"

"It's a dirndl, Mom," Meadow said, her mouth turning down.

Tawny looked disgusted. "A what?"

"It's a German outfit. All the women up here wear them."

"I guess the women up here never watched *What Not to Wear*," Tawny said. "They should never have taken that show off the air."

Meadow sneaked a look to where Olivia stood watching and her face turned crimson.

Olivia gave her what she hoped was an encouraging smile and Meadow led her relatives away.

Poor Meadow. This was what she'd had for a mother

growing up? It was a wonder she'd turned out as well as she had.

Thank God the horrible woman and her surly daughter were there for only one night. By the following afternoon she'd be gone. They could put up with her for twenty-four hours.

But could the other guests put up with them? Tawny and Arielle didn't make a favorable impression on the family sharing their table at dinner. The fortysomething couple with two well-dressed tween daughters looked as if they'd been forced to eat with lepers when the two women joined them at their table. Tawny had found a low-cut sequined top to go with her short skirt and stiletto boots. She'd touched up her make-up, slathering on the red lipstick and making sure her eyeliner could be seen from clear across the room. She looked like she was ready to stand on the corner in search of a john. Her daughter was still in her same outfit and still wearing her angry teen face.

Olivia wished she could have given them a table all to themselves. In a far, far corner of the dining room. Except there wasn't an empty table to be had.

"My daughter is one of the owners here," she heard Tawny inform her dining companions, altering her earlier story. She reached out and grabbed Olivia's arm as she tried to slip past. "Where's my kiddo?"

Olivia smiled tightly. "Brandon and Meadow are getting ready to serve."

"Don't they get to eat?" Tawny looked horrified. Her daughter, one of the owners, having to wait tables?

"We always make sure our guests enjoy their meals before we do," Olivia said, smiling at the family.

"She's not even gonna eat with us?"

"I know she's looking forward to spending time with you after dinner," Olivia lied, then escaped to the kitchen, where Brandon and Eric were busy setting up carafes of wine.

Meadow came in and saw them. "Oh, shit. You're not going to give my mom wine, are you?"

"We serve wine at every table," Olivia explained. "We'll also put out sparkling cider."

"Good," Meadow said, relieved.

But Olivia noticed when she was setting out rolls on the nearby table that Meadow's mother had no desire for the sparkling cider Meadow was about to pour for her. "What are you trying to pull, Meadow? Give me the booze," she said, and snatched the wine carafe out of Meadow's hand.

The look her daughters exchanged predicted trouble.

Oh, dear, Olivia thought. This was not going to go well.

Sure enough, it didn't.

Brandon stopped by the table to introduce himself and Tawny looked him up and down and said, "Forget the food. I'll take you."

Olivia was disgusted, but he managed a laugh. "Sorry, your daughter got to me first."

"Well, she did okay."

"She's a piece of work," Olivia observed as she and her son returned to the kitchen to bring out more food.

"You can't pick your parents," he said with a shrug.

There were many wine refills at the table where Tawny was sitting. With each one her laughter got merrier and louder and the family stuck with her got quieter, the kids blinking at the spectacle and the parents glaring.

"Cut her off," Olivia said to Brandon.

He did, apologizing to Tawny for running out of wine and switching her to sparkling cider.

The ruse worked...until she pulled out a flask and spiked her cider.

Dinner was served family-style, with platters of turkey at each table along with bowls of dressing and mashed potatoes with gravy. In addition to that, Olivia had provided cranberry sauce, roasted vegetables and pickles and olives. It was a beautiful feast, served with the ambiance of individual centerpieces of greens, lit candles and fine crystal and china. And usually congenial company.

Tawny was, in her own way, congenial, freely sharing her opinion on everything. "This isn't dressing from a box," she informed her fellow diners at her table. "I can tell. It's too soppy," she added in disgust as she helped herself to seconds. She went to set the bowl back down and set it on the edge of the table, from which it immediately toppled.

Olivia, who had been hovering inconspicuously, quickly moved to pick it up.

"Jeez, Mom," muttered Arielle. "Watch what you're doing."

"Well, excuse me," Tawny said and grabbed her wineglass. "I didn't know it was a crime to be clumsy."

"It should be a crime to be drunk," muttered the woman seated at their table.

"I heard that," Tawny snarled.

The woman called Olivia over. "Isn't there somewhere else we can sit?" she asked in a lowered voice as Tawny continued her drunken rant.

If only. "I'm so sorry," Olivia said. "Come speak to me at the front desk tomorrow. I'd love to give you a gift card for a stay at another date."

The woman glared at Tawny. "That woman is ruining our whole meal."

When a guest got too out of hand, James usually escorted said guest from the dining room. Unfortunately, this was a little trickier since this guest was a family member. Sort of.

There was only one thing to do. Olivia stepped over to Tawny. "Tawny, I have a wonderful idea. How would you like to join me someplace special for the rest of the meal?"

Tawny looked intrigued. "Yeah? Where?"

"Let's have this meal just us girls, in my apartment. That way we could get to know each other a bit, being mothers of the newlyweds and all."

The offer of exclusivity appealed. Tawny gave the family frowning at her a superior sneer. "Good idea. I don't need to sit around with a bunch of assholes who think they're better than me." She stood and leaned precariously over the table, fixing the woman with a soused glare. "I've met women like you before, bitches who think they're so much better than the rest of us."

"I'm done," Arielle announced. She threw down her napkin and stormed from the room.

Tawny waved her off with a flick of her hand. "She just wants to call her boyfriend. Let her go."

Olivia certainly had no intention of forcing the angry teen to stay. She picked up Tawny's plate with one hand and slipped her other under Tawny's arm to steady her. "Come on. Let's go."

"Fine with me," Tawny said and grabbed her glass.

"Thank God," the woman murmured, and Tawny flipped her off. "What's wrong with people, anyway?" she demanded of Olivia as they wove their way out of the dining room.

"That's a great question," Olivia said. This woman was a mystery, that was for sure. What had made her the way she was? Perhaps her own mother hadn't parented her very well. One thing Olivia knew for sure—when she was a little girl, the woman hadn't said, "I want to grow up to be an embarrassment to my children."

Back at the apartment, Olivia settled Tawny on her couch and started some coffee going.

Muffin hopped up on the couch to check out the newcomer. "Oh, you've got a cat. I love cats."

Okay, someone who liked cats couldn't be all bad.

"What's your cat's name?"

"Muffin."

"Aww, come here, Muffin." She hauled the cat on her lap, but Muffin decided she didn't want to stay and jumped down. Tawny shook her head. "Cats are such snobs. We had one when the girls were little. He was a snob, too, but they loved him, anyway. The damn thing ran away after just a couple of months. We never did find him."

What to say to all that? Nothing, Olivia decided.

"So, you guys live right here in the hotel, huh?" Tawny said, taking in her surroundings.

"We do," Olivia said. "It makes it easier to run the inn living on-site."

Tawny picked up her half-eaten roll. "I love these brown-and-serve rolls."

Olivia made all her rolls from scratch. She told herself not to be insulted.

"I don't like this dressing, though," Tawny muttered and stuffed a forkful into her mouth. "You know, I haven't heard shit from Meadow ever since she got married and moved up here. What's with that?"

Olivia could see exactly what was with that. This was why Meadow hadn't wanted to invite her mother up for Christmas and Olivia didn't blame her one bit. If she'd been Meadow, she'd have emancipated herself.

"Things change when kids get married," she said in an effort to smooth ruffled feathers. "They get busy, move away."

"They moved in with you," pointed out Tawny. "I can see why, though. This beats my old dump. But hey, when you're on government assistance, you have to take what you can get."

"Everyone needs assistance now and then." Olivia felt sure that Tawny's government assistance was not temporary.

"Damn straight. It wasn't my fault I couldn't work. I have a disability."

"Oh."

"I worked for a while, but I got back problems. That's all behind me. I'm doing good now."

Olivia wondered what had happened to change Tawny's circumstances, but she didn't ask. Most likely Tawny would get around to sharing that, anyway. She brought over a mug of coffee and set it on the coffee table. "Do you take anything in your coffee?"

"Yeah. Whiskey."

And that was going to happen. Not. "All I have is cream and sugar." And schnapps for hot chocolate. No way was Tawny getting any of that.

"Oh. Well, then sugar. The stuff's so bitter you have to put something in it."

Olivia fetched her sugar bowl. Tawny ignored both that and the coffee. "If I had a place like this, my life would have been a lot better. Hell, if I'd ever met a decent man. Guess I followed in my mom's footsteps. Not that I saw much of her once I was in foster care."

It looked like she'd had some strikes against her. For the first time, Olivia actually felt sorry for the woman. And even sorrier for Meadow.

"Meadow's dad was a real dick, let me tell you," Tawny continued. "Arielle's wasn't much better. No, it's mostly been me and the girls." She shook her head. "Every time I think I've got a good one, he turns out to be a loser. This last one..." Another head shake. "But hey, things have a way of working out and I'm doing okay. I've still got some money left from my settlement."

"Settlement?"

"Didn't Meadow tell you? I slipped on some spilled pop at Burger Babe's. Had me a hell of a lawsuit. I wound up with a buttload of money. Of course, it goes fast, doesn't it? A couple of trips to Vegas, a new car for Arielle, the little ingrate. And speaking of ingrates, did that bitch, Gina, appreciate me loaning her money to get a boob job? Did she even pay me back one penny? Nooo." Tawny glared at her plate and set it next to her on the couch. "Well, you learn who your friends are, is all I can say, and I'm not helping any more losers. At least I got my Hummer out of the deal and a nice little apartment. And I got Meadow launched. She'd always wanted to learn to ski like those rich kids. And now look at her. She's one of them."

Olivia and her family weren't exactly rich, but she supposed wealth was all relative.

A knock on the door announced Meadow's arrival. "Mom, what are you doing here?" she asked anxiously.

"I'm talking with your mom-in-law. What does it look like I'm doing? And she's a lot more fun to talk to than those stuck-up people I was sitting with, I can tell you that."

Meadow wasn't smiling, and the cockiness that was so embedded in her personality was missing. She was clearly embarrassed. "How about we go back to your room?"

"What for? Olive and me are having fun." Tawny grabbed her glass and drained the last of her spiked cider. "You know, I'm not a big wine drinker, but this cider is pretty good stuff once you add something to it. You got any more?"

"You've had enough," Meadow said firmly, striding to the couch and taking her mother's arm.

Tawny pulled away. "Where do you get off telling me when I've had enough?"

"Arielle's all by herself," Meadow said, obviously trying a new tactic.

"Arielle could care less," Tawny scoffed. "She's been pissed all day," she confided to Olivia. "She wanted to spend the night with her boyfriend. And he's *really* a loser."

"Mom," Meadow begged. "Come on. Olivia has to get back to the dining room. They need help serving dessert."

Tawny shook her head. "What a rip. You own the place and you have to wait on all those stuck-up people."

"I'm afraid so," Olivia said and stood. She'd never imagined she'd find herself feeling grateful to Meadow for anything, but right now she was. "It's been nice visiting with you," she lied.

"You, too." Tawny stood and swayed slightly, and Meadow grabbed her arm to steady her. "You're all right." She took a step toward Olivia and then embraced her, losing her balance in the process and almost toppling them both. "Oops." She giggled. "I guess your wine and my Jack Daniel's don't get along."

"I guess not," Meadow said in disgust. "Come on."

She eased her mother out the door. "Sorry," she whispered to Olivia.

"It's okay. I'm sure she'll be better in the morning," Olivia assured her.

"I doubt it."

Oh, boy. Olivia could hardly wait for Christmas morning.

Chapter Seventeen

What can compare with the joy of gathering with family at Christmas?

—Muriel Sterling, *A Guide to Happy Holidays*

Olivia woke up dreading Christmas Day. She hadn't felt like that since the Christmas after her first husband died. This, she reminded herself, was only going to be an awkward day. No one had died and all the kids were well. There was no need for this desire to crawl back under the covers. Still, that was what she wanted to do. And if she wanted to, what was poor Meadow feeling?

James's side of the bed was empty and she could smell coffee. A moment later he came into the room, still in his pajamas but wearing a Santa hat and carrying a steaming mug, the cat trotting after him. "Merry Christmas," he sang.

"And to you," she said, smiling up at him.

He handed her the mug and sat down on his side of the bed. "Are you ready for the big day?"

"As ready as I'm ever going to be," she said with a

sigh. "I hope we all survive Christmas morning with Meadow's family."

"I'm sure we will," he said. "Meanwhile…" He pulled open his nightstand drawer and took out a small box from Mountain Jewels wrapped in red ribbon. "Merry Christmas to my darling wife."

"Oh, James, you're the sweetest man," she said, taking it.

"Who's married to the sweetest woman. Open it."

She did and found a mother's ring with the birthstones of her two boys surrounded by tiny diamonds. "Oh, James, it's lovely," she breathed. "I thought we weren't going to exchange presents this year," she scolded.

"I agreed to not exchanging presents," he said. "I didn't agree to not getting you one."

"Well, I agreed to not exchanging presents, also, but…" She leaned over and took a present from her nightstand drawer, another box from Mountain Jewels.

He shook his head at her. "You didn't keep our bargain."

"I kept it the same way you did. Open it."

James opened his to find an old-fashioned pocket watch with a Santa etched on it. "Oh, Olivia," he said, teary eyed. "This is a wonderful present."

"Read the inscription," she urged.

He opened the watch and read. "'To Santa from Mrs. Claus, with love.' I'll treasure it always."

"You're the best Santa I've ever seen," she told him. "I'm glad I got back to the dining room to see you in action, giving away all those little presents."

Ever since his first stay at the lodge, James had donned his Santa suit and doled out small presents for all their guests. The women usually got soap, while the men received smoked salmon or hot sauce from Local Yokels, a shop that specialized in products made in the Northwest. The young children usually received bubble solution and slightly older children were each given a five-dollar gift card to spend on a smoothie or latte at Bavarian Brews. It was an extra expense but he loved doing it and the guests were always touched by the special show of kindness.

"I'm glad, too," he said. "My night definitely was more fun than yours."

"And we still have to get through the day."

"If it's any consolation, I doubt they'll stay for dinner. So all you have to do is get through opening presents."

A new thought occurred. "What if they decide to extend their stay another day?"

James chuckled. "We'll give them dinner and then send them off with Meadow and Brandon."

Olivia shook her head. "My poor son."

"It's the price of marriage. You usually get the family along with the girl. I was lucky. Both the girl and her family are great," he added and kissed her.

Now she really didn't want to leave her bed. But duty called. They shared one more kiss, and then she got dressed and made her way to the kitchen to make coffee cake and put her egg casserole in the oven. In addition to the casserole and coffee cake, she would serve a fruit salad.

After that, guests were on their own. Several restaurants in town served Christmas dinner, which allowed Olivia to spend the rest of the day with her family—something she normally looked forward to. She wasn't so sure about today.

Brandon made it down to help with breakfast. "Meadow's in bed eating crackers and trying not to puke, but she'll be down in time for cleanup."

"How about her mother and sister?" Olivia asked.

"Haven't seen 'em, thank God."

And they didn't. Olivia did dispatch Brandon with coffee and some coffee cake. "Tell them we'll be having our own party around eleven," she said.

"Maybe we'll get lucky and they won't want to come."

Olivia wasn't holding her breath. She had a strong suspicion that Tawny was determined to embed herself as deeply as possible into her new family.

True to her word, Meadow came down to help with the postbreakfast cleanup at ten. She looked both tired and embarrassed and could hardly meet Olivia's gaze when she came into the kitchen with a load of dirty plates.

"How did you sleep?" Olivia asked.

"Okay," she said and hurried over to the commercial sink.

Olivia followed her. "Meadow."

Meadow kept her back to Olivia. "I'm sorry about last night."

"There's nothing for you to be sorry for."

"Yeah, there is. She's my mom."

"And she loves you. She's very proud of you."

Meadow focused on scraping leftovers off a plate. "I wish I could say the same about her."

"None of us is perfect."

Meadow swiped at her eyes. "I wish she hadn't come."

So did Olivia. "I know. But she is your mother."

"I wish you were my mother," Meadow said softly.

The words pierced Olivia's heart. This irritating, needy girl was no one she'd have picked for a daughter-in-law, but for the first time she felt true empathy for her. How sad that Meadow felt the way she did about her mom. How sad that Tawny hadn't earned the love and devotion of her child.

How sad that Olivia hadn't had the grace to welcome her with open arms. "I may not be your mother, but I'll be here for you," she promised and slipped an arm around Meadow's shoulder.

Meadow nodded and wiped away fresh tears. "Thanks. And thanks for putting up with her."

"She's not so bad." Uncouth, ill-mannered, low class, yes. But she loved her daughter enough to want to be with her at Christmas and that had to count for something.

Right at eleven she was at Olivia's door, wearing pajama bottoms and a long red sweater, dragging along her designer purse and a bottle of gin with a red bow stuck on it. Arielle had also dressed for the occasion in ripped jeans and a T-shirt under her jacket that asked WTF? She wore a red bandanna over her hair and—surprise!—a scowl.

If Olivia had Tawny for a mother, she'd scowl, too. She forced a smile and a "Merry Christmas."

"Yeah, merry, merry," Tawny chirped, entering the apartment, her daughter slouching in after her. She handed over the bottle. "I always like to bring a hostess gift."

"Thank you," Olivia said and hoped Tawny didn't expect her to open it right then.

"Hey, Olive, do you have any aspirin? I've got a bitch of a headache."

"Of course," Olivia said and went to fetch aspirin. For both Tawny and herself.

"So, what's the plan for today?" Tawny asked, flopping on the couch.

"Well, we'll be snacking and opening presents," Olivia said. She couldn't bring herself to mention that after all the presents had been opened, the family would be sharing a meal together.

Arielle eyed the plate of Christmas cookies on the coffee table and helped herself to one of the sugar-cookie trees. "This is good," she said, crumbs spilling from her mouth. She almost smiled.

"I'm glad you like it."

"Oh, yeah." Arielle helped herself to another. "Mom doesn't bake."

"I do too bake," Tawny insisted.

Arielle made a face.

"Just not a lot," Tawny added. "It takes a lot of time to make cookies. And if I have 'em in the house, I'll just eat 'em. And let me tell you, I don't need the extra pounds."

Tawny wasn't carrying any extra pounds that Olivia could see.

"You know how it is, Olive. A minute on your lips, forever on your butt." She dug in her purse and pulled out a vape pen.

Oh, no. Olivia drew the line at that. "I'm sorry, but we don't smoke in here."

Tawny frowned. "Oh. Well, then, I'll just go outside for a minute. You got a deck?"

Olivia nodded to the sliding glass door off the kitchen. "We have a patio."

Tawny nodded. She slid the door open, then stood in the doorway, blowing out smoke and letting in cold air. "It's a bad habit," she called back to Olivia. "I'm gonna quit in the New Year."

She'd just shut the door when Eric and Brooke arrived. "Merry Christmas," Brooke said, kissing Olivia and her father as Eric put their presents under the tree.

"Merry Christmas, dear," Olivia said.

"Who's this?" Tawny asked.

"This is my son Eric and my stepdaughter, Brooke."

"I think I saw you last night," Tawny said to her. "You look ready to pop."

"I'm due next month," Brooke said.

"And they still make you work? Olive, you're a real meanie," Tawny joked.

"I want to help," Brooke hurried to say.

"You ought to take it easy while you can," Tawny advised her. "Once you have kids, you never get any rest, believe me."

"That's okay," Brooke said easily. "We're looking forward to the baby."

"Yeah, well, don't count on ever looking good in a

bikini again," Tawny advised just as Meadow and Brandon entered. "Well, here's my lazy-butt daughter," she said, hurrying over to give Meadow a hug. "You got up later than me and I had a hangover."

"I didn't feel good, Mom," Meadow said irritably.

"Not because you had too much to drink," Tawny said in disgust. "Couldn't convince her to have a nightcap with me," she told Olivia.

"Well, it's not a good idea for her to be drinking right now," Olivia said in Meadow's defense. She didn't see the desperate look Meadow was giving her until the words had already escaped. Oh, no.

"What do you mean right now?" Tawny asked. She looked at Meadow, brows knit. "Hey, wait a minute. Are you knocked up?"

"You didn't tell your mom?" Brandon asked, surprised.

Meadow bit her lip.

One moment later it was apparent why she hadn't. "OMG, Meadow. What's the rush?" Tawny demanded.

"I think it's cool," Arielle said from where she sat on the couch.

"Yeah, well, that's because nobody's gonna be calling you Grandma." Tawny shook her head at her daughter. "You should be having some fun before you settle down."

"I don't want to have fun," Meadow retorted, her cheeks flushed. "I want to have a baby." She moved away from her mother and went to sit next to the tree, where Brandon had been setting out their presents.

"We'll have fun with the baby," he assured her and gave her a hug.

"Yeah, easy for you to say," Tawny said with a snort. "You had your fun. Now she'll be the one doing all the work."

"That's not how we do things in this family," Brandon said, his easy smile hardening into a straight line.

"Yeah, you all look like you've got your shit together," Tawny admitted.

High praise, indeed. "So, what does everyone want to drink?" Olivia said, forcing holiday cheer into her voice. "We've got coffee, tea and cocoa," she hurried to add before Tawny could suggest they break open the gin.

Happily, conversation moved away from babies and lost figures. With everyone supplied with cocoa, coffee and pastry, the present opening began.

Eric and Brandon were happy with their gift cards from the nearby ski resort, which they could use for lift tickets and whatever new ski paraphernalia they needed, and Brooke was delighted with the cuckoo clock Olivia and James had picked out for her.

Meadow was nearly speechless when she opened her present and found the Hummel she'd admired when she and Olivia had gone shopping for her dirndl. "Wow," she breathed. "Really?"

Olivia smiled at her. "I thought you'd like it."

"I do! Thanks!"

"I saw something like that at Goodwill the other day," Tawny said. "Didn't know you were into that stuff."

"I bet you didn't see this at Goodwill," Meadow shot back irritably. "It cost a ton."

Tawny merely shrugged. Then she reached into her purse and pulled out an envelope and handed it to Meadow with great flourish. "Merry Christmas."

She had another one for Arielle, who opened the envelope, pulled out a fifty-dollar bill and—check it out, folks—smiled. "Thanks, Mom."

"Don't spend it all on pot," Tawny told her, making her daughter blush and erasing the smile. "Go buy yourself something like that little knickknack your sister got." As if fifty dollars would cover it.

Meadow also received a fifty-dollar bill. "Thanks, Mom," she said. Her response was polite, if not brimming with enthusiasm.

"You're welcome," Tawny said. "Good old Mama Claus came through again, huh? Who says I don't do anything for my daughters? Good thing I slipped on that Coke at Burger Babe's. Otherwise you'd never have been able to have that ski lesson you'd always been dying for and you'd have never met Mr. Beefcake here." Mr. Beefcake's face turned red but Tawny didn't notice. "Too bad the gravy train's about to end."

"Maybe you can find someone new to sue," Arielle sniped. "Or a new boyfriend to throw pop at."

"Hey, it doesn't matter who threw the pop. I slipped on it and fell and Burger Babe's was responsible."

Brandon's eyes grew wide and Eric looked disgusted. Brooke swallowed a gasp.

Now Meadow's face was red. "Guys," she begged.

Mother and sister ignored her. "And just because you didn't get to spend the night with your boyfriend, you don't have to get snotty," Tawny snapped at Arielle.

"The only reason you dragged me up here is cuz you don't have a boyfriend. You could have come by yourself." She had the grace to mutter, "Sorry, Meadow. It's not like I didn't want to see you. But I'd promised Tony I'd hang with his family."

"I get it," Meadow said.

"I don't," Tawny said, frowning. "We're family, too."

James and the boys watched the train wreck in shocked silence and Brooke squirmed in her seat. Meadow looked pleadingly at Olivia.

"Well, let's open some more presents," Olivia said. "Shall we? James, I think we have something under the tree for Tawny and Arielle." Too bad it wasn't gags for their mouths.

"Good idea," James said and dived for the tree.

"Would you like some more coffee?" Brooke asked Tawny.

"I'll take some more of that pastry," Brandon said. "I love this stuff, Mom."

And so the awkward moment was smoothed over, with everyone chatting away with determination. But Meadow stayed quiet.

Olivia had gotten an iTunes gift card for Arielle, who brought out another rare smile and thanked her.

Tawny was also quick to thank Olivia for her gift, a scented candle. "This will be perfect for New Year's Eve. I'm having a party and we're playing that white-elephant game. You know, the one where you steal presents from each other?"

"Jeez, Mom," Meadow muttered.

"I mean, not that it wasn't nice of you to get me

something," Tawny added. "I'm just not into candles. Too easy to catch your place on fire, you know."

"More presents," James said quickly.

Brandon was more than pleased with the knit scarf Meadow gave him. "I made it myself," she said. "Your mom taught me how."

"It's great, babe. I love it," he said and kissed her. The look of gratitude he gave Olivia then made her heart fill. He was clearly happy that she'd made the effort to connect with Meadow.

Meadow was equally pleased with the ring Brandon gave her. "I always wanted a ring with my birthstone," she said and threw her arms around his neck. "You're the best husband ever."

"I'd have gotten you one if you'd said something," Tawny muttered with a frown. She did lose the frown when Meadow handed her and Arielle their presents. More knit scarves. "Don't tell me—let me guess. You're learning how to knit," cracked Tawny.

"I worked hard on those," Meadow snapped.

"Don't get me wrong. It's great," Tawny said and donned hers.

"Thanks, sis," Arielle said. "This is awesome."

"Yeah?"

"Yeah."

A sweet moment. Good. Now, how long could they stretch it out?

Not long. Olivia opened her present from Meadow— a set of cake-decorating tips.

"I thought maybe we could decorate some cakes together," Meadow said shyly. "I always wanted to learn how to do that."

"Of course we can," Olivia told her.

"Cake decorating, what a waste of time," Tawny said with a flick of her hand. "You do all that work and people just eat it and then poop it out. So all your hard work turns to shit," she finished and laughed at her cleverness.

Dear Lord, save us. "It was a very thoughtful gift," Olivia said to Meadow. "They'll be fun to use."

Meadow's face was now so red Olivia was sure the poor girl would burst into flames any minute. She gave her what she hoped was an encouraging smile.

At last the opening of presents was finished. "Mom, can we go now?" Arielle asked, and everyone in the room held their breath.

Tawny rolled her eyes. "I know. The boyfriend. Yeah, I guess we should hit the road."

No one urged her to stay.

"I'll help you with your things," Brandon offered.

"This has been great, Olive," Tawny said to Olivia. "We'll have to do it again sometime."

Dear God, please, no. Olivia merely smiled and said, "Merry Christmas."

"Thanks for the gift card," Arielle said and gave Olivia another fleeting glimpse of a pretty smile as well as the kind of woman she could be with the right influence.

And then, after hugs and kisses for everyone from Tawny, they were gone and the family let out a collective sigh of relief. Except Meadow, who was sitting in her chair, looking at her feet, tears slipping down her cheeks.

Brooke came over and knelt in front of her. "It's okay, Meadow."

Meadow shook her head. "No, it's not. I hate her."

Olivia slipped into the chair next to her, where Brandon had been sitting. "I don't think you mean that. You know your mother loves you in her own way."

"I never realized…" Meadow stopped and bit her lip. She looked at Olivia with teary eyes. "I never realized what I was missing until I met you. I don't want to be like her. I want to be more than that. I want my life and my kid's life to be better than what I had growing up."

"You already are, and it will be," Brooke assured her.

Olivia should have been the one to say those words. "Brooke's right," she said as much to herself as to Meadow. "Now, we have a lot of Christmas left. Let's make the most of it. Shall we?"

Meadow bit her lip and nodded and wiped at the tears.

"Come on," Olivia said to her. "How about helping me in the kitchen?"

"I'd like that," Meadow said.

"Good. Come on, girls, let's get ready for a wonderful day." After what they'd all just endured, Olivia was determined to make everything as pleasant and memorable as possible. Especially for Meadow.

Sienna had spent Christmas Eve at Rita's house with the family and Leo had returned home high on sugar and the anticipation of Santa's arrival. It had taken forever to settle him down. Tito had come over later and helped her set up the train set from Santa, and come morning, she'd made sure to capture the moment of discovery on her phone and sent it to her parents.

"This is the best Christmas ever!" he'd declared as he'd plopped down in front of the set. Other presents had been ignored as, together, they set the little train racing around the tree. They were still at it when her parents checked in for some phone face time.

She insisted Leo pull himself away from the train set and open his present from his grandparents. Legos. He was delighted. For her they'd sent a Visa gift card as well as a silver necklace.

"I wish we were there with you," said her mother.

"You are, thanks to technology," Sienna reminded her.

"What are you two going to do today?" her father asked before her mother could continue her lament.

"We're just going to hang out."

"Tim's coming over," put in Leo. "Him and me are gonna play with my train," he added.

"He and I," Sienna corrected as her son bounced off the couch and back to the tree.

"That nice man you met?" her mother asked.

"Yes."

"I don't want you getting involved with any man I haven't met," her father said sternly.

Sienna thought back to when her father had threatened the last disaster man in her life with a baseball bat. It was probably a good thing they weren't living in Icicle Falls.

"Don't worry, Papi," she said. "I've gotten smarter when it comes to men."

Her father grunted. "I hope so."

They chatted a few more minutes and then it was just her and Leo again. And the train set.

And the cinnamon rolls Mrs. Zuckerman had brought over the day before. Yes, it would have been nice to be with all her family, Sienna thought as she helped herself to one, but she had both family and friends here. And the hope of a relationship that might actually work. That would be the best Christmas present of all.

She coaxed Leo into eating a cinnamon roll and then got him dressed, promising him he could play with his train set as soon as he brushed his teeth. With Leo presentable for company, she went to work on herself, showering, then putting on leggings and the new red sweater she'd bought online. After adding makeup and her favorite dangly earrings, she felt good about how she looked.

She felt good, period. Tim was looking forward to coming over and she was looking forward to having him. It wasn't going to be a fancy Christmas meal—she and Leo had had that the night before. Today was going to be guacamole and chips, pork-and-chorizo pozole and quesadillas. And for dessert, the *tres leches* cake she'd promised Leo and made the day before.

Everything was ready, including her. Tim would be arriving soon.

Meanwhile, though, Leo had to be entertained. This wasn't hard, although she got bored watching his train endlessly circling the Christmas tree.

When Leo's pal Jimmy showed up at the front door with his new sled, wanting Leo to come help him try it out on the small hill next to his yard, she said yes. Burning off some of his holiday energy would be a good thing.

"Don't go out on the street, though, you two," Sienna cautioned once Leo was bundled up and raring to go.

"I know," Jimmy told her. "My mom told me. I'll make sure he doesn't."

She watched from the doorway as they trotted off down the sidewalk past Mrs. Zuckerman's and smiled. Look who else was making his way down the street. The bottle-shaped gift bag made it easy to figure out where Mr. Cratchett was headed. And he was whistling. Now, there was a true Christmas miracle. God bless that angel, Mrs. Zuckerman, for helping the guy rediscover his heart.

"Merry Christmas, Mr. Cratchett," she called.

He didn't say anything but he managed a quick wave. That in itself was impressive.

Sienna smiled as she shut the door. It looked like everyone had someone special to be with this Christmas. But her potential someone special should have been here by now. He'd had to deliver his girls back to their mom this morning. Maybe he was running late.

She made herself an eggnog latte and settled down to listen to her playlist of Christmas songs and read the last bit of Muriel's book. Half an hour later she finished.

I hope this book has been helpful to you, Muriel wrote, *and my wish for you is that you'll have a truly happy holiday.*

She was having a happy holiday, one of the best she'd had in a long time. She glanced at her clock. It was now almost one. Where was Tim?

She was about to call and see when her doorbell rang. Ah, no need. He was finally there.

And now he was banging on the door, which seemed a little like overkill.

"Hurry up!" yelled a voice.

That was not Tim. A feeling of foreboding threw its net over Sienna.

She opened the door to find Cratchett on her porch, holding a barely conscious Leo, Mrs. Zuckerman at his side.

Chapter Eighteen

Christmas morning always brings surprises.
—Muriel Sterling, *A Guide to Happy Holidays*

"Leo!" Sienna cried. *"Madre de Dios!"*

Cratchett brushed past her and staggered into the living room, depositing Leo on the couch. His face was so red from exertion he looked ready for a heart attack.

Sienna fell onto the floor next to her son. "Leo, Leo!" She turned to Cratchett. "What happened?"

He was still trying to get his breath but he managed to speak. "Sledding with the other kid across the street. He hit a tree."

"With his head?"

"He wasn't going all that fast."

"But with his head?"

"He'll be fine."

How did Cratchett know?

"Quit standing there jabbering, woman," he snapped. "Get some ice."

"I'll get the ice," Mrs. Zuckerman offered.

"I'm calling 911," Sienna said, grabbing her cell.

Meanwhile, Leo was whimpering. And then he was throwing up. The mess hit the couch, the floor and Cratchett's shoes, something that should have made the old guy's head pop off. Oh, no.

"Concussion," Cratchett said calmly. "It's okay, son. We'll get you feeling better soon."

Sienna should have been amazed by Mr. Cratchett's kindness. She should have apologized for Leo barfing on him. Instead, she begged the 911 operator to get someone to the house right away. "My address?" What was her address?

"Give me the phone," Cratchett commanded, snatching it from her. He then proceeded to relay the necessary information even as Leo once more upchucked on him. "Stay calm," he instructed Sienna as he handed the phone back to her.

Calm? Leo's eyes were closed now. Was he conscious? "Leo, bambino."

"Kids are tough. Hell, I got a crack on the head when I was a kid. Trying to play Tarzan and swung from a tree. I landed right on my bean."

Mrs. Zuckerman was back with the ice now, wrapped in a towel. She laid it gently on Leo's head, and Sienna choked back a sob. "He's going to be fine," she assured Sienna.

Of course he would. But emotion and logic rarely danced close in a mother's heart when her child was hurt. "He's all I've got," she said in a small voice, and Mrs. Zuckerman hugged her.

"Don't you worry," Cratchett said brusquely. "Your

boy's going to be all right." He walked to the living room window and looked out. "Where are those idiots?"

Yes, where were they? It felt like the ambulance was taking a million years to get to them.

Sienna was ready to climb out of her skin by the time the ambulance arrived. She stood by, wringing her hands, as the paramedics got busy checking Leo's vital signs, looking for head lacerations and neck or spine injury.

He moaned under their ministrations and Sienna whimpered.

"His vitals are good, but we're going to take him to the hospital to get him thoroughly checked," one of the paramedics told her. "You can ride with us."

"Lila and I will stay behind and clean things up for you," Cratchett told her as she followed the stretcher out the door.

She was so upset his kindness barely registered.

The ride with her son to the hospital was the longest one of her life. Waiting in the emergency room for the doctor was torture. She began to feel like she could breathe normally again only after he had examined Leo and assured her he'd be fine.

"I'd like to keep him here overnight for observation, though," he said, and that wound her up all over again. She called Rita for moral support.

"I'll be right there," Rita promised.

It was only after Sienna hung up that she realized the person missing from this holiday picture was Tim. He'd never showed up, never called to explain why. His crotchety uncle had been more help than he had.

And now she'd found his flaw. The man was unreliable.

He eventually did call...right before Rita arrived at the hospital. Leo was getting settled into a room with ice and pain meds, Sienna hovering while the nurse worked, when her cell phone rang. She took his call with an irritability that rivaled his uncle's.

"Sorry I'm not there yet," he said. "My ex's water heater was leaking and I got stuck dealing with the mess when I got there this morning. I'm on my way now."

"Don't bother," Sienna told him.

"Look, I'll be there soon."

"No need. We're not home. I'm at the hospital."

"The hospital! Are you okay?"

"Not really. Leo had a sledding accident. He ran into a tree and got a concussion. They're keeping him for observation."

"Oh, no. The poor kid."

"He'll be okay." Which was more than she could say for her relationship with Tim.

"I'll come keep you company."

"No need. My cousin's on her way."

"Oh." He was silent a moment, digesting this. Then he asked, "Are you sure you wouldn't like me to come there?"

"No, I'm fine. Look, I need to go," she said in clipped tones.

"Of course. Take care."

She intended to. She was going to take care not to let this go any further. She'd seen the writing on the wall. She and Leo would always come in second after his first family. She understood it, but she didn't need that kind of life and neither did Leo.

Rita arrived to hear the tail end of the call but made no comment. The nurse finished up and left and the two women took up positions on either side of Leo's bed. He looked as helpless as Sienna felt.

"My head hurts," he announced.

"I know." She took his hand and squeezed it. "You'll feel better soon. And look who's here, Tía Rita."

"Hey, Leo," Rita said and laid a hand on his arm. "Looks like you had a big adventure."

"You got to ride in an ambulance," Sienna added. "Pretty cool, huh?"

"I want to go home," Leo said.

"I know, but we have to stay here for a while. The doctor wants to make sure you're all right." Leo didn't have the energy to protest beyond sticking out his lower lip. To cheer him up, Sienna grabbed the remote control and turned on the TV. She found a million-year-old cartoon about Frosty the Snowman and set that playing and the lower lip slipped back into place.

Rita came around the bed and joined Sienna. Leaning with her back to Leo, she asked, "Who was that on the phone?"

"No one important."

Rita cocked an eyebrow. "Was it Tim?"

"Yes."

"No one important already? Just last night it sounded like things were going good with you two."

Sienna frowned. "That was last night."

"So, what happened? Come on, spill. I'm pulling teeth here."

"He was supposed to spend the day with us."

"I know. You told me."

"Well, he didn't show up."

"So he was running late. That's why you gave him the ice-storm treatment just now?"

"It's not going to work out," Sienna said. "He's got his kids and his ex."

"Ex, Sienna. That means she doesn't count."

"She does enough to sucker him into doing things for her."

"Like what?"

"Like dealing with a broken water heater."

"So he's not hard-hearted. So sue him." Sienna remained silent and Rita shook her head. "I think you're crazy to let one little thing bug you."

"It's not one little thing. It's a sign."

"From God?" Rita scoffed.

"I've got enough to deal with. I don't need to add another unreliable man to that list."

Rita sighed. "Okay. Have it your way. But I think you're making a mistake. You ought to give the guy more of a chance."

Maybe, but she wasn't going to.

Rita stayed another hour and then, at Sienna's insistence, left to go spend the rest of the day with her husband and daughter. She'd been gone only a few minutes when Tim walked into the room, bringing flowers for Sienna and a Matchbox car for Leo. She wasn't happy to see him.

Leo was, though. "Hi, Tim," he said. The greeting was lacking Leo's usual energy but the happy expression on his face made up for that.

"Hey there, buddy. I hear you had an accident."

"I don't like sledding," Leo informed him.

"Sledding is fun," Tim said. "It's those trees that get in the way. Maybe we need to find a place for you to sled where there aren't any trees. Meanwhile, though, I brought you a car."

"Thanks," Leo said.

"And something for your mom," Tim added and held out the flowers to Sienna.

She took them and laid them aside. "Could I talk to you?" Without waiting for an answer, she left the room, and he followed her out. The door was barely shut when she said, "Tim, what are you doing here?"

"I thought you could use the company."

She shook her head. "I told you not to come. I'm fine on my own."

"We were going to spend the day together," he reminded her.

"Yeah. We were."

"Okay, I get it," he said. "You're mad."

Yes, she was. "Tim, this isn't going to work. We need to stop this before we go any further."

"You can't be serious."

"I am."

"Because I was late?"

"Because you have an ex."

"So do you," he reminded her.

"Mine's not in the picture," she said.

"Mine's not either, not really."

Sienna shook her head. "After today, I find that hard to believe."

"Look. I went to drop the girls off and found that mess. No one was going to come out on Christmas Day. I'd have felt like a rat to just go off and leave. As it is, they won't have any hot water. I figured I could take a few minutes to help, that's all."

All very noble, but still...

"If I'd known what was going on with you and Leo, I'd have been here in a heartbeat."

"Would you? Really?"

"Yes. Sienna, I'm not psychic. I didn't know anything was wrong. You didn't call me, did you? I mean, there were no missed calls on my phone."

"No, I didn't," she admitted. "I was a little busy myself."

"Sienna, come on. Be reasonable."

She was being reasonable. "Oh, can't you see? This isn't going to work." He needed to get the message so she could stop repeating herself, because every time she did, she got increasingly more depressed.

"You don't know that," he said. "I like what we've started here. Don't you? Let's not give up so quick."

"I don't need this kind of hassle in my life," she insisted.

"You've got hassle in your life with or without me. That's why we're here right now. Stuff happens." She was still trying to come up with something to say to that when he continued, "Do you really want to give up after one bump in the road? I don't. I don't want to spend my life alone. Do you?"

"Coming in second place isn't much better than being alone."

"Don't say that. Don't think it. You're the best thing that's happened to me in a long time. I thought you felt the same way, too."

"Maybe I've changed my mind," she said hotly.

"And maybe you haven't." He pulled her up against him and kissed her.

Standing there in the hallway, with hospital staff walking past and the smell of antiseptic all around them—it was the most romantic kiss she'd ever had.

And bittersweet. She pulled away. "I'm sorry, Tim. I can't do it. I've been hurt too many times."

"What about your kid? Doesn't he want a father?"

That was a low blow. "Of course he does. But you already have children. Remember?"

"You think I'm so small I can't love another kid?"

"I think you don't know what you'd be getting into."

"Oh, and once I found out I'd cut and run. That's the kind of man you think I am?"

"I don't know what kind of man you are," she said. "That's exactly my point!" Yes, he seemed wonderful. But seeming wonderful and being wonderful were two different things. She turned to go back inside the room.

"Sienna, wait."

She didn't.

"Where's Tim?" Leo asked when she came back.

"He's gone." And that was that.

"I can't get my car out," he said, handing her the package.

She took it. "I can do that. We don't need Tim."

We don't need any more heartache.

It was a long night. Keeping Leo entertained and keeping her mother from panicking when she called to tell her about the accident left Sienna exhausted. Nonetheless, she found it impossible to sleep on the room's pullout single bed. She tossed and turned, chased by worry and regrets. She was still awake when the new day dawned, bringing clear skies and sunshine. Her mood remained gray.

The doctor had discharged Leo and she was waiting for the discharge nurse to come with the papers she needed to sign when Bob Cratchett entered the room.

"It looks like you're going to be okay," he said to Leo. "So's the tree you tried to take out, by the way. Here, something to make you feel better," he said and dropped a giant candy cane onto the bed.

Leo gaped at him, completely at a loss. Sienna could hardly blame him. This had to feel like having the bogeyman pop up at his bedside wanting to be friends.

"What do you say?" Sienna prompted.

Leo gulped and managed a weak "Thank you."

"What are you doing here?" Sienna asked Cratchett. *And where's the real Cratchett?* He seemed to have disappeared lately.

"What do you think? I came to take you home. You don't have a car. Remember?"

"I was going to call my cousin."

"Now you don't need to. I've got a cab waiting."

Rescuing Leo the day before and now this. It was all so un-Cratchett-like. "A cab?"

The famous Bob Cratchett frown returned. "That irritating nephew of mine took my keys and hid 'em somewhere, so I had to take a cab. Of course, it should have been him picking you up in the first place. You can thank Lila Zuckerman that I'm even here. She made me call him this morning. Otherwise I'd have assumed you had a ride."

"I would have," she insisted. "There's no need."

"Yes, yes," he said, shushing her. He turned to Leo. "You ready to get out of here?"

Leo managed a nod.

"We have to wait for the discharge nurse," Sienna told him.

He shook his head. "Disorganized. Well, you get your things together. I'll go find the nurse and hurry her along."

Scare her was probably more like it.

"Look what Mr. Cratchett gave me," Leo said in awe as Cratchett walked out the door.

"That was very nice of him." Mr. Cratchett had obviously been taken over by aliens. "Let's put it in the bag with your things and you can have some of it as soon as we get home. Okay?"

Leo said a wistful "Okay," and handed over the treat.

Cratchett returned a moment later with the discharge nurse and soon the paperwork was done and the nurse had Leo in a wheelchair and was pushing him down the hall, Sienna and Cratchett walking along beside.

After their many unpleasant encounters, she felt

awkward having Bob Cratchett escorting her and her son home. She felt even more awkward about thanking him for what he'd done, but she knew she needed to.

"Thank you for helping us yesterday," she said.

He waved away her thanks. "I was at Lila's waiting for her family to show and happened to see it all. There wasn't anyone else around, so what was I going to do, let the boy lie there and freeze to death? And, speaking of being around, why isn't my nephew doing this?"

"I don't know why you'd think he should be," Sienna said stiffly as they all got on the elevator.

"Because you two have been as thick as thieves lately."

"You're wrong."

"So you're not seeing each other?"

When did Robert Cratchett get so nosy? "No."

"Well, why not? You need a man."

Sienna was aware of the nurse pretending not to hear them. Great. Now he wasn't content with being rude and impatient with her. He had to move on to new territory and embarrass her.

"No, I don't," she replied, sounding as snappish as a Cratchett in training. "Not that it's any of your business."

He grunted and dropped the subject.

But he picked it up again once they were in the taxi. "You know, Tim's not a bad sort. I always liked him, even as a kid."

"I like Tim," put in Leo.

"Smart boy," said Cratchett. "He seems to like you, too. Both of you. And I've got to admit, you're a step above that dingbat he was married to," he informed Sienna.

"Gee, thanks. But I'm not in the market."

"Well, maybe you should be." Then, surprisingly, Cratchett's voice softened. "Everybody needs someone."

"Excuse me, Mr. Cratchett, but you're a fine one to talk," Sienna said irritably. Where did this old guy get off, anyway?

He looked out the window at the snowy lawns. "Yeah, I've been pretty stupid most of my life. But a person doesn't have to stay stupid."

"Thanks for the advice." Not.

"You should be grateful. I don't give it very often."

"So why are you bothering now? You've never liked me. Since when do you care about who I do or don't see?"

"Since you started making a pest of yourself," he growled. "You and your snow shoveling and your poison cookies and that candy. I figure I owe you," he finished awkwardly.

"You helped Leo. We're even." Now she was the one sounding cranky. Good grief.

"I guess we are. And I guess my nephew will have to keep bumbling along on his own. Anyway, when people want to be stupid, there's no stopping them."

The old guy was really beginning to bug her. "You should know, Mr. Cratchett. I think I liked you better when you were a recluse," she couldn't resist adding.

He barked out a laugh. "That's a good one, huh, Leo?"

"That's a good one," Leo agreed, sure that if grumpy Mr. Cratchett was laughing, there must be something to laugh about.

They were at the house now and, to her surprise, Tim was out front, shoveling her walk. "What's he doing here?"

"How should I know? I asked him to come shovel my walk. Guess he thought he should do yours, too. Okay, you two, get out so I can pay the cabbie. Turn your meter off," he growled at the cabdriver. "You already made enough waiting for me at the hospital."

"Hey, buddy, how are you feeling?" Tim called as they came up the walk.

"Good," Leo said.

"Tim, what are you doing here?" Sienna asked.

"Uncle Bob wanted me to come over and shovel his front walk. And yours."

Cratchett had caught up with them. "What are you doing standing around in the cold? Let's get this kid inside. Come on," he added. Like an avalanche, he swept all before him, moving them into the house.

They were getting Leo settled when Mrs. Zuckerman arrived with a plate of cookies. "How's our Leo doing?" she asked, setting them down on the coffee table.

"I rode in an ambulance," Leo informed her.

"You did, indeed," she said.

"Thank you for cleaning my carpet," Sienna said to Mrs. Zuckerman.

"That was mostly Robert," she replied.

Mr. Cratchett? Sienna looked at him in amazement and his cheeks turned russet.

"I'm good for some things, you know," he said.

"Yes, you are," Mrs. Zuckerman agreed and slipped her arms through his.

"Come on, Lila, these kids don't need us hanging

around. What do you say we go over to your place? You did save me some of those cookies, didn't you?"

"I did. You get better soon, Leo, then you can come over and play with Bandit," she said, ruffling Leo's hair. She gave Sienna a hug and then she and Cratchett were gone.

Tim made no move to leave.

"Can I have my candy cane now?" Leo asked.

"Yes, you may," she said. She broke off a piece for him and unwrapped it, all the while aware of Tim standing on the other side of the couch. She should tell him to leave. She should thank him for shoveling her walk. She should see a shrink.

"So, Leo, looks like Santa brought you a train for Christmas," Tim said.

"Want to play with me?" Leo asked, and for the first time since the accident he had some energy in his voice.

"No playing today," Sienna told him. "The doctor wants you to take it easy." That brought the lower lip back out. "But I'll tell you what. You can watch *Cars*."

"Okay," Leo said, and she put on the DVD.

That took care of Leo. What to do about Tim? Her emotions were in a swirl and words were failing her.

"Did my uncle talk to you?"

"You mean did he lecture me? Yes, he did. Did you put him up to it?"

"More like he put himself up to it. I have to admit, I whined a little. He was very supportive. He told me I'm an idiot and don't know the first thing about women."

Sienna couldn't help smiling.

"I guess I don't," Tim said.

Maybe they were a match, because she'd proved more than once that she didn't know the first thing about men. What should she do?

She should hang up her coat. She snagged it and Leo's from the chair where she'd dropped their coats and hung them up in the closet, stalling for time.

She turned to find Tim standing next to her. "Maybe you could teach me."

She should tell him to go home.

"Do you still feel the same way you did yesterday?"

Attracted? Miserable? Unsure?

"Because if you do, then I'll leave."

She bit her lip.

He slipped his arms around her. "But I wish you wouldn't give up on us so quick. I don't want to."

"I don't know." Except she did know. She wanted this to work. She was simply afraid.

"I think we could be good together. I think our kids could be good together."

"I don't know."

"Look, it's early days, but let's give this a fair shot. People blend families all the time. We could make this work."

She still hesitated.

"Trial run. How about getting together on New Year's Eve? We'll have a big old family party—play games, watch movies, eat popcorn. What do you say?"

A new year, a new beginning. With a good man.

She said yes.

The twenty-ninth found Olivia and James and Muriel and Arnie at Pancake Haus, placing breakfast orders.

"It's nice to relax after our stressful Christmas," Olivia said once their waitress had left.

"I can imagine," Muriel said. Olivia had already filled her in on every cringe-worthy detail of their holiday.

"At least it ended well. James's son came up and spent the night and we all had a great time. I must say, everyone was relieved that Tawny didn't stay for Christmas dinner. But you know, I finally understand why Meadow is the way she is. It's so much easier to see past her faults now that I know what caused them."

"Anyway, none of us is perfect," James added.

"You're close," she told him, which made him smile.

"There's your cue, Muriel," Arnie teased.

"You, too," she said with a smile. "My daughter was right. Here I was able to see the potential in a silly tree and I couldn't see what a wonderful man I had right in front of my nose."

"Better late than never," Arnie said.

Dot chose that minute to join them. "Happy New Year, everyone. Have you missed me, Arnie?" she added, sliding in next to him.

He put an arm around Muriel. "Well, not so much."

"Ah," Dot said. "Guess we can let go of the charade."

"Yes, you can," Muriel said.

"I'll have to find a new travel buddy," Dot continued with the phoniest sad face Olivia had ever seen.

"It sounds like you already have," Muriel said. "Maybe now you can explain that text you sent. Who's the mystery man you're falling for?"

"You didn't tell her?" Dot asked Arnie.

"I don't blab. Anyway, I figured you'd want to tell."

Dot smiled. "Believe it or not, it's Arnie's old friend from the Yakima bank. We really hit it off. He's got money to spend and I'm gonna help him," she cracked.

"Honestly, Dot," Muriel chided.

"Okay, it's more than that," Dot admitted. "I'm crazy about the man. He's a hoot."

"Have you seen him since you got back?" Olivia asked.

"Oh, yes. He spent Christmas Eve with my family and I spent Christmas Day with his. We each got the kids' stamp of approval."

"Not always an easy feat," said James.

"No, it's not," Muriel agreed.

Olivia knew she was thinking of her second husband, Waldo. Her daughter Samantha had been anything but happy after they married and he got involved in the family business.

"But Arnie's had my girls' approval for years," Muriel added, taking his hand. "It's wonderful to find someone to be happy with at this point in life."

"You can say that again," said Dot.

"So, tell us more about this new man," Olivia prompted.

"He's younger than I am, but I always wanted a boy toy," Dot cracked.

"You need someone young enough to keep up with you," Arnie told her.

"What else?" Olivia prompted.

"He likes to travel. We've already booked our next cruise. Come summer, we'll be on the Baltic."

"That does sound glamorous," Muriel said, and Olivia hoped that Arnie would try again to get her to go on a trip with him. She suspected that next time Muriel wouldn't turn him down.

"What about New Year's Eve?" Muriel asked Dot.

"Oh, he's got that covered. We're going to spend the night in Seattle with some of his friends."

"You're not wasting any time," Muriel said.

"You shouldn't, either," Dot told her. "At our age we don't know how long the equipment's gonna keep working."

"Speak for yourself," James told her. "There may be snow on the roof but that doesn't mean there still isn't fire in the chimney."

And Olivia was glad there was. "What about you two?" she asked Muriel. "What are you going to do for New Year's Eve?"

"I think we'll spend a quiet evening at home," Muriel said, smiling at Arnie.

"Building a fire in the chimney," Dot teased, and Muriel frowned at her.

"I'm in favor of that," Arnie said, and Olivia wasn't sure whether he was referring to staying in or building that fire. She suspected it was both.

"Anyway, I've got my open house the next day. That will be plenty of party," Muriel said. "You are coming, right?" she asked Olivia.

"We wouldn't miss it," Olivia said. "We're packed out, but we don't offer dinner on New Year's Eve and we're only offering a continental breakfast on New

Year's Day this year, so we'll have light work. People are usually too hungover for a big breakfast, anyway."

She was actually looking forward to having a quiet New Year. After Christmas, she deserved it. Thank God things were settling down in her family.

Their orders had just arrived when Brandon called her.

"Mom, you've got to get back right now. Meadow's having a problem!"

Chapter Nineteen

The best present we can give is to be there for
people when they need us.
>   —Muriel Sterling, *A Guide to Happy Holidays*

Oh, no. What kind of problem? What on earth was
going on now? "What's wrong?" Olivia asked.

"She's bleeding. She thinks she's losing the baby."

The panic in her son's voice infused her with the
same emotion. "We've got to go right now," she said to
James. "It's Meadow and the baby."

He nodded and scooted out of the booth and began
to dig for his wallet.

"Don't worry about paying. Just go," Dot said. "And
keep us posted."

"Thank you," Olivia said. "Pray for us, Muriel."

"You know we will," Muriel said.

Olivia barely heard. She was already halfway to the
door. Poor Meadow.

They made it to the lodge in record time and hurried in to find Brandon in the lobby, watching for them.

"I'll man the desk," James offered, since Eric and

Brooke had taken off for the day and were visiting friends in Wenatchee. "And I'll let the kids know what's going on."

"Thanks," Olivia said, and she and Brandon hurried to the apartment.

"I wanted to call 911 but she wouldn't let me. She says there's nothing we can do, anyway. Oh, God, Mom, this is all my fault. I just had to go skiing last night. And I pushed her too hard. I know I did."

"This is not your fault," Olivia assured him. "If she is having a miscarriage, it simply means the baby wasn't developing properly. It's nature's way of starting over. It's not going to be easy on either of you, but it was most certainly no one's fault."

"It sucks," he said bitterly.

"Yes, it does," she agreed. "But let's not go there yet. Okay? Everything will be all right," she added, not so much because she believed it but because she needed to quell her son's panic.

"I should have called 911," Brandon fretted. "She didn't even want me to call you."

"Why not?"

"She's embarrassed. She says she's already been a big enough pain."

"She shouldn't feel that way."

The fact that Meadow hadn't wanted him to call her spoke volumes about their relationship.

Olivia could have cried. Of course Meadow had to have picked up on the fact that she hadn't wanted her as a daughter-in-law, and even though she'd been trying to have a better attitude, it hadn't been enough for the girl to feel comfortable turning to her in a crisis. How sad. How wrong!

"She's in the bathroom," Brandon said as they rushed through the apartment door.

He started to follow Olivia in, but he was so upset she wasn't sure how much help he'd be. "Why don't you give us a minute and wait here?" she told him.

He bit his lip and nodded.

She entered the bathroom to find Meadow huddled against the shower wall, wearing nothing but a towel. There was blood on the tile floor and she had her arms wrapped around her knees, her head buried. The sobs were heartbreaking.

Olivia opened the shower door and stepped inside. "Meadow," she said and knelt next to her.

Meadow raised her tearstained face. Her agony stirred up emotions from the worst time in Olivia's life—when she'd lost her husband, when she'd sat helplessly by his bedside and watched him slip away from her. This was life in a fallen world at its worst, Mother Nature at her cruelest.

"I'm losing the baby," Meadow sobbed.

Olivia pulled her into her arms and let her cry on her shoulder. "You don't know that yet. This might just be spotting." Although that looked like a lot of blood for simply spotting.

"I can't lose another baby. Oh, God, why can't I do anything right?"

Olivia had to force herself to stay calm. "You've done

absolutely nothing wrong. Come on, sweetie. Let's get you dressed and to the hospital."

Meadow was still crying but she did stand and let Olivia help her dress. Olivia was long past needing sanitary pads and Meadow's supplies were limited to tampons and panty liners but they made do.

"Brandon, get the car," Olivia called and, moments later, they were on their way to the hospital emergency room.

All the way, Meadow cried and apologized to her husband for letting him down.

"It's okay, babe. I just want you to be all right," he kept telling her. Olivia wasn't sure he was getting through.

Meadow was admitted immediately, and Olivia and Brandon were allowed to go into the examination room with her. They stood on either side of her, both holding her hands.

"I've never been in a hospital before," she said in a small voice. "This is creepy."

"This is where you'll get help," Olivia told her. "It's going to be all right, dear."

The nurse who took her vitals was both kind and calming. "Is this your first pregnancy?"

"No. I had a miscarriage before this," Meadow said, the tears still streaking down her cheeks.

"That happens sometimes," the nurse said. "Don't worry. We'll take good care of you."

"But what about my baby?"

"We'll do everything we can," the nurse said.

There was only so much comfort to be found in those

words. "We're gonna lose the baby," Meadow said in a dull voice.

"No, we're not," Brandon insisted.

Olivia hoped he was right.

The doctor joined them and introduced himself. He was somewhere in his fifties, his hair heavily streaked with gray. He appeared kindly and his voice was calming. He asked Meadow how far along she was and when the bleeding had started.

"Just this morning," she whimpered.

"And how many pads have you gone through?"

"I don't know," Meadow wailed. "I don't have any."

"That's all right," he said easily. "Let's take a look, shall we?"

Olivia was about to leave so the doctor could do his examination but Meadow grabbed her hand. "Don't leave me."

She nodded and remained, along with Brandon, who was looking pale.

Tears slipped down Meadow's face and he wiped them away, assuring her that everything would be all right. They were a team, working desperately to make their way together over a gigantic hurdle.

Olivia's heart ached for them and she squeezed Meadow's hand, trying to telegraph comfort to her.

The doctor completed his exam and said, "Everything looks good."

"Thank God," Olivia said as Meadow expelled her relief in a sob and Brandon hugged her.

"It's gonna be okay now," he told her, and she smiled up at him.

But Meadow's relief was short-lived. "What caused this?" she asked the doctor. "Is it gonna happen again?"

"It might. Bleeding in the first trimester happens to a lot of women. It can be caused by any number of things—hormonal changes, infections, intercourse."

"Sex? Okay, we're done," Meadow said firmly, and Brandon nodded gamely.

"There's no need to abandon your sex life," the doctor told her. "But any time you have bleeding, especially if you're having abdominal pain or cramps, you call your doctor right away. Do you have a doctor?"

"Not yet," Meadow said.

"Well, we have several good ones around here. You'll want to call and make an appointment right away."

"I will," Meadow said heartily.

"Meanwhile, go home and take it easy for the rest of the day. Have your husband make you dinner," he added with a wink at Brandon.

"Anything she wants," he said.

The doctor gave Meadow's arm a pat. "Good luck and congratulations."

"Thanks," she said. She was beaming now.

"All good news, dear," Olivia said and patted her hand. Suddenly, Meadow looked as if she was about to cry again. "What's wrong?" Olivia asked in concern.

"You called me *dear*," Meadow explained and gave her a teary smile.

"That's because you are dear to me," Olivia said.

It was no lie. She did care for this girl, could finally truly appreciate the good woman beneath the unpolished exterior. The vow she'd made at Muriel's party had played only a small part because, really, Olivia's best efforts had all been grudging. No, the change had to do with Meadow herself, slowing revealing facets of a kind heart and genuinely sweet person that Olivia had failed to see at first. All along, it hadn't been Olivia bringing out the best in Meadow. It had been Meadow bringing out the best in Olivia.

"I so lucked out with this family," Meadow said, her eyes teary once more.

"And we lucked out with you," Olivia told her. And she meant it. "Now, I'll give you two a moment and let everyone know you're okay."

"Thank God," James said when she told him. "I'd hate to see her lose another baby."

"Me, too," Olivia agreed. "She's been through enough."

The drive home was entirely different from the drive to the hospital. Brandon insisted on stopping by the grocery store and picking up eggnog and peppermint ice cream, two of Meadow's favorites.

"I'm gonna get so fat," she protested.

"Hey, you're eating for two," he said. "And both of you deserve a treat after what you just went through."

"Yeah, we do," she admitted.

From her spot in the back seat Olivia could see Meadow place a hand on her stomach as if to remind both her and her little one that they were safe. Meadow a mother—she was going to manage just fine.

They returned to the lodge in triumph and James was there, ready to hug them both and tell Meadow how glad he was that everything was all right. "Gotta take care of little James Jr," he teased.

"You mean Brandon Jr.," Meadow teased back.

"Come on, babe. I'm gonna give you a back rub," Brandon said.

But before he could lead her off, she hugged Olivia one last time. "Thanks…Mom," she said shyly.

"You're welcome, daughter," Olivia said and kissed her cheek.

The bookstore closed early the day of New Year's Eve. "There's no point in staying open late. By three in the afternoon everyone's thinking about getting ready to party," Pat told Sienna. "Me included. So, go have fun."

Sienna intended to. She took advantage of the extra free time to run to the store for goodies for her party with Tim and his girls. Safeway was packed and it seemed she could barely make it down an aisle without running into one of her new friends.

Charley Masters had decided she needed more eggnog for the specialty drink her bartender was concocting and was making a last-minute raid on the refrigerator case. "If you want some, you'd better grab it quick," she told Sienna.

"Are you doing something fun tonight?" Bailey Black asked her when they met in the chips aisle.

"A small party at home." With the new boyfriend. He'd promised to come no matter what kind of crisis occurred in his ex's life.

"I should be so lucky," Bailey said. "My sister's watching the baby while I babysit a bunch of grown men over at The Man Cave. If we don't have to call Tilda to come over and break up a fight, it will be a miracle."

She shook her head. "Sometimes I wish Todd would get rid of that place. But oh, well. Unless we win the lottery, we're probably stuck with it. Anyway, you have fun."

She would, for sure.

Muriel Sterling was coming in as Sienna was going out with her grocery bags full of goodies. "I finished your book," Sienna told her. "It really made a difference in my outlook, and following your advice has made a difference in how I'm getting along with my neighbor, too."

"I'm glad," Muriel said. "It's always nice to hear when someone appreciates your work."

"I sure do. What's your next book going to be on?"

Muriel's smile faded a little. "I'm not sure."

"Well, whatever it's about, I'll be sure to buy a copy."

"I appreciate that. Happy New Year, Sienna."

Yes, it was, indeed.

This time nothing prevented Tim from coming over for a holiday celebration. He arrived bearing a giant pizza and fireworks. "Leo will love it. And don't worry, they're safe and I'll be the one handling them."

His daughter Amy was carrying a decorated tin. "We made you cookies, Leo."

This had Leo jumping up and down with delight. And he pretty much remained in that ecstatic state all evening. They devoured pizza, drank hot cocoa, played Leo's favorite games—Cootie and Candy Land—and then settled in to watch movies. Halfway through the second one, both Amelia and Leo were asleep and Amy was hanging on by a thread.

But at a little before midnight Tim and Sienna got

them stirring and everyone trooped out to the front of the house to set off fireworks.

They'd barely gotten started when Cratchett opened his front door. "You know, some people are trying to sleep," he yelled.

"Well, that's a dumb idea on New Year's Eve," Tim yelled back, and Cratchett slammed his door.

Sienna couldn't help smiling. "And just when I thought he was becoming human."

"Well, you know what they say. Rome wasn't built in a day," Tim said, and he set off another noisy firework.

They weren't the only ones. Soon the sky was alight with showers of brightly colored sparks and the air was filled with booms.

Tim's supply ran out but they all lingered on the front walk, watching the show other people were putting on. He slipped an arm around Sienna and said, "Happy New Year." And then, to make sure it was truly happy, he kissed her.

"I told you," Cecily had said after her mother informed her that she and Arnie were now an item. Then, before Muriel could chide her for being an I-told-you-so, she'd added, "I'm glad. He's a sweet man. By the way, Serena wants to be a flower girl."

"Aren't you jumping the gun a little bit there?"

"You have to get married. It's your third, but it's Arnie's first. Anyway, I know you, Mom. You wouldn't be comfortable just moving in together. Bad example for the grandkids," she teased.

"Well, darling, first he has to ask me." Had he been back to Mountain Jewels?

When Cecily made an effort at a mysterious smile, Muriel had known that he had, indeed.

Sure enough, they were about to pour their champagne to toast in the New Year when he produced a ring box. "Let's start the New Year right," he said, handing it to her. "I know you already have diamond rings but…" He hesitated. "You will marry me, won't you?"

"Of course I will," she said and kissed him.

"Good. Now, open the box and let's get this on your finger before you change your mind."

She opened it to find a fourteen-karat white-gold pavé-set ring with an emerald-cut center diamond. "It's beautiful."

"Not as beautiful as you," he murmured and kissed her. "I can't get enough of kissing you," he said. "I hope I live to be a hundred."

So did she.

Chapter Twenty

Every holiday celebration eventually comes to an end, but the memories last forever.

—Muriel Sterling, *A Guide to Happy Holidays*

Muriel Sterling-Wittman—soon to be Amundsen—held an open house for all her Icicle Falls friends on the afternoon of New Year's Day. Anyone who was anyone put in an appearance. After all, Muriel's family was the chocolate royalty of the town, and she was the queen. She was also the closest thing to a celebrity Icicle Falls had. But more than that, she was simply well liked.

"I wouldn't miss your party for the world," Beth Mallow told her.

"Me, either," put in Daphne Hawkins. Daphne had taken over running Primrose Haus, a popular wedding venue in town, after her mother married. She herself had married a local man, Hank Hawkins, who owned a prosperous lawn service company.

She noticed the ring on Muriel's finger. "Wow, what's this?"

Arnie, who hadn't left Muriel's side, put an arm around her shoulder. "We'll be calling you soon."

"Congratulations," Daphne said. "I'm sure we can find a date for you. But don't wait too long. We're filling up fast."

"I have no intention of doing that," Arnie said. "She might change her mind."

"Never," Muriel said with a smile.

Olivia arrived with her two daughters-in-law in tow. "The men are keeping an eye on things so we can party," she said, hugging Muriel. She reached out and drew a slender young woman in ripped jeans and a jacket up to Muriel. "You haven't officially met my new daughter yet. This is Meadow."

Daughter, not *daughter-in-law*. How things had changed at the Icicle Creek Lodge. "I'm happy to finally meet you," Muriel said. She almost added, *I've heard so much about you*, but reconsidered. In light of the bumpy start she and Olivia had gotten off to, that could possibly be taken the wrong way. "Welcome to Icicle Falls."

"Thanks," said Meadow. She was smiling as if she'd been invited to the White House and not simply an open house. "I love it here. And it's epic being at the lodge with everyone. Olivia—Mom," she corrected herself with a blush, "she's awesome."

Now Olivia was blushing. "Well, maybe awesome in the making," she said.

Now Meadow was taking in Muriel's house. "You sure know how to decorate," she said, looking around. "This place is really cool." To Olivia she said, "We should redo the lodge, make it more like this. What do you think of that?"

It was probably a good thing Olivia didn't say what she thought. "We'll see," she said. "Why don't you and Brooke try some of Muriel's appetizers?"

"Okay," Meadow said eagerly. "Come on, Brooke. Let's go for it. We're both eating for two. We may as well make the most of it while we can."

"She's a work in progress," Olivia said, her cheeks pink.

"She's enthusiastic," Muriel said. "And, you know, maybe it is time to update the lodge just a little."

Olivia looked at Muriel as if she'd just stabbed her in the heart.

"Or not," Muriel said quickly. "But it's nice that she wants to be involved. And she certainly loves you."

"God knows why," Olivia said. "I've wondered more than once who the ugly tree over at our place was."

"We all have our ugly-tree moments," Muriel said, thinking of her behavior when Arnie and Dot were on their cruise.

Pat and her husband joined them now. "Happy New Year, everyone. And congratulations," she said to Arnie, who was looking like a man who'd won the lottery. As he and Ed began visiting, Pat asked, "Did I just hear you talking about ugly trees?"

"You did," Muriel confirmed.

"Well, speaking of, I've got news. Harvey Wood is selling me our building. He's even giving it to me for a decent price."

"Will wonders never cease?" asked Olivia.

"Speaking of wonders." Pat nodded in the direction of the front door, where Bailey was letting in Sienna Moreno along with her son and a large good-looking man with two little girls in tow. Lila Zuckerman was with her. And Robert Cratchett. "It looks like Sienna has finally established good relations with her neighbor," she said as they handed over their coats and scarves.

"Who's the other man?" Olivia asked.

"Not sure," Pat said, "but how much you want to bet he and Sienna are becoming an item?"

"Not taking that bet," Olivia said.

The mystery was solved when Sienna brought her crowd over to join them. She was bearing a plate of cookies and a bottle of wine. "Thank you so much for inviting me," she said after Muriel and Lila had greeted each other. "I know it was tacky to bring extra people, but Pat told me you wouldn't mind."

"Not at all," Muriel said. "I don't believe I've met this man," she said, smiling at the large man standing next to Sienna.

"Tim Richmond," he said and then introduced his daughters.

"And this is Leo," Pat added, laying a hand on Sienna's little boy's shoulders, not an easy feat considering the fact that he was bouncing up and down as if he had springs on his feet.

"Hi, Leo. Happy New Year," Muriel told him.

"Happy New Year!" Leo crowed.

"We won't stay long," Sienna promised.

"Stay as long as you want," Muriel said. Her house

wasn't big but that would never stop her from filling it with guests.

"Girls, why don't you take Leo over to the refreshment table and deposit our cookies?" Sienna said.

"Cookies!" Leo's bouncing went into high gear.

"Only one for you," Sienna told him sternly, and the girls led him away. "And this is my neighbor, Mr. Cratchett."

"I'm glad you could come," Muriel told him.

"Nice of you to have me," he said and produced a bottle of champagne.

Muriel was no expert on champagne, but even she knew an expensive bottle when she saw one. "Thank you. This is lovely."

His cheeks turned russet and he brushed aside her thanks. "Just something I've had lying around."

"Well, it was very thoughtful of you," Muriel said.

"I like to think I'm a thoughtful man," he said and gave Sienna a look that dared her to contradict him. "Come on, Lila. Those kids are like locusts. They'll eat everything on the table if we don't keep an eye on them. You two probably aren't going to," he said to Tim. "Parents these days," he added with a shake of his head and led Mrs. Zuckerman away.

"He's a work in progress," Sienna said.

"Aren't we all?" said Olivia, giving Muriel a wink.

They watched as Cratchett filled Leo's plate and then demonstrated dangling a spoon from his nose.

"He used to do that for us as kids," Tim explained to Muriel. "These days he's a changed man. You can take credit for a lot of that," he said to Sienna.

"I think most of the credit goes to Mrs. Zuckerman, but I was inspired by Muriel's book. And her ugly tree," Sienna added.

"There's your next book idea," Pat said to Muriel. "Why don't you write about how the ugly tree helped us all this Christmas?"

It was a good idea. "Maybe I will," Muriel said.

The party lasted all afternoon, with people coming and going, all of them smiling and happy and excited for whatever the New Year might bring. People talked, people laughed, people hugged. Men swapped jokes and women admired each other's outfits, while the children devoured the treats on the table.

And, adorned in all its finery, the ugly tree stood watch over it all.

* * * * *

Our Favorite Recipes from Icicle Falls

With this being the last book in their series, the gang
from Icicle Falls wanted to leave you with a good
taste in your mouth. In the following pages, they've
shared some of their favorite recipes from through-
out the series, and we hope you enjoy them as much
as they did. Merry Christmas from everyone in Icicle
Falls. May your table be filled with good things and
your hearts be filled with love!

Olivia's Eggnog Muffins

Ingredients:
1¾ cups flour
4 tsp baking powder
½ tsp salt
¼ cup sugar
¼ cup shortening
1 egg
1 cup eggnog
¾ cup candied cherries, finely chopped
¾ cup walnuts, finely chopped

Directions:
Cream together sugar and shortening. Add egg and mix thoroughly. Sift in all dry ingredients, adding alternately with eggnog. (Note: You may need to add perhaps another tbsp of eggnog if your muffin batter looks a little too dry.) Bake for twenty minutes at 350 degrees F or until a toothpick inserted comes out clean.

Muriel's Brie in Puff Pastry Appetizer

Ingredients:
1 cup apricot jam
½ cup sliced almonds
1 sheet puff pastry, thawed
1 round 14–15-ounce Brie cheese

Directions:
Heat oven to 400 degrees F. Spray cookie sheet with cooking spray. Roll pastry out to make it wider. Cut rind from Brie and place in the center of it. Spoon apricot jam on top of Brie and sprinkle with almonds. Fold pastry over, crimping edges together. Place on cookie sheet and bake 20 to 25 minutes until golden brown. Cool on cookie sheet on wire rack for 10 minutes before serving. Serve on a platter with crackers and/or sliced apples.

Cecily's Winter Salad

Ingredients:
2 cups butternut squash, cubed
4 cups baby spinach (Buy the spinach that's bagged and prewashed—so much easier.)
½ cup pomegranate seeds
handful of yellow baby tomatoes, halved
½ a red pepper, finely diced
¼ cup red onion, finely chopped

Directions:
Cook squash until tender but firm. Drain and cool, then cut into bite-size cubes. Toss that and other ingredients with spinach. Serve with oil-and-vinegar dressing.

Sienna's Enchiladas
(courtesy of Linda Barrows)

Ingredients for Sauce:
1 medium onion, chopped
1 clove garlic, finely chopped
¼ tsp cloves
½ tsp cinnamon
2 tbsp chili powder
½ tsp sugar
3 tbsp butter
½ tsp salt
1 large can tomatoes
1 small can condensed tomato soup
3 tbsp oil

Directions for Sauce:
Sauté onion and garlic in oil; add tomatoes, soup, cinnamon, cloves and chili powder. Simmer until thick (about 45 minutes). Add butter, sugar and salt.

Ingredients for Filling:
1 medium onion, chopped
1 clove garlic, finely chopped
1 pound lean hamburger

1 tsp salt
½ tsp ground oregano
dash cumin
3 tbsp oil
2 cups water

Directions for Meat:
Sauté onion and garlic in oil; add meat and fry until brown. Drain off grease. Add remaining ingredients. Simmer until almost dry (45 minutes).

Final Ingredients:
flour tortillas
sharp cheddar cheese, grated

Final Directions:
Dip tortillas in the sauce and place in 9-by-13-inch pan (lightly sprayed with cooking oil). Fill with 2 tbsp of meat and 2 tbsp of cheese. Fold in place with seam side down. When you've used up all your filling and tortillas, pour the remaining sauce over all and bake at 350 degrees F for 25 minutes.

Note: If you're in a hurry, you can omit the water from the meat and just fry your onions, garlic and meat.

Muriel's Fruitcake Cookies

Ingredients for Cookies:
2½ cups flour
2½ tsp baking powder
1 tsp salt
1 tsp nutmeg
½ cup butter & ½ cup shortening (Original recipe
called for 1 cup shortening, but everything's better
with butter! Keep the ½ cup shortening, though, as
using only butter leaves the cookies pretty delicate
and hard to work with.)
1 cup sugar
1 egg
1 cup milk
1 cup raisins
1 cup candied cherries, chopped
1 cup walnuts, chopped
1 cup dried apricots, chopped

Directions for Cookies:
Cream butter, shortening and sugar. Add egg and mix
thoroughly. Sift in dry ingredients, adding alternately with
milk. Drop by spoonful (Beth uses a soup spoon) onto a
lightly sprayed cookie sheet. Bake at 350 degrees F for

10 to 12 minutes (until lightly browned). Cool on cookie sheet. After cookies are cool, frost with rum glaze.

Ingredients for Glaze:
2½ cups powdered sugar
8 tbsp rum

Directions for Glaze:
Mix sugar and rum together until smooth. Spread a small amount on top of each cookie and let dry and harden before storing.

Bailey's Peppermint Cupcakes

(Makes 18 to 24 cupcakes)

Ingredients for Cupcakes:
2¼ cups cake flour
2½ tsp baking powder
1 tsp salt
1½ cups sugar
½ cup butter (1 stick)
2 eggs
1 cup milk
1 tbsp oil (for extra moistness)
1 tsp peppermint extract

Directions for Cupcakes:
Sift dry ingredients minus the sugar into a mixing bowl. Add the sugar, butter, eggs and two-thirds of the milk. Mix slowly to combine, then add the remaining milk, peppermint extract and oil and beat for a minute on medium speed. Pour into lined muffin tins (leaving some head room at the top) and bake at 350 degrees F for 20 to 25 minutes (until a toothpick inserted comes out clean or cake springs back to the touch). Cool slightly, then remove to wire racks.

Ingredients for Frosting:
6 ounces (½ a 12-ounce bag) white chocolate chips
½ cup heavy whipping cream
½ cup butter, room temperature
4 cups powdered sugar
crushed peppermint for garnish

Directions for Frosting:
Place white chocolate chips in a metal bowl. Microwave heavy cream until it starts to boil. Remove from microwave and pour over chocolate chips. Cover bowl with plastic wrap for five minutes, then whisk until smooth. Add butter and beat until completely mixed. Slowly add powdered sugar and beat until fluffy. Add more cream if needed.

Final directions:
After cupcakes are cooled and frosting is made, frost and top with crushed peppermint.

Happy eating and happy holidays!

Acknowledgments

Authors may write in solitary, but they don't work alone! So many people helped me as I wound my way through this story, so I want to make sure I give credit where credit is due. Thank you to Mike Chase of Leavenworth Greenhouse and Nursery for his advice on what to plant in Mr. Cratchett's yard. Huge thanks to the following women for their help and insights into the special calling of raising and working with mentally challenged children: Kimberly Anderson, Mel Christopher and Jenny Burton. And, as always, thanks to the Brain Trust—Susan Wiggs, A.J. Banner, Lois Dyer, Kate Breslin and Elsa Watson—for all your sage advice. Finally, a huge thank-you to my super agent, Paige Wheeler, and my lovely editor, Michelle Meade, for all you've done for me and continue to do. I am indebted to the whole MIRA team. You all work so hard on my behalf and I truly appreciate it.

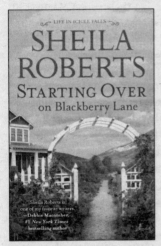

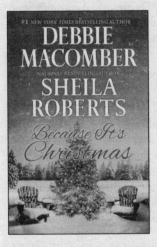

SPECIAL EXCERPT FROM

Love Inspired.

When Erica Lindholm and her twin babies show up at his family farm just before Christmas, Jason Stephanidis can tell she's hiding something. But how can he refuse the young mother, a friend of his sister's, a place to stay during the holidays? He never counted on wanting Erica and the boys to be a more permanent part of his life...

Read on for a sneak peek of
SECRET CHRISTMAS TWINS
by Lee Tobin McClain,
part of the CHRISTMAS TWINS miniseries.

Once both twins were bundled, snug between Papa and Erica, Jason sent the horses trotting forward. The sun was up now, making millions of diamonds on the snow that stretched across the hills far into the distance. He smelled pine, a sharp, resin-laden sweetness.

When he picked up the pace, the sleigh bells jingled.

"Real sleigh bells!" Erica said, and then, as they approached the white covered bridge decorated with a simple wreath for Christmas, she gasped. "This is the most beautiful place I've ever seen."

Jason glanced back, unable to resist watching her fall in love with his home.

Papa was smiling for the first time since he'd learned of Kimmie's death. And as they crossed the bridge and trotted toward the church, converging with other horse-drawn sleighs, Jason felt a sense of rightness.

Mikey started babbling to Teddy, accompanied by gestures and much repetition of his new word. Teddy tilted his head to one side and burst forth with his own stream of nonsense syllables, seeming to ask a question, batting Mikey on the arm. Mikey waved toward the horses and jabbered some more, as if he were explaining something important.

They were such personalities, even as little as they were. Jason couldn't help smiling as he watched them interact.

Once Papa had the reins set and the horses tied up, Jason jumped out of the sleigh, and then turned to help Erica down. She handed him a twin. "Can you hold Mikey?"

He caught a whiff of baby powder and pulled the little one tight against his shoulder. Then he reached out to help Erica, and she took his hand to climb down, Teddy on her hip.

When he held her hand, something electric seemed to travel right to his heart. Involuntarily he squeezed and held on.

She drew in a sharp breath as she looked at him, some mixture of puzzlement and awareness in her eyes.

What was Erica's secret?

And wasn't it curious that, after all these years, there were twins in the farmhouse again?

Don't miss
SECRET CHRISTMAS TWINS
by Lee Tobin McClain, available November 2017
wherever Love Inspired® books and ebooks are sold.

www.LoveInspired.com

SHEILA ROBERTS

33003	STARTING OVER ON BLACKBERRY LANE	___$7.99 U.S.	___$9.99 CAN.
31879	HOME ON APPLE BLOSSOM ROAD	___$7.99 U.S.	___$9.99 CAN.
31815	A WEDDING ON PRIMROSE STREET	___$7.99 U.S.	___$8.99 CAN.
31661	THE LODGE ON HOLLY ROAD	___$7.99 U.S.	___$8.99 CAN.

(limited quantities available)

TOTAL AMOUNT	$ _____
POSTAGE & HANDLING	$ _____
($1.00 for 1 book, 50¢ for each additional)	
APPLICABLE TAXES*	$ _____
TOTAL PAYABLE	$ _____

(check or money order—please do not send cash)

To order, complete this form and send it, along with a check or money order for the total amount, payable to MIRA Books, to: **In the U.S.:** 3010 Walden Avenue, P.O. Box 9077, Buffalo, NY 14269-9077; **In Canada:** P.O. Box 636, Fort Erie, Ontario, L2A 5X3.

Name: _____

Address: _____ City: _____

State/Prov.: _____ Zip/Postal Code: _____

Account Number (if applicable): _____

075 CSAS

*New York residents remit applicable sales taxes.
*Canadian residents remit applicable GST and provincial taxes.

Harlequin.com

MSR1117BL